Devoted

Devoted

A DEMON WATCHER NOVEL: BOOK 1

by

GINNA MORAN

Copyright © 2018 by Ginna Moran
All Rights Reserved.

All rights reserved under International and Pan-American Copyright Conventions, including the right of reproduction in whole or in part in any form or by any electronic or mechanical means including information storage and retrieval systems, without written permission, except in the case of brief quotations embodied in critical articles and reviews.

ISBN 978-1-942073-09-3 (soft cover)
ISBN 978-1-942073-35-2 (eBook)

This is a work of fiction. All of the characters, organizations, and events portrayed in this novel are either products of the author's imagination or are used fictitiously.

Cover design by Silver Starlight Designs
Cover images copyright 123RF

For Inquiries Contact:
Sunny Palms Press
9663 Santa Monica Blvd Suite 1158
Beverly Hills, CA 90210, USA
www.sunnypalmspress.com
www.GinnaMoran.com

For Zoë, my mostly angelic, but sometimes quite demonic, daughter.

Prologue

FIVE YEARS AGO

"**G**RANDMA, IF YOU can hear me, please—"

Taking a deep breath, I suppress a sob burning in my chest. Tears blur my eyes, seeming to never end no matter how strong or tough my grandma always told me I was. But that was before she died in her sleep three months ago, leaving me alone. It was easy to be tough with a sassy woman, who loved to dye her hair all colors of the rainbow, wear leather jackets even in the summer, and for fun had artillery in her walk-in closet instead of clothing.

She was a badass by design, though she spent most nights

watching TV or reading. She always said, "Appear unstoppable, and no one will try to stop you," but she never met the Johanssons.

I press my palms together, like the force alone could open up a door or window or whatever ethereal portal that leads to Heaven so I can make sure she's listening to my prayer. "Grandma, please. I need you to help me. Use whatever divine power you have and get me out of here."

Shouts sound through my bedroom wall and glass shatters outside my door. The social worker swore this was temporary, because she truly believes one of my aunts or uncles will come around to take me in, but I doubt it. Grandma never talked to anyone after my mom died after my birth, and we never get cards at Christmas. I only recently found out their names.

More glass shatters, forcing me to pull myself up from kneeling. How the Johanssons ever made it to the point of fostering is beyond me. Maybe desperation. Maybe they look great on paper. Either way, it's been a chaotic nightmare since I showed up with whatever I could fit in my backpack.

"Faith! Get out here," Stu Johansson yells through my door.

Cringing, I cross my room to the window. If Stu is yelling, it means he's been drinking. And when he's drinking, it means Wanda is locked in her bedroom and all his anger lands on me. If it weren't for Stu, things would be okay. Wanda is nice enough, but she never stands up to Stu on my behalf.

"Faith, did you touch my bourbon?" he asks, banging on

the door.

I squeeze my eyes shut, gripping my curtain. "No, I haven't left my room today."

"Then why's the bottle empty?" he asks. "Open this door."

"Give me a minute," I say, sweeping my gaze across my floor. Apart from a twin bed on a metal frame, a broken dresser that I can't get open half the time, and my backpack pushed into the corner, I have nothing to protect myself if I need it.

"I said now!" Stu pounds on the door, rattling it so hard I'm sure he'll break it down and then blame me tomorrow, like he blames me every day for stuff he forgets happens.

I sniffle, steeling myself, waiting for the door to break down. "Grandma, please," I whisper, turning my gaze to the ceiling. "Please."

"Fai—" Stu's words cut off, leaving me in silence. My heart pounds in my ears, my breath quickening with each passing second. It wouldn't be the first time he ran to grab his tools to remove my door. I was so thankful when he forgot to remove the lock he swore he'd get rid of.

Five minutes pass, each breath slowing as the tension slips away from my muscles. Five minutes is too long to not be back already to remove my door.

My prayers have been answered.

Releasing a small breath, I silently thank Grandma for her divine intervention. For listening to me for the first time since I arrived. I was beginning to think something was wrong with me, that I somehow got a lifetime of bad luck for surviving my birth when my mom didn't.

"F-Faith."

I freeze, my heart nearly crashing from my chest at the eerie tone of Stu's voice through my door.

"Leave me alone," I say.

"F-Faith," he says again. "Open the door."

"No."

Before I have a chance to move, my bedroom door crashes open, flying off the hinges and into the wall. I scream, bracing myself, preparing for the worst. A tingling sensation crawls over my hands, like a heat that doesn't burn me, and my mouth falls agape.

My curtains smolder in my fingers, a red energy, bright like electricity but more solid like water, gel even, lights my hands aglow. Panic rushes through me, and I fling my hands out, pelting my room with the liquid.

Stu hollers.

Spinning around, I face him standing in my doorway. He drops to his knees, his cheek blistering, glowing the same ruby red like whatever was on my hands.

A shadow, a huge, monstrous shadow, stretches across the wall in the hallway, sending a new wave of panic over me. A strange cracking sound cuts through the air, and I thrust my burning curtains open and peer at the metal bars through the glass window. The lever to open them mysteriously broke the day after I arrived when I was in the shower.

"Tell her." The smooth, masculine voice comes from a

place in the hall I can't see. The mysterious man reminds me of a few of the voiceover narrators on the documentaries Grandma used to watch. It's deep and demanding, but the kind of voice you want to listen to all day.

Stu groans from the floor. "I'm sorry, Faith. I've made some poor life choices, and I should've never mistreated you."

I frown. "What's going on?"

"Go on."

"I'm unfit to provide for you, and I have already called your social worker and told them I've abandoned you. I will pay for my wrongdoings. Will you please accept my apology?" Something weird is going on, yet my panic morphs into anger. How dare this man think a measly apology makes up for putting me through Hell these last few months?

"No," I say.

"Faith, please!" Stu yells. "Please!"

I shake my head, my blond hair smacking against my cheeks. "No."

Stu's body yanks backward as something, or someone, pulls him from my room. His screams pierce the air, sending fear right into my heart. I cover my ears, the sound growing louder and louder, and I squeeze my eyes shut, wishing I was anywhere else in the world than here.

"Grandma, please protect me. Please, let everything be okay," I pray, willing the world to bend to my desires.

A warm hand touches my chin, startling me, and I scream out and scramble back. If angels walked the earth, the man who stands before me is undeniably one of them. His jetting chin, strong jaw, and flawless skin are features found only on models in magazines. His eyes, a vibrant blue, catch and reflect a strange green in my lamplight, his pupils oddly shaped while expanding and retracting.

"Are you okay?" the man asks, keeping the space I created between us.

My lip quivers, and I nod, rubbing my hands together. The strange ruby light returns, glowing within my fingers.

I suck in a breath, hiding my hands behind my back, accidentally burning the fabric of the back of my hoodie. "Stay back. I don't want to hurt you. I don't know what's happening to me."

At the sound of my shaky voice, he steps a foot closer, holding up his hands. The same, lava-like, ruby red light glows in his fingers, bouncing off the gold in his blond hair. "I can explain."

"Are you an angel? Am I dreaming? Where's Stu?" The questions fly from my mouth faster than I give the mysterious man time to answer. The longer he stands before me, the more relaxed I feel. The more my fear lessens. But a tiny voice screams in what feels like my very soul to ask him to leave. It begs me to turn and run, to take this chance to get out of here. But my feet don't move.

The man rubs his hands together, putting out the strange orb. "Stu is no longer your concern. You are safe now. I'm getting you out of here."

I twist my mouth to the side. "I can't leave with you."

"Why not?"

"I don't know you."

"I apologize for that. Lenora was adamant about the rules in my involvement in your life, and I did not feel capable at the time to raise you. The Hunter's Alliance would have been too much of a challenge. I trusted your grandmother to keep you from that life," he says. Nothing he says makes sense.

"You knew my grandma?"

"Very well. I had fallen for her daughter," he says.

Confusion puckers my brows. "Wait, what? Are you saying—?"

He holds up his hand, cutting me off. "Come on. I'll explain things on the ride home."

"Home?"

"Well, you are my daughter. Do you really think I'd allow you to stay..." He peers around my drab room. "Here?"

"But—"

"Trust me," he says, his smooth voice digging into me. "You will always be safe with me."

I take his outstretched hand despite my better judgment, knowing in my soul he is the answer to my prayers. Anywhere from here is better, even with a stranger. I always knew my grandma wouldn't let me down. If I believed in anything good in this world, it is that she still manages to look after me.

I let the man pull me to the door. He ushers me down the hall and toward the front door without giving me a chance to look around, like he's protecting me from the place I've deemed my own personal Hell for months.

"Hurry," he says. "We must get to Moonlight Shores before dawn."

A bright red Ferrari sits next to the curb, idling. The man—my dad? My head spins at the thought. Whoever he is, he's crazy for leaving an exotic car running on my street this time of night.

I don't say it, though. There's no one even around. It's like the whole neighborhood locked themselves away, when I usually see people at all hours moving about.

"Why dawn? What's the hurry?" I ask, letting him open the passenger side door for me.

"For one, it's late and I'm sure you need your rest until you adapt to my schedule. Two, I'm sure the Hunter's Alliance is about to stake claim on you. And three, I cannot remain on this plane during the day."

He slides into the driver's seat and grips the wheel. "Did Lenora tell you about anything?"

I blink, all the years we spent together catching up to me faster than I can process. The weapons. The late nights. The old books she favored. The Hunter's Alliance. I remember the name printed on some of the papers in the safe. I thought it was a hunting organization—like for animals. I had assumed it was a hobby of hers from when she was younger.

"She said a lot of things, but they never made sense," I say. Because she did say a lot. I thought it was always her trying to be the cool grandma or trying to scare me from misbehaving. She said my father was a... "She said you couldn't come around because you were a demonic son of a b—"

The man laughs, tipping his head back before I can finish my sentence. "She was right."

The tiny voice inside me, the one deep in my soul screams out, rattling my insides, twisting my stomach in knots, begging me to get out of the car and run for my life, because my grandma wasn't joking around. She was being literal about everything.

I had no idea that I'd know more about her now than I did, like the little pieces of our lives together have finally connected to show me the big picture.

A warm hand gently touches my arm. "I'm sorry. I shouldn't have laughed. This must be so scary for you. But Faith, I want you to know that even though I'm a demon, I'm not some evil creature. I care about you. I want to protect you and teach you to live in our world before someone tries to do it for me. It's all I've ever wanted, but your grandma and I both knew that it was something that had to wait. I didn't expect the possibility of bringing you home with me to arrive so soon. I'm truly sorry about your grandmother...and for your mother. They were the best things to ever come into my life, besides you."

Tears prickle my eyes, grief and relief battling inside me to see what emotion will win. "This is all too much. I don't even know your name."

The man presses his lips into a thin line, his jaw tightening for a moment. His eyes shine briefly, and then they flash green in the headlights of a passing car and the sheen disappears. He twists in his seat, offering is hand out to me. "I'm Raphael...Blackwell."

"Wait, that's my grandma's and mom's last name."

He shakes my hand, a perfect smile crossing his ageless features. "Which they gave to me."

"Huh?"

"It was better than the ones I had made up," he says, like it is the most reasonable thing in the world.

"This is a lot to take in, Raphael," I say. "So that power back there—was that you?"

"And you. I'm surprised your power hadn't manifested sooner. I've been watching you for weeks, but tonight was the night. That foster monster of yours' soul finally fell onto Hell's path. That's all it took to give me the chance to—never mind. Let's start things off on a positive note. There's plenty of time for everything else."

I sit in stunned silence. How can I even process his words? My father is a demon, which makes me half demon. I have power. My grandma was a demon hunter, but not with Raphael. And my mom? What is happening to my life?

"Are you hungry? Maybe you could try to sleep or something," Raphael says, finally putting the car into gear to drive. "I wish Lenora had prepared you better, but I'm going to do the best I can, okay? I want you to always be happy with me."

I nod. "Can we just go home?"

His eyes light up. "Anything you want. The world is ours."

"It is?"

He nods, smiling again. "Just wait and see."

DEMON SPAWN

HOWLS ERUPT THROUGH the air, a cacophonous array that jerks my attention away from the TV and to the door. A shiver crawls up my spine, the noise sinking to my very soul, sending a mountain of fear down on me, threatening to crush me under the sudden weight of what's going on.

"Faith, you have to leave!" Aria yells, hopping to her feet to yank me to mine. "We lost track of time. The sun is setting."

Panic rushes over me, and I fling my arms around my best friend once before charging toward the door and down the hall of the Moonlight Shores' werewolf pack mansion. The air around me buzzes with adrenaline and anticipation. More howls cut through the air, reminding me that in a few minutes, nightfall will arrive to bring back the demons to earth, and not just any demon but my dad.

A wet nose nudges the back of my leg, pushing me forward to move faster. Every sunset is a race against time to get home before Dad does, but I'm usually more prepared for this. If he knew I spend my days outside the walls of our protective fortress, I'm sure he'd summon Hell right into our living room with fire and brimstone, his horns and all.

Cool beach air wraps around me, a salty breeze picking up tendrils of my blond hair. The round sun sinks halfway into the horizon, setting the puffy clouds aglow in glorious, heavenly golds that make me want to stop and watch.

But the howls push me to drag myself forward. A gray wolf matches my pace, running next to me along the crashing waves, barking and yipping, even nipping the backs of my legs so I can't slow down.

"I'm moving as fast as I can," I say, kicking up sand.

The wolf responds with a growl.

"Now turn around and go home. If my dad catches me with you, we're both double screwed."

Another deep, reverberating growl.

"I mean it, Aria. I already know you're tough. You don't have to prove you're not scared of my dad. I'm just—I'm not ready to introduce you yet."

I'm not sure I'll ever be. It's been years since Dad had broken werewolves to turn them into hellhounds to guard our house, but he's unpredictable. Things change in an instant. I know that.

One day, I was a normal kid, facing normal bad things—and then the next, my life exploded into a world I could barely process, facing unimaginable evil, having to make choices I didn't agree with, and all because I had the right reasons. Like hiding my werewolf best friend from my dad. Or how I have a life outside his demonic nights, with people he only tolerates most of the time. Like angels.

But that's a demon's life if you want to remain on earth. Everyone has a job to maintain the balance of the universe. Angels and demons must usher souls to their appropriate afterlives while the rest of the world mostly gets to live in uneventful normalcy. But demons have an evil streak. It's not their fault. Angels can also sometimes act all high and mighty. And then there's me, pulled between Hell by blood and Heaven by soul. Just because I'm half demon doesn't mean I'm evil. Though my dad encourages me to embrace my wickedness, my best friend Aria reminds me how much I love my humanity.

Aria's eyes flash in the sunset, and she skids to a stop, letting me leave her behind. I glance over my shoulder, peeking to make sure she listened to me. Another howl echoes behind me, the sound encouraging me to beat the quickly disappearing sunlight.

"Come on, Faith. Almost there. You can do it," I say out

loud, cheering myself on. "Eternity is a long time to be grounded. Just because Dad doesn't own your soul doesn't mean he won't try to take it. He's not stupid. He'll figure out how to keep you inside no matter how good at picking locks you are."

Fear creeps from my mind and down into my heart, tightening my chest. I have seconds to get inside my house before Dad materializes out of thin air. What he describes as a boring, endless land of nothing, in a realm I never want to or will ever travel to, imprisons him from sunrise to sundown with only other demons to keep him company. But few other demons make good friends. Not in a world where power matters and the balance of good and evil hovers on a fragile line.

The sun seeps into the outstretched ocean, the usual blue-green water now murky gray in the twilight. "No. No. No," I say with fifty feet to go to reach my back patio.

I'm too late.

I know it.

Slowing down, I wipe sweat from my forehead, take a few heaving breaths, and try to calm my racing heart before my dad hears it.

"Grandma, if you're bored and listening, I could really use a miracle," I say, glancing up to the purpling sky. Maybe if I can get my body to cooperate and stop sweating and if I can catch my breath, I can try to play it off like I was watching the sunset, patiently waiting for Dad's arrival.

I concentrate on listening to my surroundings. Music blares from my beach mansion, a towering glass and concrete fortress. Music is something I leave on every time I make my daily escape, because my dad and I both have sensitive hearing. Some demons get better vision, better sense of smell, and like my dad, better hearing. But it sucks. My dad helped me master the art of selective hearing years ago, even before I mastered my demonic energy, because hearing things at an alarmingly loud frequency is the most annoying thing in the world. I always thought I just hated the sound of chewing, people dragging their feet while they walked, sometimes even breathing, because they're unpleasant sounds. I had no idea it was because I heard them louder than everyone else.

Focusing on selecting the distinct sound of my dad, I push away the hum of the music from my ears. His footsteps are so light, I'd think he was weightless if I didn't know any better.

"Faith?" he calls.

I close the distance to the back door, listening to Dad. He heads toward my bedroom, his footsteps the same as always on the floor runner. I can tell where he is in the house at any moment by the change of flooring, but only if I concentrate hard enough. The fact that he thinks I'm on the opposite side of the mansion might be my only saving grace to get inside to try to fool him.

The music shuts off, and I freeze, inches away from the bulletproof glass back door. A demon's den is their most sacred—unholy? Whatever. A demon's den is not a place strangers want to enter, and sometimes the goodness of my soul sends a blip of panic through me as I turn the doorknob, but there isn't another place I'd rather live. Having a protective dad is nothing I should complain about. I've met other demons, and I'm lucky Dad gets to siphon a part of my humanity through our blood, because if he didn't, I'm sure life would be literal Hell.

Something crashes. Glass? Shoot, it's the hallway mirror. We just had it replaced two weeks ago.

I tiptoe across the entertainment room filled with gym equipment and to the hallway that'll take me past the kitchen. Holding my breath, I listen. A familiar noise sounds through the air, like two pieces of silk rubbing together. I can almost feel the breeze created by the soft whooshing of an angel's wings.

Dad didn't break the mirror because he discovered I wasn't in my room. He broke it because there's an intruder of the angelic variety in our house. One right outside my bedroom.

"You better give me one good reason why you're showing up in my house, seconds after sundown, before I even have had a chance to greet my daughter!" Dad's voice rips through the air, coming from the hallway to my room. "Business can wait."

The angel doesn't say anything. I hear another flap of wings.

"Out. Move it," Dad says. Loud footsteps head toward the front door as my Dad leads the absolutely silent angel out of our house.

I race through the house and to my room. I say a silent prayer to my grandma for looking out for me once again. She'd probably think it was hilarious I'm sneaking around with do-gooders. Even all these years later, my dad holds a grudge toward those associated with the Hunter's Alliance, though he never told me why. Grandma kept me away from them, too.

No demon wants to hear that their kid likes hanging around humans and angels, other half species like myself, and other creatures like werewolves for that matter. Because most of the people I associate with belong to the Hunter's Alliance, Heaven's way of keeping demons in check. They aren't always on the best of terms with Dad, though things are a lot better than they used to be. My dad is so overprotective because there was once a time where the alliance would've never allowed him to raise me. Something about those Heaven-bound calls to my very soul, and Dad would flip out if he knew he could never change my mind about my purpose in life. I don't want to stay forever by his side as a demon's daughter, learning demonic affairs or whatever. I'm not sure what I want to do, really. More than that, though.

Dad slams the front door like he gets satisfaction throwing an angel out, and I tense. Quietly closing my bedroom door, I run to my bathroom, turn on my shower, and jump in with my clothes on and all.

My heart pounds in my ears, and I lean against the cool tiles, watching the water steam on my hot skin. My bedroom door creaks. I purposefully over tightened a screw in the hinge so I'd always know when it opened.

"Faith? You're barely in the shower?" Dad asks from outside the bathroom door.

I tilt my chin up, trying not to laugh. All my fear washes down the drain, and I do a silent victory dance under the stream. Thank God I didn't get caught.

"I overslept," I call. "I'll be out in a minute."

"I'm waiting."

Ugh. The last thing I need to do is test a demon's patience. "Seriously?"

"Five minutes. I'll be in the hall. You know we don't have much time to spare."

I listen to him exit my room, and then I shrug out of my wet clothes and leave them in the shower to take care of later. I towel off, grab my robe from my hook, and shrug into it to meet Dad in the hall.

Dad stands with his arms crossed over his sophisticated suit. I can't think of many times he wasn't dressed for a formal affair, but it fits him. Pieces of the shattered mirror sparkle under his dress shoes, and I scrunch my face, pretending to have no idea what had happened.

"Who broke the mirror?" I ask. I peer past him, like I'm trying to see if anyone is behind him, but I know no one is there.

Dad shifts on his feet, crushing the glass into the floor runner. "Did you have any idea that a Demon Watcher was in our home?"

I blink, and then nod. I don't know why I do it, but something deep within me screams to take the blame, because whoever that angel was saved me from a night of yelling about the importance of safety and obeying the rules.

"It's rude to make people wait outside," I say, pressing my lips together.

"Rude?" Dad curls his fingers into fists, and I'm sure his true body—his scary demonic form—will rip through his human façade at any second. "Rude is coming into my home unannounced, playing on my daughter's annoyingly good grace, all before he knew I was even home. Now, that's rude, Faith."

"I—"

"Raphael? Your front door was wide open." A light, feminine voice hums through the air, and the tap of heels on tiles draws both our attentions toward the end of the hall. "You know, any demon hunter could just waltz right in, wearing something wickedly beautiful she found on her doorstep at dawn..."

The anger flashing over Dad's face vanishes, and a smile crosses his lips, a look of devilish desire lighting his handsome features. If I wasn't so relieved for the welcomed interference, I might gag a little.

Cadence Dubois, one of the few hunters from the Hunter's Alliance who doesn't mind hanging around demons, strolls into the hallway, wearing a sizzling ruby red, floor length gown with cutouts running up her sides to reveal slits of her skin. Her almost black hair shines with hints of red in the overhead light, and her honey eyes crinkle in the corners as she beams a smile.

"Hey, Faith. You look like you could use some help getting ready," she says, nodding to me with a wink. She knows I never stay home, and I bet she heard my dad yelling. Only the brave would interrupt a demon's wrath. Though she's not an angel, or any creature for that matter, I swear she can summon divine intervention. She turns to Dad. "Hey, you. Don't you look handsome."

I smirk, hearing the thrum of Dad's heartbeat pick up pace. He's such a hypocrite for wanting me to stay away from those associated with the Hunter's Alliance when he can't even manage to do so himself. Demons are known for their charm, for their ability to corrupt souls, and desire for power, but something about Cadence always has Dad on his best behavior. If it were possible, he'd have sprouted angelic wings by now.

Dad opens his arms, pulling Cadence to him. "There's no being in this entire universe whose beauty is comparable to yours, my little huntress."

Boy, he's laying on the charm thick.

Cadence giggles, flashing her perfect smile. "Keep sweet talking me like that, and I might hand you my soul one of these days."

Dad waggles his eyebrows, leans in, and kisses her. "I knew there was still hope for me," he whispers against her lips.

"God, please make them stop," I whisper.

Dad narrows his eyes at me. "Watch your language, Faith. There's enough divine interruption, annoyances, and infuriating threats around here that you don't have to pray for more."

Cadence tilts her head back and laughs, her melodic voice so sweet to my ears there's really no surprise why my dad likes her. "I'll talk to the watchers and see if they'll ease back. They should know by now that I can handle myself...and you."

I close my eyes and pout my bottom lip. It takes everything in me not to whisper another prayer. "I should really get ready," I say, taking a step back toward my room.

Cadence finally pulls away from Dad. "I'll help you." She turns to Dad. "There's still someone waiting for you outside."

Dad huffs. "And?"

Cadence loops her arm through mine and pulls me toward my bedroom door. "Just be nice."

Another sigh on Dad's part. "Only because you asked."

He stomps away and down the hall, crunching the broken mirror as he goes. Cadence doesn't say anything until she shuts my door and flips my music back on. Dad and I made a deal never to listen in on each other, and if he's ever done so before, he's never said something, but Cadence knows how demons work, even if she likes my dad. It never hurts to be careful.

"I don't want to have to be this person," Cadence whispers in my ear. "But I need to tell you that you're getting reckless. I didn't encourage you to get out more to endanger others."

I frown. "If you think my dad is so dangerous then why are you with him?"

She raises an eyebrow. "You really want me to get into this, Faith? All of that is beside the point. I'm not the one hiding the fact that I spend my days running with wolves, flying with nephilim, and secretly hiding bottles of holy water under my bed."

"You have a flask of it on your leg," I say, pointing at the slit in her gown.

"And your dad had it engraved." Cadence presses her ruby red lips together for a moment in thought. "All I'm saying is that maybe you should just tell him that you're interested in the alliance and your family history. He might surprise you."

"He won't understand."

She shrugs. "You'd rather risk him accidentally finding out?"

"He won't."

Cadence messes with a medallion on her neck, a rainbow stone infused with ancient witch magic to protect her from demonic power and charm. It's a necklace so rare that Dad's only seen another one like it once, though that one is long gone he swears.

Cadence shakes her head, her dark ruby, almost black hair, appearing completely black in my low lights. She crosses the room to shut off my music. "Okay. Just keep me out of it...unless you need someone to intervene. I like a good demon fight, especially with your dad."

"Oh, God," I say.

Cadence laughs, strolling to my closet to pull out the gown she helped me pick out for tonight over a month ago. Dad only ever allows me to leave during the day with Cadence and not all the time. He has to be in an exceptionally good mood, because most of the time, he pays for someone to bring the clothes to me. We have staff for everything, and some aren't even corrupted souls who made bargains. It's a hard habit for my dad to break, but as long as he doesn't start collecting the souls of the dead, the angelic army leaves him alone.

Screams ring through the air, and Cadence and I glance at each other. Something thuds against my window, and the hum that comes with angelic light buzzes in my ear. I race to my curtains, fling them open, and catch sight of black wings stretched across my window, blocking the view of my front yard.

Cadence curses, already running across my room, fast even in the tallest stilettos I've ever seen. Ruby light swirls within my dad's hands as he aims it at the angel pressed to the unbreakable glass. The angel's heart races as fast as mine.

"Dad!" I yell.

A giant crown of sharp, inky, bone-like horns burst through Dad's forehead, his true body revealing itself, stealing away his human façade. His blue eyes flash orange in the outside light, a snarl crossing his lips, revealing sharp teeth. He pulls back his arm, ready to throw his demonic power at the angel, and all I can do is scream.

He freezes.

"Raphael!" Cadence yells.

The angel takes the opportunity to drop to the ground. Bending his knees, he launches into the air. Dad turns toward Cadence, his roars echoing through the air. Fear slices through my stomach and up to my heart.

She raises her hands up, taking a step back. "Rein it in, Raphael. Don't think I won't dagger you."

Dad raises his hands, a deep red and orange orb flowing in his hands.

I hold my breath, wishing I had followed Cadence out.

"Raphael..." Cadence's soft voice says his name like a whispered prayer, like she's hoping to remind him of reason when Hell digs its evilness into his very being.

But demons can't be reasoned with, not like this. Not in moments where their true bodies display the Hell in their veins.

"Cadence, run!" I scream, banging on the window. "Run!"

But it's too late.

Hell has won the constant battle my dad faces, and Cadence is about to pay.

STRANGE ANGEL

DAD RELEASES THE demonic power, sending it through the air. Cadence drops to the ground, though the power flies high above her and into the night sky. She was never my dad's target. He was aiming toward Heaven's army.

Bright light erupts through the air, shining so brightly that I turn away, squeezing my eyes shut. Tears burn from my lids, dripping down my cheeks in warm trails on my skin. My heart rams so hard against my ribs, I'm sure some will crack from the force.

Devoted

The sound of Dad's yells rings through my ears, and I wish I could make the world stop. I inhale and exhale, covering my ears, keeping my eyes closed, waiting for the battle to end. This is the first time in months Dad has unleashed his true body, the last time being about a demon who threatened me—never an angel.

There's been a truce in place since I was young and new to the demonic world. I'll never forget the day it happened. How a daughter of a demon rose up to fight with Heaven's army to bring back balance in the universe. Because when the balance is at risk, so is the world. The universe even.

Now, seeing my dad like this in all his demonic glory, it scares me more than it should. Not because he's a demon, but because I'm reminded how fragile my whole life is. Heaven won't allow another demon to get out of hand again, including my dad, and I can't stand the thought of something happening to him because he's so tied to his demonic nature, especially with angels around.

My eyelids turn from bright red to dark, the light disappearing with the sound of whooshing wings. Shaking my head, I pull myself together to run outside. Cadence kneels next to my dad, resting her hand between his shoulders. He covers his face with his hands, his blackened skin smoldering from the heavenly light.

"Dad, are you okay? What happened?" I ask. Cadence stands up and puts space between us. I wrap my arms around my dad's shoulders, catching the sound of a shudder on his breath.

"I lost my temper," he says, heaving another breath.

"But why? Angels don't usually get to you like that," I say.

"It's nothing," he says, pulling himself together. His horns retract and disappear into his skin, though the once flawless façade is now damaged with blisters. His suit doesn't fare better, the sleeve torn and still smoldering from his own power.

"You're lying—"

"Faith," Cadence says from behind me. "Why don't you come back inside with me? You can't go to the party in a bathrobe, and I need to try to clean up my dress."

Dad forces a smile to me, giving Cadence an indecipherable look. "Cadence is right. I need to clean up as well."

And like that, he cuts off all my questions. An ounce of guilt pokes at the back of my mind. I shouldn't be so annoyed that he's not telling me everything, because I'm not exactly honest, either, but there was something different about tonight. About that angel. Something I don't like. I didn't get a chance to see the angel's face, but by the looks of his wings, I know he ranks high. And that can never be good.

I sigh, getting to my feet. Dad takes my outstretched hand, allowing me to help him stand. He cracks his neck, adjusts his suit jacket, and smiles—what almost felt like vulnerability to me now shifted back into his stone cold demeanor.

"Are you sure you want to go tonight?" I ask, not really in the mood to face a bunch of demons and angels.

"We can't miss it, Faith," Dad says. "It's important. Everyone's gathered."

"Okay, whatever you say. I still don't get celebrating a demon's birthday. You guys don't even age."

Cadence releases a small groan, one I'm sure I wouldn't have heard had I not been listening for the sounds of nearby angels circling. I'm pretty sure she didn't want that kind of reminder. I don't like to think about it either. "Oh, come on. You can't question a reason to party."

Dad smirks. "She's right, Faith. And after being blasted with Heaven's light, I could use some entertainment. You don't want to stay home all by yourself, do you?"

Actually... Instead of arguing, I bob my head. "Fine, okay. But I get to socialize with whomever I want. I don't think I can handle another minute of you two."

Dad motions me and Cadence to the house. "It's a deal."

Music pulsates through the open door of the Morningstar club, even through the limo window. A valet helps me out first, and I stand and wait for Cadence and Dad to follow. Whispers sound through the air. People of the angelic and demonic varieties mixed with very few hunters point out the marring on Dad's usually handsome face.

I stiffen, glaring at the closest couple—a demon woman with a man who obviously sold his soul to her. For what? Could be anything. He leers at Dad before directing his eyes to me. The woman finds Dad's holy disfigurement amusing, taking pleasure that even a demon of his power found himself on the receiving end of an avenging angel. If only I knew why.

I ignite a burst of Hell power between my fingers, my demonic instincts kicking in. It wouldn't be the first time I've stood up for Dad. Just because he carries the brand of an angel until he exits the earth realm to go into the daylight realm doesn't mean he's weak. All it means is he was caught off guard or chose his battle wisely.

A strong hand pinches my shoulder. "No, Faith. Let Marzala have her laugh tonight." Dad doesn't let go until I extinguish the blood red orb between my hands.

If it wasn't for the hum of familiar voices coming from within the Morningstar, I'm not sure I'd listen to Dad. At events involving demons, I can never let my guard down or show any weakness. If I do, my own life could end in the hands of another demon—a reality I've lived with for years. Even if a demon's job entails ushering bad souls to Hell, there's a whole lot more happening on earth that they steal what they can get their hands on—including killing competition.

Dad nudges me to walk in front of him and Cadence, and I ignore the demon-tainted bouncer as I pass by. A shudder shakes down my back, sensing the evil lacing and knotting his soul like a sixth sense that I carry around. The instinct inside of me is what makes me want to constantly surround myself with people in good grace. Maybe it's my soul's way of coping with my demonic blood.

"Cadence!" A feminine voice sounds through the air, traveling through the hum of music and crowd gathering on the dance floor. A sparkle of blue light zaps above us, and an angel-ic-looking demon nearly plows through the crowd, which can't part away fast enough. "You're late!"

Cami Anders pulls Cadence into a hug, rocking her friend back and forth. Her soft, dark curly hair cascades down her back, always a wild mass of shimmering hair I wish I had. A towering boy steps up behind her, casting a shadow over me, and I lift my hand and wave to her eternal lover, Evan. Both demons look my age, younger than Cadence, who's in her mid-twenties and Dad, who looks it. It's strange growing up while everyone around me stays the same, but that's just the life of a half human in the demonic world.

Cami releases Cadence, stepping a foot back and directly into Evan's arms. I smirk at her laced up boots under her daring white gown, glittering with a crystal bodice. Cami's bright emerald eyes catch the light from the strobes, flashing them like mirrors.

She smiles at me, and then her expression morphs into anger the second she lays her eyes on Dad. Even though her sudden rage isn't directed at either of us, I can't stop my feet from pushing me back. Dad tilts his head, directing her to follow him. Before I can tag along, a breeze picks up my blond hair from my neck, the whooshing of wings blowing from behind me to grab my attention. I spin on my feet.

"Hey, little devil girl, where you going?"

A smile lights my face, and I throw my arms around my favorite angel, one who has never looked down on me just for my existence. "Dylan! Where have you been lately? You still owe me for the lunch you bailed on two weeks ago." I pull away, summoning power between my fingers. "I should blast you, you know."

He chuckles, igniting heavenly light between his palms. "Bring it on." Dylan's power is all for show to me, and we both know it. Because my soul is firmly clinging onto good grace, all his power would ever do is leave star bursts in my eyes, maybe burn my hands a little if it comes into contact with my Hell power before I release it. My power on the other hand? It could leave him blistered like my father. I'd never actually use it on him, though.

I clap my hands together, extinguishing my power, a few stray bubbles scattering around me.

"Faith, seriously?" A gentle hand ruffles my hair before my second favorite angel appears into view out of nowhere. Zach shakes the hem of his neon green T-shirt with a happy face wearing sunglasses screen printed on the front of it. Tiny holes sizzle across the fabric, sending tendrils of smoke in the air. "This was my last shirt like this."

I raise my hands. "Well, you're better off without it."

Dylan releases a loud laugh, and fire bursts in my cheeks, my blush trailing down my neck. Sure, Zach is hot—Dylan, too, for that matter—but if Dad ever caught me checking these two out, I'd never hear the end of it. I'd be grounded. Plus, it's just not like that between us. They're more like guardians, big brothers, than anything.

I cover my face with a hand. "I meant it was ugly."

"Ouch, Faith," Zach says, pressing his hand to his chest, faking offense. "And to think I have a matching one in your size set aside for Christmas."

I roll my eyes. "I did need some clothes for—" Snapping my mouth shut, I turn to peer around the club for Dad. I catch sight of him in the VIP lounge with Cadence on his lap and Cami sitting next to him, all three deep in conversation while Evan keeps everyone else away with a single hard glance. I even want to stay away from the four of them with how intimidating they look. No wonder they run the entire demonic world. It helps that even though Cami is a demon, she has all of Heaven on her side. And Dad of course. He'll admit he's self absorbed enough to follow the most powerful demon on earth to guarantee his eternity here and not in Hell. But I think over the years it has turned into more than that. He'd never admit it to anyone, though.

"They can't hear you," Dylan says, standing close enough that his black wings graze my bare shoulder. They're identical to the ones belonging to the angel who blasted Dad earlier and the same as Zach's too, which means whatever angel came around holds a high position in the angelic army.

"Dad told you guys to shield me, didn't he?" I ask. As much as it pains my dad to ask for help from an angel, my well-being and safety is always his top priority. Bringing me to Cami's twenty-first birthday is high on the danger meter, because other demons are swarming, bowing down or aching to take the chance to test the power of the reigning demon queen.

"Don't get mad at us," Dylan says. "We know how badass you are."

I groan. "Well, you don't have to listen. I can't even social-ize in your shield, except with—" I catch sight of an attractive, beautiful even, angel across the room, standing near Dad. Dressed in jeans and a T-shirt, he gazes around the club, his arms crossed, almost like he's waiting for the perfect moment.

I've never seen the angel before in my life, and there are a lot who come and go, relaying messages to Dad about demons reported for getting out of control, normal things he handles not only to maintain his power, but to keep himself off Heav-en's bad side. It's how he's allowed to keep me without much protest, though I'd fight anyone who tried to take me away.

"Faith?" Zach asks, snapping his finger at me.

I turn toward him for a second and then back to the angel. The angel's gaze falls on me, and a smile curls up the corner of his pouty lips. I find myself smiling back. I can't help it. What else am I supposed to do when a gorgeous being does something to make my heart race in a good way, something that rarely happens.

I get lost in a staring match, losing myself in the angel's dark brown eyes, eyes like mocha but something bright glows within them. The angel straightens his shoulders, the muscles on his arms rippling. His wings expand out on his back, stretch-ing out a few feet on both sides of him, and the second the red strobe light bounces off his raven-black feathers, something dark sneaks up into my heart.

It's him.

It's the angel who attacked Dad outside our home. The one I thought gave me a miracle earlier. But maybe my not being home was the miracle. Because he was in my room. Now that I think about it, he was the one to shut off my music.

A hand waves in front of my face, and I reach up and snatch it, twisting Zach's arm out of my way. He jerks back, surprised by my move, and both he and Dylan take a step back. The angel near Dad raises his eyebrows, and I summon power into my fingers.

He does the same, igniting angelic light like it'll somehow protect him from me.

But then, he turns toward my father, standing behind him, unseen by all of the demons and Cadence, too. But I see him, and all he makes me see is red.

My body kicks into action, and I rush toward the crowded dance floor, hitting demons along the way, breaking the shield created for me to make me invisible. My power touches the back of an unsuspecting mid-level demon, one barely in control of his human façade, and he releases a guttural scream through the club and over the music. He swings out his too long arm, wrapping it around my shoulders, and yanks me to him. His sharp black teeth snap in my face, but with my arms bound to my sides, there's nothing I can do.

A blast of brilliant blue electricity erupts around the de-mon, sending his sagging skin sizzling. He explodes in a waterfall of disgusting slime, smelling of rotting eggs. I slip across the dance floor and fall right in the middle of the crowd of gathering demons.

A whip-like tentacle slaps across my arm, slashing open my skin. The wound stings, and I automatically throw my demonic power out, hitting a terrifying woman with hair made of long rope-like appendages that move as a mass all together, sharp spikes at the ends perfect for impaling. My gel-like power slides over her chest, burning through the fabric of her midnight gown, revealing a chest full of human-like eyes that widen and squeeze shut, burning under the residue left by my acidic blast.

The demonic woman wails, thrashing her head, sending her rope-hair toward me. Hands grab under my arms, yanking me back, and black wings surround me, heavenly light shielding me from the onslaught of riled up demons.

I push away the inky feathers from my face, catching sight of Dad, Cami, and Evan igniting their demonic powers. Cadence is nowhere to be seen, and the majority of the demons automatically stand down to the command of their presence.

But there's always one.

A demon, the same woman from the parking lot, the woman who laughed and mocked Dad's angelic branding, saunters through the crowd, her eyes locked on Dad's back. She summons green fire in her palms, setting her sharp features aglow. Everyone's eyes are on the wailing demon now rolling on the floor in all her demonic glory that they don't see the woman—Marzala—closing in.

"Princess!" Zach calls from across the room. I spot Dylan next to him, and I freeze. I thought I was in the arms of one of them. But clearly, some strange angel has decided to pull me from the fray of things.

Without thinking, I thrust my ruby orb of power as hard as I can from my spot on the floor. It hits Marzala directly in the chest, the force eating straight through her and to her heart. She explodes feet away from Dad and Cami, spraying them in an arc of green and black goo.

Cami claps her hands once, sending a shudder through the whole room. Most of the demons fall to the ground with her release of power. I'd have been down with the rest of them had I not already been lying on the floor.

She opens her hands to clap again, and the angel tightens his hold on me, pulling me from the ground.

"We need to leave," he says, gripping my arm.

I try to pull away. "Let me go. I'm fine."

"Don't be difficult, Demon Spawn," he says, holding me against his taut, muscular chest.

I ignite power in my hand, not giving him a choice but to let me go. I move toward Dad, suddenly needing to get far from the angel and back into the safety of Dad's shadow.

Cami claps again, and I fall to the floor, screaming out.

"Faith!" Dad yells.

But it's too late.

A huge, towering demon takes advantage of my sudden weakness and rolls on top of me. Pressing his rock like hands over my heart, the demon in his grotesque true body leers at me. Bright light flashes in my eyes, sending a wave of pure warmth over me, stealing all my senses away.

And then I feel nothing.

I am nothing.

I never expected my mortal life to end like this. Bathed in pure white light, I can feel the goodness of heaven. I should be relieved. Happy even. But with Heaven, it means I'll never see Dad again.

I didn't even get to say goodbye.

3

DEMON'S DAUGHTER

I OPEN MY eyes to vivid, sparkling clouds. Glittering puffs dance around me, reflecting light from the golden sun above. The scent of cherry blossom wafts through the air, and the soft sound of an angel's wings is followed by a light breeze that plays with my blond hair.

It's exactly how I imagined Heaven to be—all beauty and light, love and peace—but a part of me feels utterly empty.

"You're okay, Faith. It's okay," a masculine voice says from behind me. The soft tenor hum of his voice wraps around me, coaxing me like I'm a frightened animal.

I spin to face the angel. His inky wings stretch out behind him. Though dark in color, the feathers shine with an ethereal light like it comes from within. I frown, crossing my arms over my chest. If joining Heaven means I have to hang out with the angel who started this mess, I'd rather take my chances with Uncle Lucifer.

"This is not okay!" I yell, trying to summon power that doesn't come. Have I been stripped of all my demonic ways? I could see how allowing such a thing would cause Heaven problems. "I'm dead. Do you know what that means?"

He frowns. "I—"

"I didn't even get to say goodbye to my dad. I can't believe you stole my soul without giving him the chance. He didn't deserve that. You're a monster! Get away from me." Tears burst from my eyes, and I fall to my knees and sob into my hands.

"Grandma?" I ask, pulling in on myself. "Please, come for me. It should've been you to greet me."

A gentle hand touches my shoulder. "Faith, Lenora isn't here."

I snap my head up, my eyes wide. "What?" My shrill voice rips through the air. "You mean she's in..." I can't even think of the other place.

The angel cringes, shaking his head. "No, no, no. She's fine. She's at peace." The feathers on his wings ruffle, and he kneels down next to me, though I try to scoot away. "I'm sorry. I'm messing this up. This wasn't the introduction I had in mind, but Raphael, he's—"

"Don't talk about my dad like you know him. You hurt him, and then you had to go and do this? What kind of angel are you anyway?"

"A Demon Watcher," he answers, like I wasn't asking a rhetorical question, trying to belittle his supposed good morals.

"I've never seen you before, and I know all the angels who come around," I say.

"I hadn't intended on revealing myself today, but I heard your prayer and thought you could use some help," he says. "And for your information, I didn't hurt him."

I frown. "You used Heaven's light on him."

He shakes his head. "It wasn't me. You think I'd actually wait outside after his demonic outburst in the hallway? I shielded myself and returned inside. And you know what? Cadence is right, Demon Spawn. You're getting reckless. That's twice tonight I've offered my divine intervention."

My mouth falls agape. "You're twisting this on me? You were supposed to be watching my dad. And so you know, I don't need your divine intervention. I need you to just do whatever it is you're going to do to my soul so I can—" I heave a breath. "I don't even know." Tears burst from my eyes again as I break down. I can't help it. It's a good thing I'm here and not in a room full of demons, because they'd kill me all over again for showing such weakness.

Strong arms wrap around my shoulders, and black wings hide my view of the shimmering rainbow world around us. My heart picks up pace, the angel's purity washing over my soul, dipping me in every positive emotion imaginable. My tears dry, and my tense muscles relax. I think I'm about to enter Heaven at any second, but the angel releases me and smiles.

"That's much better. Are you okay now?" he asks.

I rub my hands over my sticky cheeks. "What did you do to me?"

"Your soul was in need of a little light," he says.

Oh, God. I don't need light. I need my dad. I need to be alive. "Who do you think you are to do that?"

"I'm Ezekiel."

I sigh. "You can't just mess with my soul."

"I—" he pauses. "Oh."

"You know what? It doesn't matter. Just do whatever it is you're going to do."

He frowns, his mocha eyes shining over like I've offended him by scolding him for trying to help. But I don't need this right now. I don't need divine intervention to steal away everything dark within me that makes me who I am. I'm a demon's daughter after all.

"I thought we could stay here a little longer. It's more pleasant than—"

"Ezekiel," I say, cutting him off. His words stir something within me, igniting fire in my soul. "I'm not dead, am I?"

"Of course not," he says. "I made sure of it. What kind of watcher would I be if I let the demons have you?"

I release a loud yell, clenching my fingers. "Take me back. Now!"

His giant wings unfurl, cutting through the rainbow mist in the air. They flap forward, wrapping around me, and the world turns into nothing but light before going dark.

"Faith? Faith, can you hear me?" It's Dad. "Faith, wake up."

I snap my eyes open, staring up at the look of concern sweeping across Dad's blistered face. Red strobe lights dance behind him, shadowing him in a blood-red glow, sharpening his strong features. His white dress shirt is covered in demon blood and guts, and demonic residue slickens his blond hair back.

"What has gotten into you?" he asks, folding his arms, his worry morphing into anger now that he realizes I'm going to be okay. "You nearly started a demonic war in here, throwing around your power. This was supposed to be fun, not a power play."

I groan, sitting up. The quiet club is nearly empty, the dance floor now a gory mess. I search the room for signs of Dad's Demon Watcher, but Ezekiel is nowhere to be found. Coward. I'm sure he hasn't left, but I know he's hiding behind his own shield.

I swallow, trying to find the words to explain myself. "I thought you were under attack," I manage to say.

The firelight in Dad's eyes fizzles out. "You were protecting me?"

I nod.

He sighs and offers me his hand. "You have no need to protect me, Faith. Demons can try their best, but I'm not going anywhere—but you…" His voice trails off. He's probably think-ing about my mortality just like I was. "I can't lose you. Not yet. Never if you'd let—"

I throw my arms around him, cutting him off. "Stop. I don't want to think about it. I thought I was dead right now, and as much as I want to think of coming up with an alternative plan to my existence, this is how it's supposed to be."

Tilting his head to the side, he stares at me so intently that I know in this moment he's looking past me and to my soul. He sucks in a breath, a leer crossing his face. I cringe, pulling back at the sudden shift in his demeanor.

"Zach! Dylan!" Dad hollers, twisting to look at the group behind us.

Cami steps forward before the angels can even move. Tears blur my eyes at the sight of her ruined gown. Stains run down the front of what used to be white fabric, and one of her straps hangs singed at her shoulder. Cadence on the other hand looks exactly as she did when we arrived.

"Which one of you touched my daughter's soul?" Dad ig-nites ruby energy in his hands, ready to try to throw it past Cami. Because Cami can absorb demonic power, she stands there, eyebrows raised at Dad's words, then shifts to peer over her own shoulder at the angels.

They both look at each other, expecting the other to admit fault and face Dad's wrath.

I reach out and grab Dad's hand. "It wasn't them."

Dad spins back to me. "What do you mean it wasn't them?

They were the ones watching you."

I shrug. "It was—" The words stick in my throat. I open and close my mouth, trying everything I can to spit out Ezekiel's name, but it doesn't come.

Dad throws his hands up. "Zachariel, you better get that watcher in check before I break his wings. He had no right to get near Faith. She's not a demon or Hell-bound."

Ezekiel pops up next to Zach, bringing his index finger to his lips. The lack of reaction from Dad proves the angel is shielding himself from the demons. He whispers something, keeping his eyes locked on mine. I wish angels weren't so hot. I keep getting distracted by him without realizing it.

Ezekiel disappears into thin air, though I know he hasn't left from his spot. Zach steps forward, moving around Cami to face Dad directly. All the others remain silent just watching the two of them, almost trying to anticipate what'll happen next.

Sneaking around Dad, I close the distance to Dylan. He smirks at me, running his hand over his mop of chocolate curls falling onto his forehead. I grin right back at him, but instead of saying anything, I swing my arm out and punch the air next to him where Ezekiel was last.

My knuckles collide into something hard, like I've just punched a steel door, and Ezekiel materializes in front of me. He doesn't flinch or groan or anything. He doesn't even react to the force of my punch. But damn it if my hand isn't throbbing now.

I clutch my hurt hand in the other, rubbing my fingers

over my aching knuckles. "What the Hell are you made out of?" I ask, stepping closer faster than the angel can react. I grab a fistful of his T-shirt and lift up the hem, revealing a perfectly sculpted set of abs. I'm almost convinced he's a statue come to life. Zach and Dylan are gorgeous, but they're not flawless, perfect beings. This guy though? He's—whoa.

"Heaven," he says, answering me like I'm stupid for asking such a question.

I blink, words lost to me. He's serious.

Heat crawls up from my chest to my cheeks. It takes me a moment to realize I'm still holding the angel's shirt, staring at his abs like they're the best thing I've ever seen, my demon blood pumping so fast and hot and out of control through my veins that it takes Dylan gently kicking my foot to get me to put distance between me and Ezekiel. If Dad hears my body's automatic reaction to this angel, I'll surely be locked away for the rest of my mortal life and then some.

"I'll talk to him, Raphael. It was all a misunderstanding. He thought what he was doing was right. Faith's soul was—"

I spin around to face Zach and Dad behind me. I can't see Dad's face, but I'm sure he'd pulverize Zach with a stare if it were possible.

"Faith's soul is off limits," Dad repeats. "It's none of any of your or Heaven's concern. Do you understand? If Faith shifts, that's her choice, and I will not allow you to intervene."

Zach nods. "Unless she asks."

Dad scowls. "She won't."

Now so full of fury, Dad peers around the room once more before pushing past Zach to me. He locks his fingers around mine, pulling me toward the exit. I stumble to keep up, looking behind me as the others watch me go. I'm so embarrassed I'm being dragged away like a screaming toddler, that tears burn my eyes.

Cami holds Cadence's hand, stopping her from following.

Before we reach the door, I yank from Dad and turn to face them again. "Cami," I say. "I'm really sorry about your dress...and your whole night."

She shrugs, offering me a smile. "Hey, it wouldn't be a party if I didn't leave in a disgusting gown, and my night isn't ruined. You didn't think I actually wanted to spend my birthday in a club full of demons, did you?"

Her words make me feel a teensy bit better.

"Raphael," Cami calls out to Dad. "You should stay."

He pauses for a moment in consideration. "My apologies, Cami. Please understand why I can't. I'll see you at sunrise."

Cami only nods without arguing.

Dad drags me from the club, grumbling about the angelic army under his breath, loud enough for me to hear because I'm concentrating on my surroundings. He ushers me to the limo, opening the door faster than the driver can attempt to get out.

The last thing I hear before Dad slams it shut is the sound of an angel's wings.

It's going to be a long night.

TROUBLE

A KNOCK SOUNDS on my door, jerking me awake, and Dad opens it a crack. "I have ten minutes before I must go, Faith."

I rub the sleep from my eyes. After leaving the club, Dad wanted to spend a quiet night at home for the first time in months. We sat in front of the TV, zoned out, not really saying anything to each other. Something about tonight, about the events with the demons and the angels, had Dad lost in his thoughts, acting out of character, but he refused to talk about it. He never does. So, I guess my day of staying out finally caught up to me and I had fallen asleep.

I roll off my bed, still wearing my dress. "You should have woken me up."

The door cracks open wider, and I catch sight of a frown crossing Dad's face before it disappears into an emotionless façade. "You were tired, and your presence was enough to keep me company. I sometimes wish we had more nights like this."

"You do?" I ask. It's not often Dad cracks his powerful armor to let me in, and I won't miss the opportunity to see past the Hell he claims he's made of. "I thought you liked a good party?"

"That wasn't a good party," he says.

He makes a point. Tons of demons would disagree, but Dad is unlike most demons. He has me to chain him to humanity, to see things outside himself, to really see the world as it is. "I'm sorry again. I just—you won't tell me what's going on, and after the attack, I—I know it wasn't about that angel showing up in our house. Are you in some sort of trouble? You didn't break another—"

He sighs, cutting me off. "I don't want you to worry about my personal matters. You are far too young to carry the weight of my eternity with you."

"And you're too stubborn to realize I'm not a child. I'm plenty capable of being here for you as much as you're here for me," I say.

A smile curls his lips, and he winces, his blistered cheek still bothering him. At least he'll heal come dawn when he's taken from me. "I sometimes wonder if you're not part nephilim. Do we need to work on darkening the lightness of your heart? You know, most demi-demons try to shove blessed daggers through their demon dads at your age."

I laugh, knowing full well from my lack of wings and angelic light that I'm not half angel. "If I'm a nephilim, then that'd make you an angel, and we both know there's hellfire in your eyes."

"You can thank your mom for that," he says, catching me off guard. "I do."

I open my mouth to ask him more, to try to rip open the crack in the steel wall he barricades himself in so I can know everything that makes Dad who he is, but a flash of light beams through the window behind me.

"Until tonight," Dad says, the weight of his fingers disappearing from mine with the rest of him, leaving me alone in our beach fortress.

Sighing, I glance around my empty room. Come nightfall, Dad will have rejuvenated himself and returned to the devilish man he usually is. I glare at the bright sunshine rising from the east, wishing the sun would rewind to give me a few extra hours of darkness.

I guess that kind of miracle is too much to ask for.

I turn to my bed, considering falling back asleep, but my phone buzzes from my night table. Crossing the room, I see an unknown text message pop up on the screen.

Survive the night? Is all the message says, and without having to ask, I know Aria's been waiting for the sun to rise to talk to me. It's the same as every day.

I quickly text back, *Barely.*

You need breakfast. Come over.

Be there in ten.

You have five, she replies.

Rolling my eyes, I set my phone down and head to my bathroom to get ready. Knowing Aria, if I'm not there fast enough, she'll show up at my door, no matter how often I tell her not to. If I wasn't so good about hiding evidence, Dad would definitely know a werewolf has been trespassing, even if she was invited by me.

I change from my gown into jeans and a T-shirt and step into my untied boots, not bothering to lace them up. I head through our fortress to the back door that'll lead me to the beach. A gust of wind plays with my hair, coming out of nowhere, and I freeze, concentrating on listening.

I hear feathers ruffle together before I feel a cool breeze again. A ruby red orb materializes between my fingers, the demonic power an instinctual reaction to intruders, even those of the angelic variety. *Especially* those of the angelic variety who go around trying to fix souls that aren't tainted or broken.

"I thought only demons were gluttons for punishment," I say, spinning around to face Ezekiel. I push away the noise that comes with him standing so closely, the whisper of his wings moving, the sound of his heart beating, even how his shirt sounds rubbing against his skin as he flexes his arms.

His black wings disappear on his back, and he hovers feet away, his hands clutching a small bouquet of blush colored roses. "Blast me if you must, but can I at least give you these first?"

What the? Is this angel for real? "I thought romancing demons was against Heaven's rules?"

His brows crinkle together. "You're only half."

"So, you are trying to sweep me off my feet with those scary wings of yours," I say. I hold my face completely emotionless. Ezekiel obviously isn't trying to seduce me or anything. He's an angel, basically purity incarnate. But it sure is fun to tease him.

"I—No, I wanted to apologize for last night," he says.

I smirk at him without taking the roses. "What for?"

He shifts on his feet, his boot squeaking on the tiles. He's wearing the same jeans and T-shirt from a few hours ago, but he still looks just as good as the first moment I saw him. And he's even cuter with the blush warming his face.

This is too easy and too much fun.

He inhales a small breath, his wings flashing for a split second before disappearing. "I was out of line for—"

"You saved my life," I say, cutting him off.

He clears his throat. "But I shouldn't have touched your soul."

"Is that why you're not interested in me? Because my soul? You think it's gross because I'm a demon, don't you?"

"Faith, I—"

"No, it's fine. Whatever. Dad would pluck every feather

from your wings if he knew that I thought you were hot," I say.

He freezes, staring at me with his mouth half opened. His wings flash again, and a gust of wind picks up my hair. He drops the bouquet of flowers on the floor.

I laugh. "Lighten up, Ezekiel. You're too fun to fluster."

He licks his lips, turning his gaze away from my stare, one I purposely try to lock him in. He sucks in another small breath, his heart picking up pace for the first time since showing himself. He turns his eyes back to me, a smile tugging at the serious line of his lips.

"You truly are the spawn of a demon." A second later, he disappears.

I grimace, releasing a small burst of power at the spot he was standing in. It hits the wall, crackling and burning the paint. Sighing, I cross the room, gather the roses into my hands, and bring them to my nose.

"There isn't anything wrong with being the spawn of a demon," I say into the soft petals.

"Not with a pretty soul like yours." Ezekiel whispers the words so quietly I'm not sure he intended for me to hear them.

A soft breeze brushes the hair from my shoulder, and my frown turns into a smile. I don't respond to his words, just keep the roses to my face to hide my expression. I should be annoyed. I should be angry even. But I've had time to let my demon blood cool off since my near death experience, and thinking back, he did help me from going into mental meltdown mode.

My phone chimes from my pocket, and I pull it out to glance at another text message from Aria. She's threatening to meet me halfway. I text her back and rush toward the door. I listen for a moment, just touching the handle, but I'm greeted only by the sound of the ceiling fan.

"You better not follow me," I call out, in case. "I'm not your demon to watch. This is supposed to be your downtime."

Still, no noise or response.

With one more look around, I shut the door behind me and step onto the beach. A black feather glides through the air, landing at my feet. I bend down, picking it up, watching it glow with an ethereal light in the bright morning sunshine.

I hide the evidence of Ezekiel's existence in my pocket instead of destroying it with my demonic power. Strolling away from my fortress, I smile up at the sky. "I mean it, Ezekiel."

Another feather glides to my feet.

I guess he doesn't take orders from a demi-demon.

I wish he would, though. Because for how good he is, I'm sure he's going to be a whole lot of trouble.

"Can you get him to show himself? I want—no I *need*—proof." Even though Aria doesn't say the words out loud, I can read her lips, hearing the whoosh of her breath forming the silent sentence.

I shrug. "Ezekiel?"

She scrunches her nose. "His name is Ezekiel?"

I smirk. "I know, right?" I like the name Ezekiel, but maybe I can annoy him enough to reveal himself again. It's not like we're in public or around the pack. No one would dare come into Aria's room without knocking. Not because she's scary or anything. It's because of me. I'm the daughter of the demon who had broken some of Aria's pack mates years ago before Cami had vanquished her Hell raising demonic father, stealing his power, and rose to be the most powerful demon with Dad as her right hand.

I hate even admitting this to myself now, but when I first moved in with Dad, I had no clue werewolves were people. I thought they were animals, and Dad made them into hellish guards. They were there for our protection. I was so naïve that I didn't question until I was shown otherwise.

Something like being broken into a hellhound, even if they can't fully remember it, stays with a person forever. So, I can't fault the Moonlight Shores pack for not welcoming me in with open arms. At least Joshua, Aria's uncle, is nice enough to let me hang out as long as I'm gone before sunset.

"Ezekiel?" Aria asks, getting up from her bed. "Can I call you Zeke?"

I turn over and lie flat on my back in the space she left behind. "You don't even know the guy, and you're giving him a nickname?"

"Well, yeah. I bet no one has ever done that. I bet he doesn't even have a last name," she says, her voice rising higher than a whisper.

A shadow falls over me, and I startle at the sudden appearance of Ezekiel standing over the bed, peering down at me. He brings his finger to his lips, asking me not to mention the fact that he's here, right next to me, just like I had expected.

"I don't think I like Zeke," he says, pressing his lips into a thin line.

Aria doesn't react, so I know he's chosen now to only bother me.

I grin, glancing from the angel to my best friend as she slowly moves through her room, waving her arms. Ezekiel expands his wings out, stretching them from one wall to the other, and then he surprises me by shifting to sit on the bed. It doesn't even move under his weight.

I scramble to sit up and scoot away to lean my back on the wall. "I think he would love being called Zeke," I say to Aria.

"You think?" she asks.

Ezekiel frowns.

"Absolutely."

"What about a last name, Zeke? I can come up with a great one," Aria says, like she can see the invisible angel, hear him even. Too bad she's staring at the wall and not me.

I open my mouth to respond, but Ezekiel reaches out and rests his hand on my bare foot. I pull my leg back and then kick him in the forearm. I cringe as pain radiates through my toes. Aria's basically staring at Ezekiel's clone, because I'm pretty sure the wall was built using the same materials as he was. There's no way he has blood and guts under his skin. Steel, rock, and cement fill up that muscular angelic body of his.

"What about..." Aria scratches her head, pushing her platinum hair back over her shoulder.

"My last name is October," Ezekiel says.

My nose crinkles. "October?"

Aria spins around to face me. "That's so ridiculous. I love it. The perfect last name for Zeke."

Ezekiel wags his eyebrows at me.

Someone bangs on the door, drawing Aria's attention away from me, and mine away from Ezekiel. He doesn't move from his spot on the bed, continuing to invade my personal space like he's never heard of the concept.

"Are you alone?" a masculine voice says from outside the door.

Before Aria can open her mouth to reply, her uncle pushes his way into the bedroom. I lift my hand to wave but notice the sudden confusion crossing Aria's face. She stares at the bed where I'm still leaning against the wall with Ezekiel in front of me.

He's shielding me from the werewolf pack leader.

Joshua glances from his niece to the window, before moving to stare at the ocean stretching out for miles. Lacing his fingers on the back of his head, he doesn't move or say anything, but a strange scent catches in the breeze from the ceiling fan and wafts to me. I tense, noticing sweat on Aria's uncle's neck, and I lean forward and listen. Joshua's heartbeat starts racing, his breathing nearly panting, a sound I never really hear outside of his wolf form.

"You're scaring me, Uncle Josh. Has something happened?" Aria asks, breaking my concentration on the pack leader's body language.

Another strange smell, almost like wet dirt, drifts my way. This time coming from Aria. I blink my eyes, clearing the sheen suddenly blurring my vision. The scent isn't normal. It's the scent of fear. Something I don't usually smell unless it's powerful. Because demons prey on fear, and since I'm half, it sets me off a little.

A cool hand slides into mine, and I draw my gaze away from the two werewolves. Ezekiel's playful expression from a moment ago morphs into steel, his eyes narrowing, his jaw clenching. The sudden change in everyone around me screams for me to leave. To get out of here. Because something is wrong.

"Uncle Josh," Aria asks again, her voice trembling.

He straightens his back and finally turns away from the window. "Robert and Jenny are missing."

While I don't know Aria's entire pack well, I have met both young wolves in passing over the years, though they've never given me a chance to get to know them. Very few werewolves acknowledge my existence, except come dusk when all of Hell starts to break loose from the sunlight realm.

The thing about being a demon's daughter is that I'm bound to Dad by blood. He can find me anywhere through our bond, and everyone knows that. Being here at sundown would lead him right to the pack. And that wouldn't fare well for me...or them...with the shaky, horrifying history between werewolves and demons.

"What do you mean?" Aria asks. "I saw them at sunrise."

"I don't want you to get freaked out, but Jenny's boss called, wondering where she was. She didn't show up for work. I sent Lola into town, and she—" Joshua closes his eyes for a second, sucking in a deep breath. "Robert's car was found abandoned, still running. She smelled a demon."

"But it's daytime."

He sighs. "That doesn't mean anything. Demons use humans all the time for daytime affairs."

"So, what now? What do we do? I can ask Faith to—"

Joshua shakes his head. "Absolutely not. I know Faith is your best friend, but if it came down to you or her dad, she'd pick Raphael. And until we know what happened or who took Jenny and Robert, you have to stay away from her. Got it?"

"But—"

"Aria, this isn't up for discussion. I've already called it into the Hunter's Alliance, and they're handling it from here. You must stay away from Faith until further notice. Call her and tell her you're leaving town for a few days and that you won't have your phone. Don't tell her what's going on."

Aria's worry morphs into anger, and she struts to the door and opens it. "If that's it, get out."

"Aria, please. You have to understand."

She points again. "Just leave, Uncle Josh."

With one more look around, the pack leader leaves, and Aria slams the door behind him. I tug my hand from Ezekiel, realizing I've been squeezing it so tightly I've left a red imprint on his fingers from my body heat and strength. All he does is move his fingers and leans back to watch me stand from the bed.

I reach out and grab Aria's shoulder.

She releases a small yelp before covering her mouth with her hand to muffle the sound. "What do we do?" she asks, throwing her arms around me. "Do you think he was right about demons?"

I frown. I hope not. Because if werewolves are missing and demons are involved, that could only mean one thing—someone is collecting a pack of hellhounds. And not just any demon. Someone as powerful as Dad.

"I don't know, Aria. But I'll try to find out, okay?" I say.

She nods. "I'm coming with you."

"Josh said you couldn't see me—"

She glares at me. "Is that angel still here?"

I glance at Ezekiel over my shoulder.

He shrugs.

Aria releases a loud gasp, her hand flying to her heart. Tears burst from her eyes, staining her cheeks in wet trails. Then she drops to her knees, full on sobbing.

"What the heck?" I ask, kneeling down to my best friend. "What happened? What's wrong?"

"I—I don't know," she says, her words catching in her throat. "I—I—Zeke's so—"

I tilt my head back and release a loud laugh. My eyes widen

at the noise, and I slap my hand over my mouth. I swivel and turn to Ezekiel. "Put your damn wings away. Aria's never seen a full-blooded angel before, and they're messing with her soul."

Ezekiel smirks at me, and his wings disappear. "I was only doing what you wanted, Faith." The way he says my name sends a whole lot of conflicting emotions through me. I almost wish he'd continue to mock me by calling me Demon Spawn. I hate the way I like how my name sounds on his soft voice.

Aria rubs the tears from her eyes, composing herself. She heaves a few shuddering breaths, glaring at me as I grin at her. Aria might be a tough werewolf, but when it comes to anything angelic, she's just as human as the rest of the world in her reaction to celestial beings. Where Ezekiel makes me nervous, she would of course start thanking Heaven for such an opportunity. She'll deny her desire to do so, though.

Scooping up a pillow from the floor next to her, she chucks it at Ezekiel, catching him off guard. It hits him in the face, smacking the grin off his mouth while sending white feathers from the stuffing through the air.

"Give me some warning next time before flashing your wings, Zeke October, or it'll be my fist instead of a pillow in your face," Aria says, getting to her feet.

I laugh. "She's not joking." Dad might protest if he knew I was best friends with a werewolf, but a comment like that would win him over. Punching angels might possibly be his second favorite pastime apart from punishing demons.

Ezekiel stares in surprise for a moment and then says,

"You've hung out with Demon Spawn for far too long, Wolf Pup."

I snort. "Are you sure you're not some demon in disguise, Ezekiel?"

He frowns, not getting that I'm insinuating he seems to like punishment like most demons out there. Dad loves the constant idea of a threat.

Aria cracks her knuckles next to me. "I'm going to let your nickname slide, but only because we need you."

I grimace. "We do?"

She nods. "He's sneaking us out of here."

BAD BLOOD

A FEW HOWLS sound from the living room with a variety of other noises like panting, whimpering, and the occasional growl. Because werewolves fear the night, they tend to remain in their animal form during the sunlight hours while they're in their den—home.

A wolf comes barreling into the hallway, and I swing my arm out and knock Aria into the wall, covering her body with mine. She growls under her breath, probably because I hurt her in the process, but she doesn't push me away.

"Damn it, Faith," she hisses. "What was that for?"

I pull away when the hallway is empty. "If someone touches us, it'll break the shield. You want the whole pack blocking our exit?"

Aria once told me the werewolf pack communicates telepathically while in their wolf forms. If one wolf sees us, we're screwed. Aria isn't afraid of her pack, and I don't like to think I am, but facing a mouth full of sharp teeth isn't how I wanted to spend my morning. Joshua might have forbidden Aria from hanging out with me for her protection, but I'm pretty sure he was thinking of mine as well. I might be half demon, but I'm still mortal.

"Zeke, you can't do better than that? I'm sure people run into you all the time," Aria says.

I glance at him. I'd like to know, too.

"They don't," he says simply, only responding to the second part of her question.

I thrust myself back without thinking, cringing as I'm about to slam into the bone-hard chest of the angel to prove him wrong, but the world flies by me. A second before I crash into the wood floor, a firm hand grips my wrists, catching me.

"I don't lie, Demon Spawn," Ezekiel says, righting me on my feet. He stands awfully close, my chest touching his every time I suck in a breath to calm my nerves from the surprise of failing in my plan to prove a point.

Aria clears her throat. "Can we just get out of here already? We only have so much daytime left."

Ezekiel doesn't make the first move, forcing me to pull myself together to stop getting trapped in his angelic stare.

I shake my head, sending blond hair into my face to obscure my view. "You better not be glimpsing my soul or something. That's private."

Ezekiel's eyebrows lower on his head, his jaw tightening, making him all pouty and brooding, like my words offended him. Guess he can't take a joke. "You demons and your way of sullying everything. I know Raphael got it into your head your soul is something you possess and it's an object to be played with, but that's because he lost anything resembling a soul. You are your soul, Faith, and I can't stop looking at you, even if it sometimes pains me."

This is the most Ezekiel's ever said to me, and his words hit me like a falling boulder from the sky. I hate to admit he's right.

I glower. "Don't you lecture me about souls, Demon Watcher." So much for coming up with an insulting name. God, I'm lame.

Aria growls. "Guys!"

It takes her stepping between me and Ezekiel and pulling me away to get me to drop it. She's right about not having any time to waste, but the presence of Ezekiel does something to me. My demon blood wants to fight back, to prove he's wrong about everything. That he knows nothing about demons or half demons. About my soul or me. And then there's my soul, basically trying to throw itself at him so he can shine all that heavenly light on me.

I huff, wishing more than anything I could portal to the

sunlight realm to visit with someone who understands. Cami knows what it's like to have Hell in her veins and Heaven in her soul, but she's more powerful. Immortal. And I don't know of any other demi-demons around like me. Dad keeps me far away from those left with the Hunter's Alliance.

Maybe I can call—

My cell phone rings from my pocket, pulling my attention from my thoughts. I peek at Cadence's pictures smiling at me and then peer over my shoulder at Ezekiel, wondering if he just granted me yet another miracle. He's going to start requesting something in return if that's the case. *He's an angel. He wouldn't.*

Aria drags me toward the back door, not giving me a chance to answer my phone. It's not until we're on the beach and out of the chaotic mansion that she releases a breath. Sunlight shines from above us, turning the sand into little specks of glitter every time we kick it up.

"Okay, Zeke. Let's fly," Aria says. "We can start in town first and then maybe Faith can figure things out."

Ezekiel crosses his arms over his chest without saying a word.

"There is no way I'm riding in the arms of an angel," I say. "He could purposely drop me."

"I'd ne—"

"Oh, come on," Aria says, cutting Ezekiel off. "I don't have a car. The bus will take too long, and I'm not walking."

"Well, I'm not flying," I say.

"I have to agree with Faith," Ezekiel says.

I turn to glare at him. "What? Am I too hot for you to handle? Scared I might corrupt you if you hold me too long?" Why did I say that? Now a million ideas on how to corrupt him fly through my mind.

He steps back, expanding his wings out, and I tense. Okay, maybe no corrupting. "I thought you didn't want to treat me like a form of transportation, Demon Spawn."

"Well, that's beside the point. The face you're making insinuates that you want nothing to do with me catching a ride in your arms."

He sighs. "Fine, if you want—"

"Of course I don't want to, but—"

"Heaven help me," Aria says.

I turn to her. "Stop asking for divine intervention. We don't need Ezekiel. I have an idea."

"You do?" Ezekiel and Aria say in unison.

She glares at him. "It better be a good one."

"Her ideas are never good," Ezekiel mutters.

I place my hands on my hips. "He's right. It's not good. It's awesome. My dad's not home until dusk, which means..."

Aria grins. "You evil, evil, demi-demon."

I turn toward Ezekiel. "Thanks for getting us out unnoticed, but you can leave now. I don't need your little halo head getting in my way."

"I don't have a—"

"Bye, Zeke October," Aria says, cutting him off.

Without arguing, Ezekiel bends his knees and launches into the air to disappear on the wind. Howls sound out behind me, and I grab Aria's hand. We run side by side on the beach, racing as fast as we both can. About halfway to my house, it turns into a competition, like most things between us, and Aria shoves me before taking off ahead.

I blast the sand in front of her, forcing her to jump, and she topples to the ground and somersaults. She nearly catches my leg as I hop over her. A pinprick of fear pokes at me, passing by a walkway that leads to the private street of my neighborhood, and I slow down to let Aria catch up.

This is the closest she's been to my house without actually going inside. And I'm not taking her in now.

"Meet me out front. I have to run inside and grab the keys," I say, pushing her toward the pathway, knowing if I don't, she'll argue she's not afraid to come with me. "My dad can't know you're here, especially with what's going on. I mean it."

She raises her arms. "Hey, I wasn't going to argue...much."

Shaking my head while rolling my eyes, I wait for her to pick up her pace to head to the front of my house. I jog to my back patio and open the door to go inside. Dad keeps the keys to his bright red Ferrari in the garage on a hook.

I've never actually driven his car, and the only reason I can drive is because Cadence taught me in her Jaguar, but it shouldn't be that hard to figure out. I think.

Rushing into the garage, I hit the button to open the door.

It hums to life, allowing sunshine to filter in. A silhouette stands just on the other side, hands on hips, and I snatch the keys from the hook.

"I told you to wait on the street, Aria," I say, hitting the key fob to disable the alarm, like anyone would dare steal a car from Dad or any demon for that matter. It's more for show than anything.

"She is," a familiar voice responds. "And I want you to put those keys back and go tell her goodbye. I talked to Joshua a bit ago, and he told me you're supposed to stay away from Aria for a few days."

I glower. "It's not fair. They're punishing us because I'm half demon."

Cadence steps into the garage so I can see her without the shadows covering her face. Her stilettos tap on the textured tiles, and she meets my eyes with a pout. "No one is punishing you, Faith, but the pack is concerned. Can you blame them? Their history with your dad isn't a good one."

"Neither is yours but you got over it," I snap.

"I know it's not fair," Cadence says, coming closer to sling her arm over my shoulder. "It sucks. I know what it's like to be forbidden from seeing your best friend, but you have to think things through. I'm sure it'll pass, things will get figured out, and you can go back to sneaking behind Raphael's back."

"What am I supposed to do with myself?" I complain. "I promised Aria I'd help her look into the disappearances. You damn well know that you did your own thing when you were my age. I was there, remember?"

She releases a soft laugh, breathless almost. "And I almost died on more than one occasion."

"I'm not afraid of dying."

"Well, I am. I like hanging out with my favorite people in the universe. No need to cut our times short, right?"

She makes a point. An annoying point but still a point. "Fine. But if I can't go with Aria, then I want you to help me. I want to go into town and see things for myself. That's all. Maybe I can help."

Twisting her red lips to the side, she considers my request. I stick out my bottom lip, staring at her expectantly, and she heaves a sigh.

"You know that crap doesn't work on me, but since I was planning to hang around until sunset with you anyway, I guess we can go for a little drive."

"Me, too?" Aria asks, peeking her head from the side of the open garage. "Everyone still thinks I'm in my room, and Uncle Josh knows he better stay away until things are under control."

Cadence shakes her head, her long, reddish black hair pelting me in the face. "Sorry, Aria. I'll already have Hell heating my back if Raphael finds out I took Faith out. I'm not adding an angry werewolf pack to that list."

I cross the garage and hug Aria. "I'll text you later, okay?"

"Zeke October is way cooler than your dad's girlfriend," she mutters loud enough for Cadence to hear. "I bet I could still convince him to fly me."

I laugh. "Good luck with that."

I wave Aria off, watching her head to the side of my house to take the pathway back to the beach. I swear I hear feathers ruffle, but if Ezekiel is nearby, he's definitely not showing his annoyingly gorgeous face again.

Cadence pinches my arm, making me jump. "Who in the Hell is Zeke October?"

I roll my eyes. "The most annoying angel in existence."

Cadence bares her teeth in a smile. "Raphael's Demon Watcher?"

I nod. "But he doesn't like to be called Zeke. It's Ezekiel."

Cadence peers around like she can somehow rip the angelic shield from Ezekiel to meet him in person. "Zeke's better. I had asked Dylan about it last night, but he refused to give the angel up. Brother code or some bullshit. But now I have a name."

I laugh. "That you won't be able to say after sunset."

She sighs. "Damn angels. Have a demon for a best friend and then also date one, and you get put on the naughty list for life." A smile crosses her face. "The naughty list is great, okay? My soul's still heading to Heaven, and I'm having an awesome life. Have you thought about the fact that maybe I'll turn them good instead of them corrupting me?" She's practically yelling, like all the angels in Heaven can hear her if she tries hard enough. Doubt it. I'm going to be the one with the headache. "I didn't think so!"

I wince. "Pretty sure they tuned you out when you said damn."

She laughs again. "You're probably right. Now come on. Give me the keys."

I tilt my head to the side. "You're going to drive my dad's car?"

"Might as well make teasing with his fury worth it."

I stroll around the empty parking lot for the millionth time in a row. The werewolf's car was already moved when we got here, and there isn't much to go on from the looks of things. I can't sniff the lingering odor of a tainted human like a werewolf can, but I was hoping to see something maybe they missed.

"See anything?" I ask Cadence, who stands near Dad's rumbling Ferrari. I wish she'd shut the engine off, but she wants to be able to quickly get away if someone else shows up.

"Like I said five minutes ago, the Hunter's Alliance cleaned up and took anything they found already. There's nothing here. We're better off waiting."

"But night is coming."

"I'm sure my dad is on it," she says. It's always weird to me to think that Cadence's dad leads the Hunter's Alliance. I'm sure he hates that his only daughter is knowingly dating a demon. Maybe he doesn't know. I'm sure he'd call a hunter intervention or something. "The Moonlight Shores pack and he go way back. He'll make sure things are good."

"I think you just don't want to get involved."

"Well, if you must know, I don't. I know you love Aria and she's your best friend, but it's hard to forget the bad blood. I understand everyone does things for what they think is the right reason, and I'm telling you, Faith. We have no right or wrong reason to get involved. If the Hunter's Alliance can't handle it, Cami and your dad will."

"Listen to the hunter," a masculine voice says from behind me.

I spin to meet Ezekiel's dark eyes. "I thought I told you to get out of here."

"Huh?" Cadence asks.

I turn around to face her. "Nothing, it was—"

My cell phone ringing sounds through the air, cutting off my words. I glance at Aria's smiling face for a second before I answer it.

"Hey, there's nothing he—"

A scream rips through the line, causing me to wince.

Dropping my phone from the sudden noise piercing my ears, I yell as it clatters to the ground. I scramble to pick it up, and my heart crashes to my feet, seeing the shattered screen.

"Aria?" I ask, holding it to my ear.

Silence. My phone's dead.

"Faith, what was that about?" Cadence asks.

I grip my phone to stop my hands from trembling. "I—I don't know. I think something's wrong. It was Aria."

"What did she say?"

Tears burn my eyes. "Nothing. All I heard was her screams."

MORTAL BONDS

"STAY BEHIND ME," Cadence says, straightening her shoulders. "Your dad will release Hell on the world if something were to happen to you. And we all know how that went the last time that happened."

"That would be the reason no one will hurt me," I say. It wasn't long ago that demons were out of hand—well, they can still be out of hand, but not without consequence—and disrupted the balance of the universe by collecting and imprisoning Hell-bound souls on earth. The war between Heaven and Hell still leaves people reeling. I know I'll never forget it.

Cadence side-glances me. "Still, I'm not going to put you in danger."

She says it like I'm not the one capable of summoning the power of Hell into my hands to protect myself. Cadence is human—badass—but still human. Her life is more fragile than mine, because I heal quicker, though she'd argue until the end of time that it doesn't mean anything. She's been wrestling and cuddling with demons and still manages to keep her soul in good grace. I'm pretty sure no one else in the universe can say that. But I still worry she would put her safety before mine.

Cadence raises her hand to ring the doorbell of the Moonlight Shores pack's mansion. It swings open before she even touches the button, and Joshua stands tall, blocking the entire entrance with his sheer size.

His hard eyes soften when he sees Cadence, but the second they land on me, they narrow. "Faith, Aria was supposed to tell you that she was heading out of town. You shouldn't be here."

"But—"

"Go home, Faith," he says, cutting me off. "And Cadence, you know better than to bring her here."

Cadence steps forward, stretching to try to get into the pack leader's face. "Knock it off. You're wasting time."

"Time?"

"Aria snuck out," I blurt, jumping into the conversation I'm clearly not invited to participate in. "We were going to investigate the disappearances—"

Joshua growls, the sound sending goosebumps over my

skin. "What!" His loud voice sends me reeling back, and I hit a wall behind me, knocking the breath from me. But it's not a wall. Walls don't have muscular arms with veins that bulge with the movement.

"Calm down," Cadence says.

Joshua points to me. "Where is she? I swear to God, Faith, if something happened to Aria because of you, you'll—"

With one quick motion, Cadence slides a dagger from a hidden sheath under her jacket and aims it right at the pack leader's heart. "You won't do anything. Aria wasn't with us. I intervened before their adventure and Aria was supposed to head straight home."

Joshua backs away from Cadence's aimed knife. Peering over his shoulder and into his mansion, he yells, "Aria! Aria, get out here, now!"

A few werewolves appear in the foyer behind Joshua, now interested in what's unfolding between us. Fear trickles through my mind, dripping down my neck to pool right in my chest, cooling the fire of my half-hellish heart.

"Josh, something happened to her," I say. "She called my phone."

"What did she say?" he asks. "Give me your phone."

I tug out my broken phone and hand it to him. "She didn't say anything. She only screamed."

Joshua swears under his breath, jerking his arm to chuck my phone over my head. It smashes right into the side of Dad's car. I wince, knowing that fury is going to rain down on me and

Cadence in waves of hellfire and ash the second Dad realizes we damaged his car. Not like I can blame Joshua. Dad might come to the door, yelling, causing more problems than any of us need.

Cadence jerks her arm out, and I expect her to clock the werewolf for putting us in a dangerous position, but she only squeezes his arm. "We will find her. She would've been walking between here and Faith's along the beach."

If I didn't know any better, I'd think Joshua transformed into a demon. I swear his eyes glow red with the glare he gives me. "You took her to your house? That was possibly the stupidest thing you could do. You both know better than that."

I cringe away. "I couldn't stop her."

A growl erupts from behind Joshua, and someone pushes him out of the way. Things happen so fast that I can't even manage to summon my demonic power into my hands. A giant, black furred wolf lunges from the house, plowing into Cadence to get her out of the way, and charges me.

I scream, stepping back, but I can't move out of the way with Ezekiel's angelic form standing too close behind me for my liking. The wolf launches, heading straight for my chest to tear off my face, and I elbow Ezekiel, wondering if he's punishing me for just existing.

I squeeze my eyes shut, bracing myself, my power finally in my hands. My stomach rises into my throat, thinking about how I'm going to have to hurt a werewolf to protect myself. It'll stain my soul like every other bad decision I had to make because I ran out of options.

Wind whips through my hair, the world dropping out from under me. I snap my eyes open, watching the wolf skid in the grass of the front lawn before Joshua tackles the beast. The world shrinks below as Ezekiel ascends, the cool moisture of the clouds steaming on my warm skin, making me shiver.

I release a haggard breath, the shudder shaking me in the angel's arms. Ezekiel holds me tighter, his arms digging into my stomach below my ribcage, his chin resting on the crook of my neck. He's so close to me that I catch the scent of cherry blossoms emanating from his ethereal skin.

"I didn't need your help," I say, trying to ignore the fact that my shirt bunches, and his arms touch my bare skin, his fingers clamping to my sides.

He flaps his wings, shooting us even higher. "No, but that wolf did."

As much as I want to lie and tell Ezekiel he is wrong about me, I can't. Because he is right. I was fully prepared to have the werewolf's blood on my hands. Choices, even ones made out of desperation and fear, still have consequences. Ones I've hardened myself to live with.

Tears blur my eyes, spilling onto my cheeks. Sniffling, I bring my hands to my face, glad I'm facing out instead of toward the angel. There is nothing more embarrassing than crying, and doing so in front of Ezekiel is mortifying.

"Faith." His soft voice, nearly a whisper fighting against the noise of the wind in my ears, wraps around me in a tone I've only heard him use with me once.

I expect him to say more, to point out the fact that he got to me, but all he does is descend, holding me to him so tightly his heartbeat thrums into my back in quick beats that distract me enough to get myself under control moments before his boots touch the ground, bouncing the both of us a few times as he adjusts to solid ground.

I close my eyes, listening to the sound of his feathers coming together as he retracts his wings, hiding them without me having to see that he's done so. He doesn't release me right away, holding me for a moment like I'll spill to the ground if he lets me go.

I roll my shoulders, pushing him back with the movement. Neither of us says a word, but I can feel him standing behind me. His breath cools the warmth of my skin on my shoulder since angels run cooler than demons, even half demons like me.

I can't handle the intensity of his closeness for a moment longer, so I take a step forward and away. We're a few blocks away from the Moonlight Shores pack's mansion, and as much as I want to run back and face them all over again, try to reason with them that their unwarranted aggression toward me will get us nowhere if we're going to find Aria, I don't. I don't need the pack to figure things out. I don't need anyone.

I'm going to find my best friend, even if it means I have to tell Dad I've been lying to him. That I've been sneaking out and going against his wishes. Because facing his hellish wrath is nothing compared to the fear of something bad happening to

Aria. To never seeing her again.

"Faith?" Ezekiel asks from behind me.

I don't turn to look at him. "Yeah, Ezekiel?"

"What are you doing?" he asks.

"What do you think I'm doing?" Anger replaces my worry, and I spin around to face him. "I'm going to find my best friend. The sun sets in—" I pause and look up at the sky. "In an hour. If a tainted human took her, I have to find her before demons return. I can't let my best friend be turned into a—" I squeeze my eyes shut. Damn these tears.

A cool hand touches my cheek, smearing my tears across my skin. The thud of Ezekiel's heartbeat thrums in my ears, and I realize I've been concentrating on listening to him long enough that I pushed away all the other sounds in the world.

His wings flash for a split second, sending a wave of peace over me at the sight. The intensity of his gaze, locking with mine, keeps me frozen so I can't turn away as much as I need to, even if I don't want to. There's something about the angel that burrows deep to my soul, scratching at the armor I've built around myself. And the problem with his persistent presence is that my armor cracked from the inside to let him sneak in.

"Please," I whisper, finally finding my words. I don't know what I'm asking. Maybe for him to step back, to stop looking at me. To stop trying to shine his heavenly light over me. I don't need Heaven or the good grace he possesses. I don't need my fracturing soul to be mended. I need him to back off. I need to hear my own heart pumping my demon blood through my veins. I need to feel the hot power his cool presence unintentionally keeps at bay.

I need the fury of Hell on my side. Because the goodness of my soul doesn't stand a chance when it comes to demons. And if Aria has been taken, I need all the Hell I can summon. I need my armor. I need to be me.

"Let me help you," he says, surprising me.

"You're not going to suggest I go home and try to be good?"

The corner of his mouth twitches up, but he refrains from smiling. "I know you better than that."

"You know that's creepy, right? Just dropping that kind of information. How long have you been hanging around in the shadows?"

He shrugs.

"Angel secrets, huh? Or is it because you really want to lie about it and can't, so you're going to say nothing?"

"I don't hang around in the shadows," he answers.

I roll my eyes and step away from him, finally getting myself to move. The light shining in his eyes dissipates, but darkness isn't left behind. Nothing about him could ever be dark. He's so pure and good and everything holy that it hurts something inside me just a little. Like a nagging ache warning me that he's celestial while I'm demonic. We play on different teams but neither of us can ever win or lose.

"So what now?" I ask, changing the subject. Angels love their secrets. They'll never admit more than they have to. I'm surprised Ezekiel's talking to me at all.

Ezekiel rubs his lips together and scratches his neck. "I don't know. I have a feeling you wouldn't listen to anything I say."

"You're right, but it's not like you would listen to me, either," I say. "But if you offer your help..."

"Are you asking?"

I nod. "Please, Ezekiel."

Something flickers in his eyes, a shimmering light that softens his features, making him look more boy than angel. Young. Not the powerful watcher assigned to watch a powerful demon like my dad.

He releases a tiny breath, a sound so subtle it competes with the whisper of his invisible wings. "If I can't persuade you otherwise, then yes, I'll help, but I must ask you to promise me something."

"Deals are for demons," I remark.

He closes the distance between us and takes my hand. It's such a strange gesture. Angels, unless close to someone like Dylan and Zach are to me, don't usually touch people. It messes with their shields protecting them from being seen. Allowing me to see him, letting me in his space, stirs both light and dark in me, and I don't like this sort of confusion. "It's not even close to a deal. It's a promise, and I'm not making you do it. You can say no and I'll still help."

"I'm listening," I say. Might as well play nice.

"Will you forgive me for last night? I know I messed up,

and I know you're holding it against me. I can feel it."

"Um...okay?" That was unexpected. And sweet. Dad would blast me for thinking I'd be okay with him getting cozy with my soul if he was this awkward and cute all the time. I'm so used to bone and steel and fury that it's nice to have someone actually care how I feel instead of telling me I shouldn't feel anything at all. "I think I can do that, since I'm going to take advantage of you and all. Possibly corrupt you while I'm at it."

The softness in his eyes disappears and his jaw tightens. "Unlikely, Demon Spawn," he says, his voice deepening. He gazes at me, boring his eyes into me for so long I shift, now the one awkward and uncomfortable. "Go ahead and try if you'd like."

I don't know why I'm ever surprised by an angel's ability to joke, but damn it if I left myself open for it. My cheeks burn. "Are you new or something? I'd think you'd know better than to tempt me."

He doesn't respond.

My eyes widen. "You are new. Why on earth would my dad get a newbie? What happened to the last watcher?"

Again, no response.

I sigh. "Whatever. It doesn't matter. Let's go. The night is coming, and someone has Hell to pay."

"Let's hope not," Ezekiel mutters, striding to walk next to me. "There's already enough of that going around."

The beach leading to my house remains undisturbed as the

werewolves refuse to get within a mile of Dad's demonic fortress. Less than an hour before sunset doesn't give them much time to comb the beach, and if they want to pass onto Dad's stretch of private beach, they'd have to request permission through the alliance who would go through Cami and then to Dad. Like everything, there are rules.

But these rules don't apply to me.

"I bet you're breaking all sorts of angelic army rules being here right now," I say, staring at the ground, taking in every inch of the sand in case there is some sort of sign. We entered the beach from the public parking lot not far from the pack's mansion, slowly working our way closer to my house in time for sunset.

"You would like that, wouldn't you?" he asks.

"Possibly. If you're already breaking rules, your demonic corruption is just around the corner," I say. My first defense to deflect my fear is with humor and mindless chatter. I'm glad Cadence remains down the beach from us, because I'm pretty sure Ezekiel wouldn't say anything if she were here. There's something about learning about Dad's Demon Watcher that makes his sudden arrival less creepy, especially since he won't admit how long he's been around—just saying long enough.

Ezekiel chuckles, the smoothness of his voice helping to ease the tightness clenching my chest. I'm both frustrated and relieved I haven't found anything on the beach, but that still leaves me with so many unanswered questions and fears. What happened to Aria? Who took her? Was it someone working for demons? Is she okay? Is she—

"You talk a lot when you're scared," Ezekiel says, cutting off my thoughts.

"I'm not scared." Sweat prickles on the back of my neck. If Ezekiel was a demon, he'd surely smell the fear all over me. "I'm—" I can't believe I'm admitting this. "I'm terrified. Aria's my best friend. Do you even know what that is? To have someone who gets you and loves you despite everything? Who would fight for you, with you, and even help you hide a body? That's Aria to me. Everyone in this world thinks I have this horrible side to me lurking below my skin, waiting to come out."

"Because you're half demon."

"God, you're so obvious. It kills me."

Ezekiel's shadow stretches in front of me, blending with my own shadow. Every time I put space between us, he closes it.

"I'm not God, and I'd also be the last person to cause your death, Demon Spawn. I saved you from getting your heart ripped out, remember?"

I ignore him, definitely not needing the reminder that he saved my ass in The Morningstar.

Ezekiel stands next to me, his gaze taking in the side of my face as I refuse to look at him. "As for a best friend, I understand the power of mortal bonds—all bonds really. I wasn't born yesterday. I didn't ascend then, either."

I want to ask him when he was born, because I can't really tell his age considering he's immortal, but instead, I say, "I guess you would know, huh? Since you live for saving humanity and all. Don't get me wrong, I love my dad, but with him, I sometimes feel like—" I sigh. "You know, if my dad prayed for anything, it'd be that my evil side would surface. But Aria, she swears that even if I have demon blood in my veins, I will never be what everyone expects or hopes I will be. The only other person in the world who ever thought me to be just me was my grandma. I like to pretend that's why she named me Faith. She had a whole bunch of it in her for me."

Ezekiel stares off into the distance, watching the ocean turn from blue to gray as the sun hovers over it, igniting the colors of fire on the glittering surface. Hooking his arm around my shoulders, he surprises me with a hug, spinning me around so that I have to face him. He pulls me closer, forcing me to rest my cheek on his taut chest, and I don't move or pull away. All I do is listen to his heart racing in my ear.

"They're not the only ones who have faith in you, you know," he says, nearly whispering.

I pull away. "You're required to say stuff like that, right? Trust in yourself, let the light shine in your dark, little devilish soul. Blah."

I expect him to grimace, maybe even flash his wings, but he chuckles instead. "It's rule number one."

I roll my eyes. "This isn't a joke."

He reaches out, pushing the stray blond strands of my messy hair out of my face and behind my ear. "I'm sorry. I didn't mean to laugh. It's just, you don't have a dark soul. Shockingly, there isn't even a blemish on it."

Warmth flourishes up my cheeks, surely turning me as red as the setting sun next to us. I both hate and like that he talks about my soul again. "Ezekiel, knock that crap off. My dad will cut your wings off if he heard you."

He smiles. "He won't hear me, and if he did, I'm not afraid of him. Not with you around."

"Me? You think I'll protect you?" I ask.

He nods. "I do."

I point to the sun. "If we don't hurry back to my house, we might have to test your theory."

"I have faith."

"I'm not a possession," I quip, grinning.

Ezekiel shakes his head, a strange expression crossing his face. Slowly, he pulls away from me like the gesture is painful for him to do, and I suddenly wish that he wouldn't. I've always known I loved to be around Aria because of her good soul, but damn, the more Ezekiel is around, the more I realize how much I don't just like being around someone close to Heaven. I need it. I crave it.

I stroll away from the angel, speeding up to keep the distance between us. It's not only Ezekiel's good grace I like...

Oh, unholy Hell. What is going on in my head? This can't be happening.

I suck in a deep breath, trying to get my desire and demonic blood under control. I cannot like an angel like this. It's against the universe for me to have a crush on a celestial being. He's off limits, not only because of Dad but because he could never like me back in any other way but pure, devoted, safe love. I'm just setting myself up. I'd never, ever—and I mean ever—want that from him. I'm sure I'd go straight to Hell, and that's an eternity I'm doing my best to avoid.

"Faith, slow down," Ezekiel says. "Did I do something?"

"Yes!" I yell over my shoulder, trying to remember why I'm out here in the first place. And I thought demons were charming. He made me open up in ways I shouldn't have, and now I'm losing the day by the second, and I'm no closer to finding Aria. "You distracted me and messed with my emotions, you evil angel. Now, I'm going to have to come clean with my dad."

I bet he's grimacing because I called him, the embodiment of everything good in the universe, evil. "Faith, please. Just stop," he calls from behind me.

I don't stop. I run faster. I'm so confused and embarrassed by his presence. About what it has done to me in my moment of weakness, because I'm scared for my best friend. I joke about corrupting him, but I'd never want that.

A shadow streaks across the sand in front of me as Ezekiel takes flight. His expansive wings glitter in the setting sun, and instead of trying to cut me off, he picks up speed toward my house. My breath heaves, and I slow down. There's no escaping a Demon Watcher. If only he'd get a clue and disappear.

He holds up his hands, palms out, motioning me to stop. His black wings spread out on his back, blocking the view of the beach behind him. Fear rises in my chest, sending my heart crashing against my ribcage. He isn't cutting me off to continue our annoying heartfelt conversation. He doesn't want me to go any closer.

"Faith," he calls. "Stay where you are."

I swallow the burning in my throat. "What are you hiding?"

"Your dad will return in seconds. Please, wait for him."

Dashing forward, I close the distance between me and Ezekiel, igniting a glowing red orb of demonic power between my hands. I thrust it at him, forcing him to launch into the air to get out of my way.

And then I freeze.

The edges of my vision shadow, my stomach heaving.

"Oh, God." I press my hand to my chest. "God. God, please. No."

A soft thud sounds next to me, and a hand hooks around me, stopping me from falling to the blood stained beach.

The body of a wolf lies in the sand, covered in so much blood. Too much blood.

"Faith?" Dad's voice echoes through the air. "Where are you?"

The wolf whimpers in front of me.

I scream.

HEAVEN'S ARMY

"WHAT IN THE God-forsaken Hell?" Dad's voice cuts through the evening air, sounding so loud I'm sure everyone in Moonlight Shores can hear him. Ruby light explodes from his hands, sparkling across the bloody sand as he releases his power at nothing in particular.

Dad crosses the beach to my side, his shadow falling over me. Ezekiel lets go of my arm, so I hit the sand, and I know he's done so to protect himself from Dad. I can still feel his presence, but he's shielding himself from the wrath radiating from my demonic father, begging to break free.

"What happened, Faith? Are you hurt? Did the beasts attack?" Question after question flies from Dad's mouth. He leaves my side and goes to the dying wolf only feet away. He kicks it, flipping it over, causing it to whimper again.

Flying from the sand, I scream and launch at him, power bursting from my hands. I collide into my dad and smash my hands to his chest, pushing him away. "Don't touch her!"

Dad freezes, letting me hit him with wave after wave of power, smoldering his dress shirt. He flies off his feet from the force of my fury and lands in the sand not fighting me back at all, just accepting all I give. Tears burn from my eyes, dripping onto his face. The droplets steam from his skin. He grimaces and reaches out and locks his hot hands around my wrists. "Faith, stop. You have to control yourself."

Instead of lashing out again, I begin to sob, unable to control the emotions simmering to the surface to overflow from my soul. I lean forward and hug Dad, and he wraps his arms around me, squeezing me against him.

"Take a breath and tell me what happened. Did the beasts attack? Did you do this?"

My breath shudders, and I sniffle, turning to glance at the bloody wolf. Pulling away from Dad, I crawl through the sand and touch my fingers to the dirty wolf's muzzle. "This wasn't me. She was fine when I left her here."

"What do you mean? Who are you talking about?" he asks.

"Aria. Dad, I've been keeping secrets," I admit. "I've been

hanging out with the wolf pack down the beach during the day. Aria is one of them, and she's my best friend in the entire world. And someone hurt her. Other wolves have gone missing, too. The pack leader says it was a tainted human." Once I start talking, I can't stop. Confessing everything to Dad makes me feel slightly better. I need him. I need his help if I'm going to survive this, because Aria...

My stomach heaves at the thought.

"Faith." I don't meet Dad's fiery gaze. I expect him to start yelling. I expect the ground to open up to reveal Hell beneath me, to unleash fire and brimstone and doom and darkness on the world. I expect my whole existence to implode.

A hand touches my back, rubbing smooth circles between my shoulder blades. Now this, this wasn't something I expected. "The wolf isn't Aria, Faith," Dad says. "It's male."

I blink away tears, hope rising through me in a bright light to push away the darkness threatening to consume me. "What?"

"It's not Aria," he repeats.

"Thank God!" I yell, glancing at the starry sky. Dad grumbles under his breath, and I release a shaky puff of air. I sit back in the sand. "I'm sorry, Dad. I'm just—" Another wave of fear rushes over me. "If this isn't Aria, then where is she? Oh, no. Dad, do you think it was a demon? What if..." I don't even want to think about a fate worse than death for my best friend. Because being demon-broken and transformed into a hellhound is exactly that.

Dad gets to his feet and peers around. "If that is the case, then someone will be taking a trip home to Hell very soon." He walks over to the wolf, igniting a glowing orb into his hand.

"What are you doing?" I ask.

"Ending its misery," he says. "And then I'm going to figure this all out."

"Dad, no!" I yell, dashing forward before he can release his demonic power onto the dying wolf in a mercy killing.

Bright light flashes from the sky, blinding me, and Dad yells out and stumbles away from the wolf. Three quick thuds sound through the night as people—angels—land on the beach next to me, cutting Dad off from the wolf and also me off from Dad.

Golden wings cast a glow over the bloody sand, and I blink the shadows from my eyes at the sudden shift in light. The angel closest to the wolf expands its wings and reaches down, pressing its palms to the werewolf's heart. It releases a soft gasp, a strange human sound, and then the wolf dies. The angels intervened, thinking my dad was doing something he wasn't supposed to.

A hand locks to my shoulder, pulling me back. A racing heartbeat thrums on my back before I catch the scent of cherry blossoms. If it wasn't for those things, the angel would have an elbow to the ribs and smoldering feathers.

"What is going on here? Get off my beach. This is a demonic affair and none of Heaven's concern," Dad says, igniting power into his hands. The three angels stand in formation without moving. "This is your one warning."

I cringe, turning away, afraid to see the Hell Dad's about to unleash on the angelic army. Another flash of bright light erupts in my vision, and the wind picks up, blowing my hair from my face.

Dad yells.

I jerk my attention back to him, seeing two more angels drop down behind him. He's surrounded and outnumbered. Heavenly light won't kill him, but it'll inflict a night of pain on him like last night.

The two angels behind him reach out and each take one of his arms, restraining him like he's some sort of criminal.

"Release me!" Everything happens so fast. Dad can't even defend himself, his skin smoldering under the angelic touch of Heaven's army.

I move to rush forward, but Ezekiel holds me back, preventing me from going to Dad. Anger snaps the fear out of me from seeing the bloody wolf. I stomp my foot, stepping on Ezekiel's boot. He shifts me, and I jerk my arm back and elbow him in the stomach.

"Ezekiel, let me go!" I yell, my voice dripping with dark desperation.

Dad turns his attention to the sound of my voice, his eyes flashing red. "Don't hurt her. She has nothing to do with this."

"Faith, calm down. I can't let you go," Ezekiel says.

I summon demonic power into my hands, breaking one of my arms free. Without thinking, I chuck it at the angels standing in front of me, golden wings so bright and glorious unlike the inky feathers of Ezekiel's wings.

"Let us go. My dad didn't do anything wrong. He was gone all day," I say.

"But you were not," an angel says, dusting the burned feathers I seared on his golden wings. I had hoped they'd scatter at my power blast, but they all look more annoyed than anything.

"Faith, calm down," Dad says this time.

I want to scream. Calm down? My best friend is missing, the angelic army just surrounded my house, my dad's stupid Demon Watcher won't let me go, and now the angels are trying to blame me? Oh, unholy Hell. I'm mad—furious.

My eyes widen. "Are you kidding me? I didn't do this." I thrash in Ezekiel's arms and finally manage to pull myself free. I hold power in my hands, ready to light the beach aglow. "Tell them, Ezekiel. You were with me the whole day."

Wind lifts my hair again, this time from Ezekiel flapping his black wings. "She's right. The demon spawn didn't do this. She has ties to the wolf pack. A bond with one of the young pups."

"Which gives Raphael a reason to intervene," another angel says. "Discovering the half breed with wolves could easily set him off."

My mouth falls open. "What? No. He didn't know. Why are you accusing him? This wolf was left to die here by someone else."

Dad releases a sigh, one that isn't full of anger or annoyance. It's a sigh I never thought I'd ever hear coming from him. "It's no use, Faith. This has been a long time coming, and the angelic army has finally found a reason to intervene. But it's going to be okay."

"They'll send you to Hell." My voice rises over the roar of the ocean.

He presses his lips into a thin line. "This isn't the end, Faith, and I need you to be strong."

"Dad..." My voice turns into a whisper. I don't understand. Dad's one of the most powerful demons. Why isn't he trying harder?

"I've done some unforgivable things in my eternity, and the angelic army has been waiting for a reason to intervene, so I knew this day would eventually come. But I want you to remember who I am, okay? Don't let them ruin you. You're my daughter and your mother's daughter, and there is nothing wrong with that despite what anyone says."

Tears burn my eyes. "Don't talk like this is goodbye."

"It very well could be, Faith. We both knew our eternities would part ways, and I am thankful for every second I got to spend with you."

Anger burns from my very core, snaking through my legs and arms, darkening my vision in tints of hellish red. My demonic blood pumps hard and fast through my veins, making it so I can't hear the whoosh of feathers, the shifting of sand, the hum of water behind me. All I can hear is Dad's blood racing through me, thudding in my ears, reminding me that I'm half demon, and these angels, these blessed beings who stand before me, clutching everything high and mighty within them, are not something I should ever align with.

It was never Dad who would ruin the goodness of my soul. It was them.

The ground shakes beneath me, and I thrust my hands out, unleashing power unlike anything I've ever been able to summon before. This time, the angels scatter, all of them taking flight, sending beams of light throughout the beach as they ready themselves for the Hell burning through my very skin.

"Faith!" My name rings out behind me, and a hard body crashes into my back, knocking me off my feet. "Get him out of here. I have her!"

The sound of Ezekiel's voice digs into me, ripping me open to send my insides out and onto the already blood soaked sand. Betrayal courses through me. I should've known better than to trust an angel. I should've known better than to let my guard down and let him into my life, even for a day. Look how he repays me. He's ruining my life. My world. He's destroying my entire eternity.

Bright light blinds me, stinging my eyes, searing through my already hot skin and to my soul. Dad yells out to me, but there's nothing I can do to fight against Heaven's light as it steals my senses away and leaves me defenseless in the sand under an angel who'll surely try to save my soul.

"I love you, Faith." Dad's words trickle through the pounding in my ears.

I open my mouth to respond, but sand fills my mouth and throat, stopping me from even breathing. My head swims with dizziness, the weight of Ezekiel, of the world, crushing me.

"Faith," Ezekiel says into my ear. "Don't fight. Let me in."

I thrash, pushing against the angel's solid build. If I could talk, I'd scream at him to go to Hell. To leave me alone.

I build a steel wall around me, and then ten more to keep Ezekiel out. I imagine a fiery moat, a pack of hellhounds, Uncle Lucifer himself. All these things ready to protect me from Ezekiel, to stop him from getting to my soul. Because if I don't have Dad, if I lost Aria, too. My soul is all I have left.

And Ezekiel cannot have it.

Heaven can't take it from me.

"Faith," he whispers again.

I don't respond.

"Please, forgive me," Ezekiel says. "Forgive me."

Pain burns through me, my strength and protective barricade shattering completely under his angelic influence.

I feel his ethereal presence in my soul. His bright light pushes the very darkness threatening to consume me away.

"I hate you," I whisper.

"Forgive me," is all he says.

I open my eyes to a bright beach with crystalline water stretching endlessly into the horizon. The sea air sparkles with rainbow mist, leaving a haze in my vision. The shining sun hovers overhead, suspended in the sky, yet I lack a shadow. Something's wrong.

A gust of wind blows tendrils of my hair over my shoulder.

Launching to my feet, I spin around, igniting my demonic power in my hands. I throw the glowing orb, smacking Ezekiel right in the shirt with it.

My power eats away at his shirt, turning his skin red from the heat. Without saying a word, he remains in his spot with his hands at his sides, his chiseled abs now displayed for the world—or just me—to see.

I throw another burst of power at him. "I'm in Hell aren't I?"

He frowns. "I—"

"That's the only explanation I have for you being here," I snap, cutting him off.

"Faith—"

I shake my head, chucking more demonic power at him. He steps out of the way before it spills across his jeans. "You don't get to talk. You set us up! This was all your doing. Dad was right about you angels. You think you're all holy and right-eous, but all you do is judge and look down on us."

"I don't—"

"Just because my dad's a demon doesn't mean he's destroy-ing the world. He knows his purpose. He knows what he's sup-posed to do, and he's been doing it. You guys haven't been wiped off the earth because of my dad. And this is how you re-pay him? And they say demons are evil and manipulative." Closing my eyes, I release another orb of power in his direction.

I'm hoping if I continue to do so, he'll finally leave me alone.

"I know that, Faith. It's what prevented the angelic army from taking immediate action against your father." Ezekiel closes the distance between us. Reaching out, he grasps my hand. "I'm doing everything I can to prolong his assessment."

His words snuff out the fire burning in my veins. "You're what? Why would you do that?"

"Because of you."

"Me?"

"And your soul."

I open my mouth to say more, but the world trembles. The ground splits open, sucking in the glittery sand, pulling me away from Ezekiel. I slip and fall into the sinkhole, and the world turns dark.

Gasping, I sit up, my heart racing, tears burning my eyes.

"Faith," a familiar voice says. "Faith, it's okay. It's me. Don't unleash any power, all right."

I sit up and meet Cadence's glassy eyes. "My dad."

She embraces me. "He's okay for now. I'm so sorry I couldn't reach you on the beach."

I had forgotten she was with the werewolves. "He didn't do anything wrong. You have to tell them."

Cadence leans back and purses her lips. "I have. Cami is trying to work with Zach to fix this."

I rub my palms over my sticky cheeks. "Dad said they've always had it out for him, and now whoever is behind the missing wolves is going to get away with it. Aria, she—"

"We will find Aria, I promise, but I need you to listen to me carefully. Because Raphael's been taken by the angelic army, the Hunter's Alliance thought that it would be best if you moved onto campus and into a dorm for the time being," she says.

"What? No. They can't do that," I say.

"It's for your safety. We don't know what we're dealing with at the moment. If your dad's being set up, we can't risk leaving you open for attacks. I—"

"If?" I ask, cutting her off. "You can't believe he had anything to do with this. You know him. Probably better than anyone. And my safety? Bullshit!"

Cadence cringes. "Faith, I didn't mean—of course Raphael had nothing to do with this. And you're right. This isn't about your safety. It's about everyone else's. The alliance wouldn't even agree to allow you to stay in my care. They don't want us together at all. They think—"

I chuck an orb of power at the wall. The lights flicker, and the power fades. It's then that I realize we're somewhere sacred. A church? I can't tell without the windows. I'm in a basement of sorts.

"This can't be happening. I can't lose him," I say.

A tear slips from Cadence's eye, and she swipes it away, smearing her dark eyeliner. It's the first time I've seen her imperfect. It makes things utterly real and not some twisted demonic night terror.

"We're not going to lose him, understand? Have faith," she

says.

"In the enemy?"

She covers my mouth with her hand. "Shhh! You can't talk like that here."

Of course not. How dare I say anything bad about the beings who judge my dad without real proof? How dare I point out that it's possible for a heavenly being to be imperfect?

"Whatever. I don't care."

Cadence sighs. "Please, Faith. I know this is hard, but this is the world we live in. It's never been a fair place for anyone. We both know that."

She's right. But it's come a long way since Dad saved me. I like to think he took a part in it, even if for selfish reasons he likes to keep me safe, keep what he had here.

"Well, what now? Why am I in a basement? Your dad is head of the alliance. Can't you pull some strings and convince them to let me see my dad?" I ask.

"I wish I could. I've already tried myself. There's only one person apart from angels allowed to see him, and that's Cami."

"Cami can see him? I have to talk to her. She can help us. This is what she does."

She offers me a weak smile. "It'll have to wait until tomorrow night. She's with him now."

Tears blur my eyes. I rub them away again, wishing they'd stop falling. I hate crying. I hate feeling weak and out of control. I hate that I'm forced into this position at all. I've only ever had to worry about Dad and his wants for me until now. I'm afraid he's sheltered me for too long. I don't even know how to deal with any of this.

"Cadence..." I say, my voice trailing off. I don't even know what to say anymore.

She hugs me again. "Come on. We have to go. Our escorts are waiting."

"Our escorts?"

She sighs. "Yeah, they separated us from your dad. We're at Seraphim Rock."

"The angelic army headquarters? Why would they bring us here?"

Her lips twist up to the side in a smile. "You had them shaking their feathers off. They thought you were going to summon the devil himself to earth to come to your defense, so they brought you to the holiest place on this plane."

I frown.

She laughs. "I'm kidding. I don't really know why."

I sigh. "They're going to wish it was only Uncle Lucifer coming to earth. Because if they do something to my dad, I'm going to—"

Before I have a chance to finish my sentence, the door swings open, and an angel narrows her eyes at me. She motions for us to get up without saying a word.

Cadence takes my hand. "Be strong, Faith. Your dad would want you to be."

She's right. It's one of the last things he said to me.

Nodding, I follow her from the room and behind the angel

to wherever it is they're taking us. If only being strong were easy. If only I could figure out how to give Dad a fighting chance.

8

DEMON WATCHER

MY CHEST TIGHTENS, stealing my breath at the sight of Ezekiel standing on the edge of a cliff overlooking the dark ocean. Dylan hovers next to him, and both their wings outstretch, competing for my attention as they prepare to take flight.

"Dylan!" I yell, rushing to close the distance between us.

Dylan holds his arms open, and I let him pull me into a hug. He rubs his hand in circles on my back, hushing me with a soft whisper. Dylan's probably the only angel in existence I don't want to see explode in fire and brimstone. If he were

Dad's Demon Watcher, I bet none of this would've happened. He'd have fought for me, because there was once a time where he was assigned as my own guardian before he ascended in Heaven's ranks and took the position of Demon Watcher to Evan, when the demi-demon descended to full-blooded, Hell-touched demon.

"You have no idea how glad I am to see you," I say, hiding my face in the soft cotton of his shirt. "My dad is being set up. He didn't hurt that werewolf. Can you make the angelic army realize their mistake?"

Pulling back, Dylan glances down at me with his chocolate brown eyes. "It's not so simple, Faith."

I glower. "You don't believe me?"

"Of course I believe you, but—"

Turning away, I swipe away the tears burning my eyes. Damn it. Why can't I stop crying? "Save your excuses for someone else. Out of everyone, I thought you'd be the one who stood up to help me. You went to Hell for a demi-demon, but I guess since you're not in love with me, my life doesn't matter to you."

A hand touches my shoulder. "You know that's not true. You matter a whole lot to me, little love. I just—some things are out of our control. But it doesn't mean we can't get them back into control."

"They're going to send him to Hell," I say. Why wouldn't they? The angels have been after Dad forever according to him. And the angel who attacked him yesterday? He made it clear

Dad doesn't stand a chance.

"You don't know that," Dylan says.

I cross my arms. "But I do. And you know what? If that happens, I'll—"

An arm hooks around me and a hand slaps over my mouth. "Don't."

Jerking my arm back, I elbow Ezekiel as hard as I can. He has some nerve to even touch me after everything he's put me through. Dylan glances between me and Ezekiel, who still holds me, refusing to let me go.

I ignite a ruby orb in my hands, intent on tossing it right over my head. A muscular hand shoves me from behind, and I lose my footing, stumbling forward too fast for Dylan to grab. The world whooshes around me, my eyes stinging from the wind, and I fall right off the cliff toward the rocks in the water below.

I scream, my stomach flying into my throat, the waves crashing white on the side of the jagged cliff bottom. Squeezing my eyes shut, I brace for collision, praying to my grandma that I hit the water. The drop is far, and any normal human would die on impact, but I'm only half. I'm tough. There's a chance I'll survive.

I don't get the chance to find out.

Fingers lock onto the back of my shirt, yanking me up. The side seam rips from the force. Cold wind sends steam from my bare stomach, and I manage to grip the fabric long enough for Ezekiel to hook his other hand around my wrist. He tosses me in the air in front of him, my shirt disappearing on a breeze to leave me in my bra when he catches me.

"You should've let me hit the water!" I yell, wrapping my arms over my chest like it matters to Ezekiel. Someone as pure as he is wouldn't even realize I'm mortified. It's hard to call an angel a creep. What makes it worse is he's still wearing the ruined shirt from earlier and his cool body presses into my hot skin. "It'd have been more pleasant than this torture."

I expect him to land at any moment to reunite me with Cadence and Dylan, but instead of descending back to Seraphim Rock, he flaps his wings, flying us higher and away. A figure shoots up next to us, and I spot the familiar black wings of Dylan.

"Are you okay, Faith?" Dylan shouts over the whistling wind. Cadence rests in his sinewy arms, her hands locked around his neck.

And I'm mad. Pissed. Not because Cadence is catching a ride with Dylan, but because I'm forced to be with Ezekiel. I'd have never agreed to this. I'd take a silent, uptight, judgmental angel over this guy, who my heart won't stop racing for.

"Do I look okay to you?" I snap. "He pushed me from a cliff and ripped off my shirt."

"Sounds like a good time to me," Cadence says.

My cheeks burn so much that I swear I see steam radiating from my face.

"I'm kidding," she calls. Shifting in Dylan's arms, she shrugs from her jacket. "Here, take this."

Dylan flies her closer, and she holds out her leather jacket to me. I lock my fingers around it and wiggle in Ezekiel's arms to try to put it on. The position we're in with me held in front of him like I'll try to bite his face off or something if he flips me around makes it incredibly hard to put on. The wind whips around us, and the hem catches on the breeze, flying up into my face. The world jerks and the jacket rips away. It must've covered Ezekiel's face, blocking his vision too, and his annoying reaction was to yank it away. But I wasn't holding on tight enough and now the jacket disappears into the churning ocean below.

"Oh, unholy Hell!" I scream, shivering now in the freezing wind.

"Zeke October," Cadence calls. "You owe me a jacket."

Ezekiel doesn't say anything, but he ascends higher and away from Dylan and Cadence. Swinging me to his side, he holds me on his hip, despite my protests. I'd blast him if it didn't mean I'd fall directly into the freezing sea.

With his free hand, he tugs his own dirty, ripped shirt over his head. He readjusts me, cradling me against him like a small child, and then hands me his shirt.

I stare at it in stunned silence.

"Put it on. You're shivering," he says.

His words kick me into action, and I shrug it over my head. It's so big that I manage to tie the frayed fabric in the front, blocking my skin from the cold wind completely.

"Thanks," I say, wishing I could steal the words back. He

deserves no thanks from me.

"It's the least I can do," he says.

"The least? The moment we get to solid ground, I want you to leave me alone. I don't ever want to see your haloed head again," I say, tucking my chin toward my chest.

I don't glance up to look at his face, but the sudden pounding of his heart speaks everything. My words got to him, but in what way? I don't know. He's probably swearing to high Heaven if angels swore. Because angels care. That's something I can't deny. But he could care about a lot of things that don't necessarily mean me. It could be that he lost my trust, and without it, he'll never be able to betray me for the sake of Heaven again. Or that he can't try to save my soul if I don't give him permission to get near it, and angels, more so than demons, care about the direction a soul heads.

"I hope you can forgive me one day," he finally says after a moment of quiet flying.

I clench my fists. "Oh, no you don't. You will not try to make me feel guilty. You hurt me. You ruined my life."

He sucks in a soft breath, one I almost miss over the wind.

I smack his firm, bare chest. "You have no right to be upset."

"Faith."

"You've damned me to Hell. I can't survive eternity without knowing he's okay. He doesn't deserve this no matter what anyone thinks."

"Faith," he repeats, like saying my name is the only thing

he knows how to do.

"I didn't even get to hug him. He might be a demon, but he is my dad. My blood. He took care of me when the world would rather me not exist. You said it yourself, I'm just the spawn of a demon. But you know what? I'm more. He taught me that."

"I know, and I wish your weren't put in this position. I had no idea what I was getting into when I was given this assignment. But you're coming to a point in your life—"

I finally look at Ezekiel, though his eyes stay trained on the dark world in front of us. Pressing my fingers to his lips, I cut off his words. "This assignment? You said you were my dad's Demon Watcher."

His jaw tightens.

"You lied to me? Angels can't lie."

"Technically, I did watch your father...when he was with you."

Anger bubbles through me, rising to the surface, steaming my skin in the icy ocean air. Why on earth would a full-blooded angel be assigned as my guardian? My soul wasn't at risk of turning Hell-bound. I wasn't causing problems with anyone. I was being a good little demi-demon.

"I—I can't believe this." Ruby power ignites in my hands, swirling and moving, begging for me to hit Ezekiel right in his godly bare chest. Maybe if I can blast open his heavenly façade I can glimpse his intentions. See what the angelic army is up to. Maybe I can set his pure little heart aglow in flames and show him what it's truly like to be me. A good soul with a hellish heart.

Before I get the chance, Ezekiel tosses me away from him and into the air. The world blurs around me, the light of the stars above turning into white streaks the faster I fall. And people say demons are known for their love of punishment. I bet Ezekiel will take every opportunity and excuse he has to continue to torture me. *You can't expect an angel to take your demonic crap. Only demons like those games.*

I push the thoughts away. I don't want him to like it. My life isn't a game. Ezekiel can't just expect for me to open my heart and let his light in so I forgive him for being a manipulative jerk.

I scream, the water seemingly rising up to catch me. I thought he dropped me to teach me a lesson and that he'd grab me at the last second like before. But now, oh crap. Oh, unholy Hell.

"Oh, God!" My voice explodes through the air, and I squeeze my eyes shut.

Arms wrap around me a moment before my boots hit the water, and I scream again at the sudden motion, my stomach dropping to my feet. My heart crashes against my ribcage, and if I had a true demonic form under my skin, I'm sure horns would slice through my head right about now.

"Not God," Ezekiel says, his breath tickling my ear. He holds me against him, his hands locked around my waist, my chin on his bare shoulder. My blond hair flies around, veiling the world from my view apart from his ethereal black wings shining brighter than ever in the dark of night. "And you have to stop that. Other angels won't be so understanding."

"I don't care!" I yell.

"Faith, please," he says, his voice lowering so much that it's just a breath coming from his throat.

"Stop. Stop pretending you care. If you cared, you wouldn't be doing this. You wouldn't stand by and do nothing. You'd do more. You'd help me."

"I—" Ezekiel snaps his mouth shut.

He loosens his grip on me to hold me out in front of him so my face can't hide in the crook of his cherry blossom scented neck. His mocha eyes meet mine, his face so close that I can't see him clearly. But I still see him. I see his full lips hovering right in front of mine as he takes in my face, as he looks past me to my soul. His heartbeat thrums louder than the soft breath he releases, a breath like a whispered kiss against my mouth though our lips don't touch.

"Please, forgive me," he murmurs.

He looks right at me, but the words travel on the wind, his voice meant for someone else.

A tear splashes on my cheek, and I realize it's not from my eyes. The tear glitters, reflecting heavenly light from my face and into Ezekiel's glassy gaze.

My heart threatens to stop beating. My lungs, they've given up on breathing. If I died right now in this moment, even though the world around me falls apart, I'm most certain every broken piece of me will fall together.

Ezekiel tilts his head forward, pressing his forehead to mine, closing the space between us. But the kiss I crave, the one I imagine happening, the one my whole body begs for, doesn't come.

My whole world turns white, and then everything turns dark.

My body shifts in cool arms, and I refuse to open my eyes, wishing the darkness would stay with me. I can't face the world. Not now. Not when my very soul hurts with all horrible emotions summoned from the depths of my being. The cool, reassuring arms release me and my body shifts again, but to someone warmer. Burning hot, actually.

Warm lips press against my forehead. "Your mercy will not be forgotten, Ezekiel." Dad's voice hums in my ears, sending a shudder through my whole body. I squeeze my eyes tighter, afraid I've fallen into some twisted dream. "Faith, please wake up. We only have minutes."

Snapping my eyes open, I stare into my father's blue ones the same color as mine. I swallow back my tears at the sight of him. The angels stole every piece of humanity from his human façade, leaving him in his true body as a demon. His skin smolders, glowing with fire from his veins, his black boned horns jutting in a deadly sharp crown. No matter how hard it is, how much it hurts my soul to see him like this, I don't turn away.

I reach out and press my palm to his cheek, holding his

gaze. "I thought I'd never see you again."

He cups his blistered hand over mine, burning my flesh with the heat radiating from him. I don't wince or pull away. I let his fire warm the ice freezing my veins as dread and fear clutch me, trying to force me to submit to them.

"They will try to see to it that you don't," he whispers. "And I'm sorry you must pay for my eternity of sins."

I lean into him, pressing my face to his blackened chest, his dress shirt frayed and barely held together at the seams. "Sins can be forgiven, can't they? I just—I don't understand, Dad. You had nothing to do with that werewolf. You weren't even there. Cadence said—"

Dad hugs me tighter, and I snap my mouth shut before I begin to cry. "Who knew that beautiful, dangerous little huntress would ever stand up for me." He sounds almost dreamy, like he'd prefer to lose himself in his thoughts in this moment.

"Dad," I say. "We're going to fix this. Cami, she'll help."

Dad kisses my head. "I'd like for you to hold onto that hope, Faith."

I crinkle my nose. "You should, too."

"For you, I will. I'm just—" He sighs, and I don't think I've ever seen him so weak in the form he's most powerful.

"I love you, Dad," I say, knowing he doesn't want to talk anymore. That maybe he can't do it.

Someone clears their throat from behind me. "Faith, it's time to go."

I hug Dad tighter. Ezekiel will have to drag me away kicking and screaming before I leave my dad here in the blessed arms of angels. "No."

Dad shifts me, and to my utter horror and dismay, he kisses my forehead once more and hands me over to Ezekiel.

I slap my hands against Ezekiel's hard chest. "No! I don't want to go. No. Please."

He sucks in a small breath through his nose. "The sun is rising. You can't follow him where he goes. His watchers will be here any second. If they—"

"Go with the angel, Faith," Dad says.

I press my lips together to stop my mouth from quivering. "I won't let them do this. This isn't the end."

"I love you, Faith."

Ezekiel adjusts me in his arms, forcing me to look into his eyes again. "You can't speak a word of this to anyone, okay?"

"What happens if I do?"

He closes his eyes. "Please."

"Heaven help me," I whisper, my lips nearly brushing his.

Dizziness washes over me, the edges of my vision fade as he unfurls his huge wings. "I'm trying."

THE HUNTER'S ACADEMY

"WAKE HER UP, and gently. The last thing we need is for someone to get hurt because she thinks she must fight," a masculine voice says, stirring me from the fog of my mind.

"Be good, Demon Spawn," Ezekiel whispers so quietly he might only be mouthing the words to me. "Don't give them a reason to isolate you. They will do so until you calm down."

I squeeze my eyes shut. Maybe if I fake sleep, they'll leave me alone. I'm not ready to deal with the world. With who I'm assuming is the Hunter's Alliance, waiting to try to mold me into one of their little demon fighters. While the alliance doesn't actively hunt demons unless they cause huge problems, they still remain the fighting force for the angelic army. Whatever makes them sleep better, is what Dad used to say.

"Come on, we don't have all day," the man says.

"Give her a break. She doesn't exactly have the fondest memories of you, Dad." It's Cadence.

Relief rushes through me, and I slowly ease my eyes open, trying my best not to startle anyone. I purposely groan and cover my face, but I don't say anything.

"Faith," Cadence says. "I know you're scared and had a rough night, but I'm begging you to stay calm. No one here will hurt you. We're going to do our best to make sure you're comfortable until things get sorted out."

I know she's trying to make the best of this horrible situation, but she's not doing a very good job at disguising the nervousness in her voice. I'm not even sure she believes her own words. I am a demon's daughter after all. There aren't many of us around. With the Hunter's Alliance's treacherous history with demi-demons, I was thankful every day to be with Dad, and that says a lot.

I sit up and take in the small room. Ezekiel's body stands over me with his back facing me while Cadence and Aston Dubois, her dad, look at me from a foot away. I realize that Ezekiel shields himself from them, and the old hunter was talking to Cadence all along.

Cadence smiles, showing her teeth. Her eyes water, but she

only blinks, trying to keep her expression perky, most likely for her dad's sake. "Hey, kid. Remember me?"

I blink, clenching my teeth without a response.

Her eyes beg me to go along with things. "It's been a while, huh?"

Yeah, like a few hours. "Where am I?" I don't know why I ask. I know exactly where I am, because Cadence told me we were going to the Hunter's Alliance, and the only full-blown facility near my house is the academy a couple hours south, where hunters go through training to deal with the demonic world.

"The Hunter's Academy. The divine think you're at risk with the captu—removal of your demonic father."

I'd call the academy the safest place for humans and other species to be if it weren't for the fact that it's been destroyed by the hands of demon-tainted humans once before during the Demon Uprising my dad participated in to save me years ago. It's because of that, I'm not so sure it's a good idea I'm here—bad blood and demonic associations considered.

"Okay," I say. As much as I want to yell, to protest, to shoot my demonic power all over the place, I know better than to give the hunters or angels a reason to punish or hurt me—or worse—try to save me.

After seeing Dad, hugging him again, just being with him once more, I know now that I'm at the mercy of everyone who has been raised against me no matter what anyone says or tries to make me believe. This isn't the first time I've been here.

Hunters kidnapped me just months after I first met my father, and if it weren't for Cami, I'd have never been reunited. She'd have never transformed into a demon either. This place, it does nothing but leave a bitter fire in the pit of my stomach no matter if times are different now.

"Okay?" Aston says, surprise raising his voice in pitch.

I sigh. "Would you prefer me to protest while burning the building down? Because I'm not in the mood to fight anymore. It's a losing battle, and I'd much prefer to be left alone."

Aston presses his lips into a thin line. "Well, I do hope you'll at least check out what our facility has to offer. I understand that our history is a little shaky—"

"That's an understatement," I say. I can't help it.

Clearing his throat, he adjusts the sleeve of his leather jacket. "Please, do try to make yourself at home. A suitcase of some of your belongings has been delivered, and if you would like anything else, write it down, and I'll pass it along."

I blink, trying to suppress the rage sneaking up on me because a stranger went into my house and touched my stuff. "I will do that. Now, if you don't mind. I've had a long night."

Aston looks at Cadence. "Please, fill her in on anything she needs to know. Introduce her around. Go over the rules—"

"I have it under control," Cadence says, cutting her dad off. "Go do whatever it is you do."

He smirks, reaches out, and touches my shoulder. "Don't hesitate to come to me for anything. If you'd prefer someone like yourself, Hunter Garcia can be found in the Alana O'Neil

Community Building on the west side of campus.

With one more look around, Aston exits my small room—complete with a twin bed, nightstand, dresser, and tiny closet. No TV or computer. Not even a landline phone. Maybe they're trying to let boredom take care of me so they won't have to.

I hop up and hug Cadence. I open my mouth to tell her I saw Dad, but one look over my shoulder at the ever-silent Ezekiel, I'm reminded of the promise he asked me to keep. And even though I'm still angry with him, I won't forget about his gesture of mercy for me and Dad. Surely it broke some sort of angelic code, but I doubt he'd ever tell me.

"Thanks for not giving me up to my dad. You'd think at twenty-four and in love with a demon I wouldn't be scared of anything, but—no need to give anyone else a reason to judge. The angels are bad enough."

My eyes water at her admitting she loves my dad. I don't think I've ever heard her say it, and I don't think Dad realizes that anyone apart from me could ever love him. Clenching my fingers, I summon my power and chuck it right at the wall. To my surprise, Ezekiel flies in its path, blasting it with his own heavenly light.

Cadence's mouth drops open. "What the f—"

Ezekiel expands his wings, creating a gust of wind in the small room that blows me and Cadence back, cutting off her words.

She startles, unsheathes her knife, and points it at Ezekiel. "What a creep! First you disappear with Faith for over thirty minutes and bring her here knocked out. Now you're hiding here? I thought you left at the gate. You angels. What are you planning?"

I release a laugh, Cadence's reaction far funnier than it should be to me. And boy does it feel good to laugh, like it breaks up the rock in my chest into grains of sand that are annoying but bearable to live with. "He's planning to stay with me for the rest of my mortal life."

She frowns. "Whoa. You must make the angelic army nervous if you get a full-blooded angel." Turning to Ezekiel, she places her hands on her hips. "If Faith's soul binds to Hell, it would be your fault, but you know she isn't at risk of descending as a demon. Cami won't bring her back. No angel would either. It's been made clear to Raphael."

"If Dad's heading there now, might as well join him," I mutter.

Both Cadence and Ezekiel turn their attention to me, horror crossing their faces, my sarcasm lost on them. Hell is no joking matter to hunters or angels. But they don't know what it feels like to have Hell in their veins. With the way people treat me on earth, why would I want to hang out with them for the rest of eternity?

"Oh, Faith, don't talk like that," Cadence says. "You don't mean it."

I turn away. "You're right. I think I need some alone time."

"You sure?" she asks. "I thought we could get some lunch, check out the new facilities. You should see the gym."

"Shouldn't you be going back to Moonlight Shores? What about the pack?"

Cadence jerks her head to Ezekiel. "Ask him. I'm on lockdown until Cami and Evan return for the night."

Ezekiel steps back under the weight of my stare.

"Seriously?"

He doesn't respond.

"This blows," I say. "I don't want to be here."

"Let's try to make the best of it," Cadence says.

I sigh. "I'd rather be miserable...and alone."

Cadence nods. "I understand. How about I make some calls and come back with lunch in a bit?"

"Okay."

Cadence hugs me and moves past Ezekiel to leave the room. I know she wants to be here for me, but I don't want to treat this as a girls' day out. I want to treat this like it is. I'm being held prisoner in a nice room with a view of the sprawling lawns with people who pretend to like me because they're afraid of what I could do to them.

The door closes with a soft thump, and I move to sit on the edge of the twin bed, wishing it were my California King one at home. Through my window, I spot people moving through campus—all hunters, all probably preparing for the coming night. Even though demons are supposed to follow new laws, they still cause havoc on the human world. Trading in souls is still a big deal in the night. As long as no demon collects the souls of the dead, my dad never intervenes. In the grand scheme of things, Hell still runs through a demon's blood, and hunters still need to keep the damned and tainted away from the good in the world.

The bed bounces next to me, and Ezekiel's knee touches against mine. The feathers of his wings glide across my back, and before I can elbow him, his wings fold and disappear.

"Are you really doing this?" I ask, trying not to let his closeness burrow under my skin. I train my eyes on my dirty jeans, though they really want to glance at Ezekiel's bare stomach. *Stupid humanity. Control yourself.*

"Doing what?" he asks, bumping his shoulder to mine. He knows exactly what he's doing. He's attempting to use his angelic presence to subconsciously make me feel better. I can't see or feel his wings, but I'm pretty sure I've grown so used to the sound that I can hear them whooshing even with his angelic shield around them, and I know he's trying to wrap me in them.

But I don't want to be wrapped in his wings.

His bulging, muscular arms on the other hand...

Shifting, I swing my legs up and rest them right on his. He doesn't move them or stiffen or anything. His lack of reaction pokes a hot iron right into my devilish little heart. Now I want to really test him. If I'm stuck here, at least I can find a way to take my mind off things—angelic corruption might just do the trick.

"Faith, whatever it is you think you're doing..." His voice trails off.

"What am I doing?" I ask, smirking.

He brings his gaze up to meet mine, one eyebrow raised, and stares at me with his soulful mocha eyes. We both know what I'm doing, and we both know it won't work, but we also know that I'm going to keep trying anyway.

He shifts his arm behind my back, leaning closer, sending my heart racing. I freeze, feeling like I'm going to die if he doesn't break his gaze. This was a stupid, stupid idea, trying to test an angel. Because my poor little half demon heart can't handle him. His overpowering presence no longer makes me want to touch him, torture him—corrupt him. I'm pretty sure he's about to unleash Heaven upon me to cleanse my wicked thoughts.

Smiling, he reaches up and touches the backs of his fingers to my cheek. He brushes strands of my blond hair behind my ear.

I break. I can't fight this losing battle.

Shoving him back, I jump from my bed and scramble to get as far as possible away from him. I raise my hand and point at him. "Not cool."

His smile widens. "What did I do?"

I wave my hand at his bare chest. "Oh, you know what you did. You're playing with my humanity. And they say demons are bad. You're a wicked, wicked angel."

"And you're cute when you're flustered."

His words leave me stunned silent, mouth open and every-thing. I shift on my feet, glancing from Ezekiel, to my window, and then to my door. The small room shrinks by the second, fire rushing through my veins, turning my warm cheeks as hot as Hell.

I run my fingers through my hair. "Don't call me cute," I manage to spit out.

"Okay, Demon Spawn," he says. "But just so you know, you're the one playing a dangerous game."

I hold my hand up to my chest. "Me?"

He responds by unfurling his huge wings, knocking over a lamp in the process. I cower, hitting my back on the door, suddenly afraid he's turned into an avenging angel. A gust of wind blows my hair in my face. When I brush it away, Ezekiel's gone.

I release a tense breath, the residue of his good grace still lingering in the air along with his cherry blossom scent.

Keeping my eyes on my empty bed, I feel behind me until I touch my hand to the door knob. I fling it open and rush from my room and through the hotel-like hallway. A few of the doors display tidy dorm rooms, and the hum of voices drifts in my ears as I try to listen to any possible angelic noise.

I nearly collide into a boy as he steps from his room. He spins me around, and I hit my back into the hallway wall. It takes everything in me not to blast him away with my demonic power. The second he realizes I'm not going to fall over, he releases me and steps back.

I can't bring myself to look up past his black T-shirt stretched across his broad chest. "I'm so sorry," I say, nearly gasping for air I won't find until I'm out of the building. It's like the blessed walls of the entire academy poke at me, pushing through my good soul to sear the demon blood inside me.

He shifts his scuffed up boots. "Is everything okay? You look like you've seen a demon for the first time."

"Try an angel," I say, tilting my head back against the wall. "If you think demons like souls, angels are a hundred times worse." I'm pretty sure I've freaked him out by the sound of his silence. "I mean, they just expect you to hand your soul to them willingly with nothing in return and—"

"You must be Faith," the boy says, ignoring all the crazy pouring from my mouth.

I finally summon the courage to bring my gaze to look at the boy. He offers me a closed-lip smile, like he's already formed an opinion about me without actually meeting me. And it annoys the Hell out of me so much that I have to snuff out a small ruby orb of liquid power that erupts in my palm. Luckily, he's too busy inspecting every inch of my face to notice. Maybe he's trying to see if I have horns under my skin.

I force myself to smile. "Um, yeah. That's me. I'm sure everything you've heard you'll think is true regardless, so I'm just going to go."

I turn toward the stairs to leave, and the boy rushes to cut me off. He could've grabbed my arm to stop me, but I'm pretty sure he was taught about not surprising someone with power like mine.

His eyes narrow, though his lips part in a wider smile. "You say that like you know me. Talk about judging someone."

"I'm sorry if I don't have the best experience with people from here," I say, trying to shift past him.

He lets me by, but instead of watching me leave, the boy follows me to the stairs. "That used to be the case for me, but things change."

"Not always for the better." I take the stairs two at a time.

He keeps up my speed. "I hope that changes for you. Aria always said how awesome you were."

Hearing my best friend's name coming from this strange boy in a place far from Moonlight Shores breaks my concentration, and I miss a step, flying forward. I tuck in my head, somersaulting for a softer impact with the floor.

I land on my back, staring up at the shiny light fixtures above me. The boy stands over me, haloed in light, and he offers his hand out. As much as I don't want to, I let him help me to my feet. I straighten my shirt, realizing I'm still wearing Ezekiel's ripped and filthy shirt. I silently curse the damn angel.

Adjusting my top again, I fidget, considering asking the universe for help, but I'm afraid it'll just yank more unwanted divine intervention my way.

"I'm Christopher," the boy says. "Aria's my cousin."

I crinkle my nose, my heart clenching at the sound of my best friend's name. "She—"

He tilts his head slightly, his sandy blond hair falling onto his forehead. It's in this moment I realize he might not even know something happened to Aria, and I'm about to be the one to tell him.

"Are you okay?" he asks.

I shake my head. "Excuse me. I need some air."

I move past him and run toward the nearest exit across from what sounds like a laundry room. The hum of a dryer drowns out the sound of even my own heart, and I consider locking myself in there so I can just concentrate on cacophonous noise and nothing else.

"Faith, wait," Christopher says from behind me.

His footsteps force me to turn to the door instead. The last thing I want is to be trapped in another small room with a person who'll surely hate me the second he realizes my demon dad has been accused of foul play against his pack.

"Leave me alone!" I yell. "Please, just leave me alone."

Warm sunshine engulfs me the second I exit the building. I don't know where to go or where to run. It's not like I can get far.

I stand frozen, tilt my head to the sky. "Please. Please, let this be a dream."

Wind picks up my hair from my sweaty neck, and all I can look at is the shadow of wings.

THE TRAITOR PACK

EZEKIEL SETS ME down in the middle of a lemon grove, the zesty scent overpowering everything around me. I spin and press my palms into his bare chest.

I close my eyes, sucking in a deep breath. "You seriously need to put a shirt on," I say, bracing myself against him, feeling the twitch of his angelic muscles under my fingers.

He wraps his hands around mine and laces our fingers together so I stop touching his chest. Like holding hands is much better. "You're welcome to give mine back."

I summon demonic power in my palms. He jerks his hands

away and rubs them together. Placing my hands on my hips, I glare at him. I don't even know what else to do. He's the one who swept me off my feet and dropped me into the grove on the outskirts of the academy.

I pull the hem of the shirt up. "Fine."

His eyes widen. "I was kidding. Don't do that."

I grin. "Why? Afraid I'll ruin your purity?" Would serve him right for joking.

He blushes for the first time ever. He's been so unfazed by everything I've thrown at him until now.

I release a loud laugh that echoes through the quiet orchard. "You are! Oh, my God, Ezekiel. Is my humanity rubbing off on you?"

He expands his wings, hitting them against the lush greenery of the trees, sending citrus fragrance into the air. I expect him to take flight or to hit me with angelic light at any second. He crosses his arms over his chest instead.

He narrows his eyes at me. "It's not your humanity or you, Faith. I know you're acting this way toward me because you have no one else to direct your emotions toward."

I glare right back at him. "Shut up. You don't know me. If you did, you'd know I bottle my emotions up."

Something flickers in his hard gaze softening his expression. "No you don't, Demon Spawn. Your emotions are written all over your face. In every word you say. You can try to disguise them, but it doesn't work on me."

My breathing quickens. "Why are you doing this?"

"Because I want you to know you don't have to be made of steel or Hell's fire around me. I can see you're hurting, Faith. I want to help you."

Help me? If that were true, he'd have done something more to get the angels away from Dad. He wouldn't have brought me to the Hunter's Academy to suffer, knowing that I've lost all power given to me by birthright. I lost the safety of Dad's shadow, and Ezekiel's angelic light isn't blinding people from seeing me. It's shining a spotlight right on me.

"You can't help me or save me, Demon Watcher. I don't even want you around. You're playing games with me, trying to appeal to my good grace," I say.

"Is that why you keep threatening to corrupt me? Because you secretly enjoy my presence?"

I stare at him in shock. "I—" How do I even respond? He keeps lightening the heaviness of my thoughts, igniting the darkness threatening my essence. I hate that he can do that. That he's not letting me fall into the despair of my inner thoughts.

"And so you know, nothing you can do will ruin my so-called purity as much as the idea pleases your fiery little heart, but you can try. Whatever makes you feel better."

I groan, unleashing Hell power at his feet. "Just shut up and leave me alone. You win. I can't take this."

He chuckles, the musical tone of his voice sending another good wave of unbidden emotions through me. "You can handle the wrath of demons but a little teasing is what gets to you?"

"Coming from you, yeah," I say.

His smile melts away, and he gives me that terrible, world destroying look. The look that gives me a glimmer of hope while simultaneously screaming that I'm screwed. "I'm sorry."

"Good. You should be."

Ezekiel rubs his hand along his smooth jaw, looking more boy than angel, as he thinks for a moment. "I know this is all an adjustment. It is for me too, but we'll figure out how to compromise and work through whatever we have to."

I hate admitting that to myself—that maybe Ezekiel isn't so bad despite everything. He could be worse. He could be like one of the golden winged angels, the soldiers who don't get involved with humanity while protecting it. Ezekiel's black wings mean he's worldly enough to handle demons and humans, he has a higher understanding. But why was he assigned to me? I'm not exactly a risk. Am I?

"Or you could just disappear and creep around like normal Demon Watchers do," I say.

"Why? You're not a demon. I have no reason to hide from you. And, this is more fun isn't it?"

Fun? No. I don't say so, though. "Cadence was right, huh? You were assigned to make sure I don't ever try to descend and rise as a demon."

"Something like that," he says. "But I don't think you're at risk. If I did, I'd—"

"Save my soul?" I ask, cutting him off.

He shakes his head. "Your soul doesn't need to be saved,

despite all the demonic threats you keep shouting into the universe. What I was going to say was that I'd have never showed my face or answered any of your prayers. But I thought you should know you're not alone, especially now. I'm here."

Blah. Angels are unintentionally cheesy. I'm annoyed how I like it. Dad prepared me for an eternity of evil at the hands of demons. What he never prepared me for was stuff like this. Stuff that fills my soul with everything he glowers at. He was worried angels would hurt me not protect me.

I sniffle, blinking unwelcome tears from my eyes brought on by my thoughts of Dad. What I wouldn't give to share what Ezekiel said to me to see how demonic his reaction would be. Rule number one in life should be never provoke a demon, but Dad isn't an ordinary demon, and I'm not terrified of him. His reactions have always made me laugh.

The sound of someone stomping through the orchard draws my attention away from Ezekiel and my sorrow and toward the trees behind him. He brings his index finger to his mouth, motioning for me to remain quiet. His angelic shield stops humans and demons from seeing him but never angels. If he wants me to be quiet, he might have a good reason. I would've preferred a stoic, hardened angel to bring me here, but it doesn't mean I want one getting in my business now after everything. Ezekiel got to me in a good way, and even if I'm still mad at the angelic army, I can't keep blasting him. Not when he feels like the only heavenly ally I have.

Closing my eyes so I don't have to look at Ezekiel any

longer, I listen for any identifying sounds, especially of the angelic kind. Every person makes their own distinguishing noise I can detect if I just listen hard enough. Whoever comes through the grove hasn't been trained much in stealth, because I'm sure even a normal human could hear them from a mile away.

Another strange noise, like a child-like giggle, tinkles through the air. A branch snaps and a thud, like something hit a person, comes next.

A deep growl reverberates through the air, seeming to vibrate the dirt under my boots. I'd recognize the sound of a werewolf from anywhere after having spent so much time around Aria. "Knock it off!" Christopher yells.

Another branch snaps followed by a thunk. The child-like giggle rings through the air again. Ezekiel glances from me and in the direction the commotion sounds out. I narrow my eyes, trying to figure out what's going on. It almost sounds like someone is getting clobbered with...lemons? Yeah, I'm pretty sure a little kid is throwing lemons at someone.

Christopher emerges into view, swinging his arms around, blocking lemon after lemon that whizzes in his direction. Ezekiel picks a lemon from the tree and tosses it at Christopher, surprising me, and I can't control the laugh that escapes my mouth.

I slap my hand over my lips but realize Ezekiel's shielding me from the werewolf. "What did the werewolf ever do to you?"

Ezekiel plucks another lemon and tosses it. "He's trespassing. It's in my good conscience to assist the forest nymph trying to get him out of here."

My eyes widen. "A forest nymph? Dad told me about those. He said they are little pests."

"Because they hate demons," Ezekiel says. "Anyone not in good grace, really."

"Looks like she doesn't like werewolves either, apparently," I say.

Ezekiel shakes his head. "No, I think she doesn't like this particular one. Says a lot."

I roll my eyes. "Well, aren't you all righteous and judgmental? I'm sure if you let me be seen, she'd try to chase me away as well. I'm the spawn of an oh-so-evil demon."

Ezekiel responds with a smirk and shrugs.

I turn back toward Christopher to watch everything unfold. He crashes right into me, knocking me onto the ground. Rolling back to his feet, he yanks a dagger from his belt. I hold my hands up in surrender, forcing my demonic instincts not to show him that his dagger is a butter knife in a fight against me. Instead, I fake fear and step back.

"Don't hurt me," I say.

Ezekiel sighs but doesn't reveal himself. Christopher broke Ezekiel's shield by plowing into me.

The young werewolf immediately drops his arm, pointing the dagger at the ground. "Faith, I didn't know you were—" A lemon pelts him in the back of the head, cutting off his words. He growls. "Quit it, already! I'm almost out of here."

Another lemon flies through the air, and I jerk my hand

out and catch it. "Hey, you almost hit me," I call out, expecting a dozen more lemons to follow.

Musical laughter sounds through the air, and the cutest girl with red hair wrapped in ivy vines and a flowing dress made out of who knows what, almost like she wove the clouds together into a material that moves more than she does, steps out from behind a tree and into the open.

"Oh, my. Aren't you confusing?" the girl says. She looks to be in her early teens but sounds child-like. "The night clings to you, but you're a star in the darkness. And loved by Heaven. Where is your angel? I can feel him. I bet he's handsome. Or is it a she? No matter, I can feel good grace shining from you." The girl dances forward and twirls around me. She reaches out and touches my hair. "But if you are loved by Heaven, why are you so sad. Your smile can't hide the ghost of tears now dry from your eyes."

"I—"

"Come on, Faith. Don't let her musings get to you," Christopher says, nudging me with his hand.

The forest nymph twirls away, picks up a lemon off the ground, and chucks it at Christopher. "You cannot take my new friend away from me. She just got here. But you? I don't like you. Get out of my home."

I step between Christopher and the forest nymph. "That's not being very nice."

"He's a tricky one. Not animal, not human. The demons love him so," she says.

I grimace, turning to look at Christopher. "The demons love me, too."

"Not like the angels. Not like *your* angel. Can I meet him? Oh, please. Tell him to show himself."

I shift awkwardly, now uncomfortable by her words. No one in this universe loves me more than Dad. This forest nymph is mistaken. Something comes over me, the nerve she struck in my soul ignites like a match, and power glows between my fingers.

Screaming, the nymph rushes back behind one of the trees. "You're a naughty little half breed. I think Heaven is mistaken with their fondness of you."

I step forward. "You have no idea what you're talking about. Now stay away so we can leave."

Christopher smiles at me and then to the forest nymph. Usually people get nervous seeing my power manifest, but not this boy. And the fact that he doesn't cower or look away, how he stands tall next to me, looking at me in amazement and intrigue—it reminds me of Aria. There's no denying they're related.

"Come on," I say, snuffing my power out. "Where are you heading? I'll walk with you."

Christopher motions to the forest in front of us. "The wall. Classes ended for the day and no one notices anyone missing unless they don't show up for dinner."

"Except me," I say. "I'm sure an army of celestial beings will swoop down to drop me off right where I started."

He holds out his hand to me. "Aria's told me you used to sneak out of your house all the time. Sounds like this might be a fun challenge to me."

I frown, sadness gripping my chest at the sound of her name. "I—before we go anywhere, I have to tell you something."

He shakes his head. "I already know, but I also know that my cousin is strong. Unbreakable. Look who her best friend is."

I puff out my bottom lip. "She never mentioned you. Why?"

He shrugs. "Maybe because I work for the Hunter's Alliance?"

"Yeah, that's pretty embarrassing," I say.

He laughs. "Says the demi-demon." Christopher continues to smile at me. "Which isn't a bad thing, though Josh disagrees."

"You don't care what your pack leader thinks?" I ask. Aria butts heads with Josh, but in the end, she'd still fall into line with her pack...like the same way Josh said I'd choose Dad. But I'd still rise to fight for Aria. She'd do the same for me.

"Josh isn't my pack leader. I'm considered a traitor, because I'm working with people who shunned us and refused to help us when we needed it and only helped us when we had stuff to offer." Christopher glances around, breaking my stare. "So, please, don't mention to anyone that me and Aria still talk."

I grimace. "You don't have to worry about me."

"Good, never know with all that Hell in your blood."

I pull my hand away from him to cross them over my chest. "That has nothing to do with—"

He raises his eyebrows. "I'm just kidding. If you haven't guessed, I like a little danger in my life, especially your kind of danger."

I roll my eyes. I can't help it. How do I even react with that kind of quip? It's as bad as Ezekiel's. "You don't even know what danger is."

Christopher holds his hand out to me again, and I reluctantly take it. "I guess I'm about to find out."

Pulling me away from the forest nymph still hiding behind one of the lemon trees, Christopher nearly drags me through the orchard. We reach a tall wall, at least ten feet in height, and there's no way I can ever climb over it without a ladder or angelic assistance. *Speaking of...*

Ezekiel is nowhere in sight, which means he must be within touching distance. I might not know everything about him, but I know he'd never let a werewolf drag me off under his watch. He's my babysitter after all.

I swing my arm out, expecting to smack him in his chiseled chest, but I hit empty air. If Christopher didn't give me such a funny look, I'd do it again.

"Just checking to make sure we won't have any divine intervention," I say, feeling all sorts of awkward.

Christopher peers around like he'd be able to see Ezekiel if he tried. "Damn angels. They always know how to destroy fun."

I laugh. "You're not like everyone around here, are you?"

"I hope that's a good thing." Christopher guides me to the wall, humming with a blessed shield my demonic blood can feel, though it can't stop me. Turning to me, he offers me a smile tinged with familiarity as he reminds me of Aria. It eases the tightness in my chest.

I smile right back, feeling good in this moment despite everything. His presence is exactly what I needed to get my mind off things. And unlike Ezekiel's intensity and angelic glory, Christopher isn't dangerous. He doesn't make me feel like I'm on the verge of whatever it is Ezekiel elicits from me. *Why are you even comparing them?* "I haven't decided yet."

He chuckles. "I'm going to change that."

"Oh, really?"

His grin widens as he accepts my challenge. Touching his hand to my back, he nudges me forward toward the towering wall. Christopher motions for me to wait at the base. He jogs a dozen feet away in a clear path to the wall, sunshine peppering through the trees in starbursts to set his sandy hair aglow in golden streaks. Though the sun's rays cast him in light, a wicked glint sparkles in his narrowed gaze, setting me off in a good way. I can't help enjoying someone's bad side as much as I like someone's good side. It allures to my very nature, and even with a Heaven-bound soul, I can't stop what being a demi-demon does to my humanity. Things would be different if I weren't raised immersed in a demonic world, but the bond I share with Dad only grows with our closeness. But if he's no longer around...

Christopher charges at the wall, yanking me from my darkening thoughts. He launches from the ground, jumping higher than humanly possible, and hooks his hands on the top of the wall. Swinging his leg up, he climbs the rest of the way and straddles the wall.

"Are you sure you don't have wings hidden somewhere on your back," I ask, smiling up at him from the ground.

"Definitely not." Ezekiel pops into view next to me, expanding his inky wings from his back, stirring the hair from my neck and into the air. "And you need to turn around and head back into campus."

"Take my hand," Christopher says from above me.

I expect for Ezekiel to steal me from sight to drag me back to my new prison in the disguise of a boring dorm room, but all he does is glance between me and Christopher's dangling hand. Ezekiel's clearly waiting for me to make the right decision. I'm not sure he can make it for me, because of my free will.

I decide not to test my theory and shove my hand into Ezekiel's chest, pushing him back, and jump into the air to grab Christopher's hand. Christopher's fingers lock around my wrist, and he pulls me up so quickly that I release a squeal before I find myself balancing on top of the wall. Ezekiel flaps his wings, launching into the air, his flight shaking me so much that I grab onto Christopher for balance. The werewolf's arm hooks around my waist, pulling me closer, and I smile, touching my hands to his chest.

"Whoa, I got ya," he says, slightly digging his fingers into my side, sending butterflies through me.

"Blame my Demon Watcher," I say. "I think you've ruffled his feathers."

"Does he follow you everywhere?" he asks.

I nod. "My own celestial stalker. Just as creepy as it sounds, too. Apparently the whole universe is worried I might summon Hell on earth because of my—"

"Your dad?" he asks, finishing my thought. "I hear he's been accused of foul play."

A blip of fear blossoms in my chest at his words. What if Christopher's being nice for the wrong reasons? If he knew something happened to Aria, then I'm sure the Moonlight Shores pack has filled him in on their accusations. But he said they shunned him...

I step back, preparing to summon a ruby orb of power in my fingers. "He's not responsible for any of this. My dad has changed."

Christopher's smile disappears. "Think demon's can really change?"

"Yes, and I know he's being unfairly judged by the angels. They've had it out for him since..." I don't actually know.

"Since your mom," Christopher says, surprising me. "I've read the files."

I grimace, crinkling my nose, wishing I was back on the ground instead of balancing on this wall with a boy who could very well try to hurt me, leaving me no choice but to fight back. And I know exactly what will happen to me if it came down to that. I'd be accused of crimes against werewolves just like Dad. And then who knows what will happen.

Christopher's hard features soften, and he frowns. "I'm sorry. That all came out wrong. Now, I'm sounding as creepy as the angels."

"Why did you research me? Are you trying to set me up?" I ask, anger sliding through me.

His eyes widen, and he holds up his hands. "No, no, no. God, I'm sorry, Faith. I can explain."

"You better," I snap, accidentally summoning power in my hands, my body automatically reacting to the dark emotions coursing through me.

"When Aria told me about meeting you, she asked me to look a few things up for her in the database," he says. "She couldn't believe someone like you could be so nice. She wanted to make sure she wasn't falling for demonic charm."

Tears sheen my eyes, my breath coming quickly. I can't believe his words. Aria and I've been best friends for two years, since the first time I ventured off my private beach and into town.

"Hey, whoa. It's okay," Christopher says.

I swallow the burning in my throat and take a breath. "I'm sorry. I know Aria was just looking out for herself just in case, it's—I wish people didn't have to question my entire existence because of who I am and who my dad is. I don't even have a bad soul."

Christopher closes the distance, surprising me with a hug. I can't believe I'm standing on a wall, now upset, being hugged by a werewolf I've just met.

"I'm sorry, Faith. I didn't mean for things to start off like this. When I heard you arrived on campus, I had all these big plans to try to make things better for you, because I know how much Aria loves you. She'll tear my face off if she finds out I—"

"I'm not crying," I say, blinking my eyes. I huff a small breath and laugh. "Don't you dare tell anyone I was either."

Christopher squeezes me once more before letting me go to peer up at the sky. "And risk the wrath of a demi-demon? Definitely keeping this to myself." He shifts on his boots and peers down at the other side of the wall. "Still want to leave with me? I'll understand if you don't. But, I promise it'll be—"

I jump from the wall before he can finish his sentence, half expecting Ezekiel to catch me mid-air, but my angelic shadow remains hidden in the orchard. I stumble forward, bracing my arms out to catch myself. A strong arm hooks around my waist, stopping me from falling.

Christopher steadies me on my feet. "For being a demi-demon, you really could use more training."

My cheeks warm with blush. "Haven't needed anything besides the basics."

Christopher takes my hand, pulling me forward and away from the wall. "Well, I'm an excellent teacher if you ever want to learn a softer landing."

I smile. "I won't be here long enough."

He shrugs. "I hope not, but maybe you'll want to visit."

A shadow cuts across the ground before us like a huge bird, and I nudge Christopher toward the trees to block us the best I can.

"Or you could visit me," I say.

"I think I could handle that."

Howls sound through the air, sending a shiver up my back. Christopher glances at me in his peripheral vision, and I bare my bottom teeth in an awkward, nervous smile. I had no idea what to expect from leaving the Hunter's Academy, but heading to a werewolf den wasn't something I expected.

Reaching out, Christopher takes my hand. "You look scared. Don't worry. My friends are harmless."

As harmless as a giant wolf with sharp teeth can be. "It's not that I'm scared. Aria and Joshua were the only ones to tolerate me in Moonlight Shores. I never really get a warm welcome."

"That's because you haven't met the traitor pack," he says.

"You're all hunters for the alliance?" I ask.

"Yup, hence why we're traitors. We all have our reasons for joining the Hunter's Alliance even though they never looked out for us...or most creatures."

"Except angels," I say, looking over my shoulder.

"And the half breed abominations," he adds with a laugh.

"I'm the abomination. They're the miracles. Get it straight."

"Hypocrites. The whole bunch of them."

He's talking about nephilim, half human-half angels who

remain in Heaven's good grace, though their celestial dads went against Heaven to get a little too involved in human affairs. I don't know much about nephilim, but what I do know is those fallen angels find a fate in Hell, according the Dylan, who was half angel before he ascended in Heaven's ranks.

I laugh. "You really want the alliance to think you're a traitor, too? They'll blame me for being a bad influence."

His hazel eyes hold mine. "If anything, you'll be a good influence on me."

Christopher tugs me toward the door of a single story, fenced in house at the end of a lifeless cul-de-sac without giving me a chance to ask what he means. The house has seen better days, the lawn brown with dead grass, the yellow-painted smoothed out stucco exterior fading. Christopher opens the chain-link gate for me and strolls next to me to the screen door. Guttural growls and howls shake the board covering the broken front window, and it takes a sharp intake of breath to keep my steps the same quick pace as Christopher's.

He releases a loud whistle, making me cringe. The front door bangs open, and a tall, muscular boy no older than Christopher stands in the doorway, blocking our entrance. The Hunter's Alliance is known for training hunters young, and it looks like they still do.

The boy tilts his head back and hollers, half howling in his human form. "Chris! You made it!" The boy's golden eyes turn from Christopher to me. I brace myself for the snarl, the swear words, the possibility he'll launch at me. He bites his lip for a moment and gives me a once over instead. "And you brought a wicked hot little friend."

I smile without saying anything.

"Malik, this is Faith. Dragged straight from a demon's den by featherheads and dropped right in my path at the academy," Christopher says. "Crappy day for her. Pretty great one for me."

Malik shakes his head and points at me. "Time to change that. You look like you need a drink...maybe a punching bag. Definitely to blow stuff up."

I step forward with Christopher when Malik motions us to enter the shabby house. Wind whips through my hair, and the whoosh of wings draws my attention behind me, but I don't look over my shoulder. I continue to smile at the werewolf wagging his eyebrows at me.

"Welcome to the Traitor Pack, Faith," Malik says. "I'm sure you'll fit right in."

I enter the small foyer connected with the living room. Four other people, three boys and a girl, hang out on a stained couch with brown stuffing seeping from a tear on the arm. Thuds sound from the hallway, and a black furred wolf comes charging in my direction. It barrels straight at me, barking so loudly it hurts my ears, and I tense.

Christopher jumps in front of me, tackling the wolf to the ground, pressing its muzzle to the filthy carpet. The wolf growls and snaps at Christopher, but he only laughs and holds it in a headlock.

Bones crack, popping and snapping, and the black wolf

transforms right before my eyes into a completely, unashamedly naked man with a black beard, dark eyes, and hair longer than mine. He releases a loud howl, shoving Christopher away.

I take an automatic step back into a cool, muscular body, and a gentle hand slides over my clavicle. Ezekiel doesn't say anything, but his tense body speaks volumes, screaming that he's more than annoyed with me for running off with a strange werewolf despite the fact that he's related to my best friend.

The man strides closer, his hands crossed over his chest. "You scared of a little wolf like me, honey?" he asks, his dominating presence digging into me. Without having to ask, I know he's the leader of this so-called Traitor Pack.

I straighten my shoulders. "Only scared of accidentally melting your face off." Ruby power sizzles in my fingers. I'm not going to stand around and give anyone a reason to underestimate me, even if they probably can smell my fear not unlike demons.

The naked man releases a loud laugh, doing a little dance that sends my gaze straight for Heaven if it were above me.

Christopher shoves a pile of clothes at the man. "Knock that crap off and get some damn clothes on, Vic. You're going to scare Faith off just when she's beginning to like me."

"You mean tolerate," the only girl yells from the couch.

I smirk at her. "You're right about that."

Christopher holds out his hand to me, yanking me away from Ezekiel without even realizing there's an angel in their midst. Ezekiel's footsteps mimic mine, and he hovers so close behind me that I could elbow him pretty hard in the stomach if I wanted. But, I kind of like knowing he's with me, stalking me, just in case. I also like how annoyed he must be that I'm here, too.

"Everyone, this is Faith. Faith this is—" He points to the girl and continues down the line. "Kristin, Randall, and Lou."

"Nice to meet you," I say. I turn to Malik. "You, too. But not you, Vic."

The older wolf laughs again. "Well, it's a pleasure to have one of Lucifer's finest among us."

"And a daddy's girl at that," the girl, Kristin, says. An amulet glows around her neck, similar to one Cadence has worn for as long as I remember. One that Dad said was so rare, that it was only one of two he's ever seen. Cadence was given the necklace by Cami, who made a deal with a witch. But this girl?

I can't take my eyes of the rainbow stone, threatening to burn my retinas if I continue to gaze at it. "You're a witch."

"And you're Raphael Blackwell's spawn," she says. "I almost don't believe my eyes."

It takes everything in me to control the sudden heat of emotion that burns through me. "Why?"

"You're supposed to be dead," she says, leaning forward to rest her elbows on her knees.

That was the last thing I had ever expected to come from the girl's mouth. "What?"

She reaches for her necklace and laces her fingers around it like it'll somehow protect her from whatever is going on in her mind. "Let's just say I knew your father from before your conception."

There is no way this girl is old enough to have been around before I was born. She barely looks older than me with her long, nearly black hair and just as dark eyes. But then again, she's a witch. A creature I know nothing about. According to Dad, demons nearly wiped witches off the universe, because demons felt there was only enough room on earth for one of Lucifer's servants, despite the fact that most witches weren't Hell-bound. But they could be. They can swear allegiance to Hell for power. No deals need to be made.

"You knew my mom," I say.

"It was unfortunate what happened to her," she responds, a frown tilting her lips down.

Grandma always told me my mom died giving birth to me. Without her saying, and after I met Dad, I assumed it was because I was half demon, even though dying giving birth to a demi-demon isn't always the case—there are exceptions, but I'm not one of them.

"You make it sound like my birth was unfortunate," I mutter.

Kristin frowns. "No, definitely not. Like I said, I thought you died...with your mom."

"Faith," Ezekiel says from behind me. "Let's go."

But I can't move from my spot while a witch dangles information about my life right in front of me. Information that doesn't make sense or go with what I know.

"I don't understand. Why? Why would you think that?"

Christopher steps up by my side and takes my hand. "You mean you don't know?"

Hot, liquid power swirls in the perfect orb in my free hand. "Someone spit it out. What don't I know? My grandma said my mom died in childbirth. She made a deal with my dad that kept me with her until she died."

The room falls silent.

Vic steps forward. "Careful, Kristin."

I point at him. "Shut up!" I look at the witch. "Tell me now or I'll—"

Christopher slides his arm around me, hugging me before anyone has even said anything.

The gesture surprises me, because I could seriously hurt him, kill him by accident even, in this moment when my world is closing in on me. Dad's situation doesn't do anything to help my fragile emotions.

"You have to remember, Faith. This was a long time ago. Things have changed," he says.

With his words, I know exactly what happened to my mom. I understand why Kristin was surprised to see me alive. It's not like I've been paraded around the Hunter's Academy. Dad has kept me away from all of it, even now when things are supposed to be okay. But bad blood isn't so easily forgiven.

"Faith," Ezekiel says from behind me again.

"The Hunter's Alliance murdered her, didn't they?" I ask, not needing confirmation, because both Christopher's and Kristin's expressions say it all.

"She betrayed them, loving a demon. Not even your dad could save her," she says.

PURPOSE

THE EDGES OF my vision darken, anger and rage coursing through me. Everyone steps back, and for the first time, I catch everyone's fear circulating through the air. I take a deep breath, but nothing helps. How could Dad keep this sort of information from me? He always warned me against the alliance and those involved, but he could've told me it was them who killed my mom. No wonder Grandma turned her back on them and hid me. No wonder she went as far as to make a deal with Dad over it.

"Faith," Christopher says. "I'm sorry you had to find out

like this."

I tense at the touch of his hand on my shoulder. "I—I need some air."

"Take her out back," Vic says.

Before Christopher can even take a step forward, I race away from him, down the hallway, and toward the back of the house. I blast the rickety door right off its hinges and then send another blast of power at the dead tree in the middle of the open field behind the house.

Christopher comes up next to me, carrying a basket of old bottles in his arms. He sets them down at our feet.

"I hope you don't hold this against me," he says, throwing a bottle into the air.

I chuck power at it, and it explodes in a cascade of brown glass that rains onto the weeds in front of us. "Of course not. You weren't there."

"But I'm fighting for an organization with a history of unjust and horrible conduct," he says.

I purse my lips. "Who's also known for letting werewolves burn under demonic command."

He throws another bottle into the air for me to blast. "Hence why I'm a traitor in my pack's eyes."

"But why? Why are you even here after everything? If I had a choice, I'd run right now and never look back," I say, blowing up another bottle. "Actually, I think I might."

He drops the bottle he's holding back in the basket, forcing me to look at him. "And disappoint a werewolf who might have a tiny bit of a crush on you?"

His words make me blush. If there's one thing I know about werewolves, it's that they're far from subtle.

"Well, if it's only a tiny bit..."

Christopher laughs. "Enough that I could get in serious trouble if anyone discovers that I'm the one to have snuck you off campus."

"Sounds like a lot."

He responds with a flirtatious smile that sends my heart racing. Who knew I could ever like a hunter, a werewolf hunter, at that? Dad will be so disappointed, but it's not like he has a lot of room to speak. If my mom was a hunter, and Cadence is a hunter...like demon like daughter, I guess.

Christopher steps away from me, motioning for me to follow him. "Come on, let's go back inside. I think you'll like it here. The guys, they—"

Christopher's words cut off, and the world falls away, before I can even hear what he's about to say. Ezekiel's cool breath tickles my neck, and my stomach flies to my feet the higher he ascends.

"What in the name of Hell, Ezekiel?" I ask, more than annoyed that he basically ripped me away from Christopher just when I was starting to like him. Talk about an angelic intervention.

"Sorry, Faith. I have to get you back to the academy before someone misses you," he says. "We've been gone long enough."

I groan. "No one will miss me. I bet no one knows I'm

gone."

"Let's keep it that way, yeah?" he asks.

"You don't want me to have any sort of life, do you? I'm trying to make the best of all this. I can't sit in my room all day, thinking about my dad and what your kind is putting him through. And now that I know about what the Hunter's Alliance had done? God, Ezekiel. I want someone to take my side for once, and I think those people would have. They are the first I've met in a long time who didn't cower in fear of me," I say. My eyes uncontrollably leak in the wind. "You ruined that."

"I'm sorry, Faith. I—" He takes a deep breath, shifting me so I have to face him. "I'm here for you, remember? I'm on your side. My entire existence is solely for you. You're my purpose, and I refuse to fail you."

His words should make my heart thump faster. They should make me swoon, make me feel things I suppress. But he doesn't mean them in any other way but pure. He's my watcher. My guardian. Nothing more.

"Are you so pure that you can't grasp that I need more than someone watching out for me? I liked that boy. He was nice. He—"

"Didn't deserve your attention."

Shock drops my mouth open, and I'm pulled between wanting to hug him and blast him. He almost sounds human, jealous even. But angels don't get jealous...I think.

I do neither thing to him. Instead, I glance down at the

world below to break the stare he's trying to lock me in. Once I get locked into his dark, brooding, soul searching eyes, I'm lost to them until he releases me. That kind of control is scary. But not because I'm scared of Ezekiel or his dark, dreamy eyes. I'm scared of what they see in me. He's so pure that one glimpse into my demonic self could ruin him.

I'm not going to be the girl who accidentally breaks a Demon Watcher. Making angels cry is something Dad would do. Not me. I can't have that sort of guilt hanging over me for the rest of my eternity. "You can't say stuff like that. Who are you to say who deserves my attention? Is that how you feel about my dad? He's a demon so he doesn't deserve me?"

"You're putting words in my mouth, Demon Spawn. There is a huge difference between that wolf pup and your dad."

"One's on the brink of being sent to Hell?"

"That's their commonality."

I suck in a breath through my teeth.

"The difference is that Raphael, while he would love for you to embrace the other half of your heritage, would never push you into it. He understands you've made your choice no matter where it takes you in your eternity. But that werewolf would enjoy dragging you so far into darkness that even my light couldn't save you."

"But he's a hunter," I say.

"And Hell-bound. Wouldn't be the first, won't be the last. Souls are tricky things."

"People can change."

Ezekiel's silence draws me back to his gaze. The intensity in his eyes softens and turns to pity, like he's saddened by my hope for possible change.

Holding me tighter with one arm, squishing me against his bare chest, he uses his now free hand to touch my face. His cool finger glides across my skin so softly, it's like he's touching my cheek with one of his downy feathers. He brushes my flying hair behind my ear, wrapping a hand to the back of my neck. I lean my head forward, and I swear his lips brush the top of my head.

Just when I don't think he's going to say anything, he whispers, "That's what I'm afraid of." I don't know if he's referring to me—or to Christopher because of me—but either way, it's not his business. He can't say these types of things and mess with my emotions.

Before I can say anything else, put my thoughts into a mass of incoherent words, because I'm having trouble processing, Ezekiel lands with a soft thud in the sprawling lawns out front of the dormitory. He runs a few steps from the quick landing, and his wings vanish a moment before he lets go of me and disappears from sight.

Sighing, I spin around to take in the lively grounds, too lively and cheery for the darkness coursing through me. I'm annoyed I'm back here in the place responsible for never giving me the chance to know the woman who loved a demon enough to have me.

For the first time in my life, I miss her. The name Grace

Blackwell repeats over and over in my mind. I've always known her name, but she felt like a story to me. A tragic fairytale. But now, looking at the buildings around me, seeing what could've been her future—our future—it hurts me to my very soul.

I need Dad. I need him to be here, to tell me everything. Because the little details that felt irrelevant in the grand scheme of things feel so utterly and completely important. Without them, I'll forever have a missing piece in my soul, one the angels precariously removed like a cancerous tumor, trying to stop it from spreading. But the piece wasn't poisonous or killing me. It was an organ I didn't know I had and now I need.

A cool hand touches my shoulder, and a breeze lifts my hair. But Ezekiel remains hidden. He doesn't speak. And I wouldn't want him to. All I want is to listen to the sound of silence, to feel like nothing. To be nothing.

Turning to the dormitory, I consider going inside, but the small room makes it hard to pretend I'm anywhere else in the world. Instead, I plop down right in the grass and curl my knees to my chest, not caring what people think. I'm just tired.

So tired.

I fall asleep right in the middle of the lawn, waiting for the coming night.

I sit in the warm sand of a desolate beach, digging my bare feet into the sand. The sun hovers frozen in the crystalline sky above the still ocean. Behind me, my beach fortress looms, but it's so blurry in my vision, I know if I stood and walked over to it, it would disappear like a mirage. This place, the dream, is my imaginary oasis after feeling lost in the hunter's world for what feels like more than hours. If a day feels like a year, I can't imagine how the rest of my life will feel.

A shadow stretches out over the beach next to me, but I don't turn my eyes away from the blue of my house. "Is there no place I can go to escape you? Even my dreams aren't safe."

Ezekiel kicks sand instead of sitting down. "You're suffering. I want to be here for you if you let me."

I sigh. "Don't you know demons enjoy suffering?"

"You're not a demon, and that's not always true. Take your dad for example," he says. "He wouldn't want this for you."

"Don't talk about my dad like you know him," I say.

Ezekiel flaps his wings, stirring up sand. "You're right. I don't know him like you do. I'm sorry. I just—I need to know how to make this better. Watching the light in your eyes dim is the most painful thing I've ever endured. They never trained me for such an experience."

It's the first time he's revealed anything about him really, about who he is as an angel, and I never knew that I craved to know more about him and his existence apart from how to get him to fix mine. "You make it sound like you went to angel school. I bet sitting in a desk with those wings was annoying as Hell."

"It's more of a journey of the soul than structured education," he says.

I tilt my head to look up at him. "They should've added

more obstacles, huh?"

He chuckles. "I don't think there would have been anything they could've done to replicate you, Faith. You're—" He
presses his lips together and glances down at me before turning
his gaze back to the frozen ocean. "You're the most insanely,
incredible, beautifully frustrating soul in the universe. Just when
I thought I was getting used to you, you surprised me."

"What's the fun in making things easy for you?" I ask,
watching his Adam's apple bob in his throat. He turns his gaze
to me again, and I hear the thrum of his heartbeat pick up. It's a
melodic sound, thump-thumping in rhythm with my own racing heart. "Haven't you learned my favorite thing is to be difficult?"

He sits down, surprising me. "I'm not afraid of the challenge. You make it worth it."

I don't know how to respond to his words. It's hard to separate his angelic tendencies from my humanity. "Ezekiel."

He shifts to look at me, but the second our eyes meet, I
can't find the words. I'm afraid to put anything out there, afraid
that the second I ask him what he means about my worth, that
this peaceful dream will implode.

"What?" he asks. "Is that so hard to believe?"

Again, more silence from me.

He reaches out and touches my knee. "When I found out
my assignment was to be a guardian for a demon's sp—for you,
I was confused. I had expected to be a Demon Watcher for a
demon of your father's caliber. I had prepared for an eternity of

watching the downfall of souls, to intervene when I could, to monitor the damned. Then I got you."

"Must have been so disappointing," I say.

"A blessing," Ezekiel says. "You have the most mesmerizing soul I've ever seen. Brighter than anyone's. And while I know you are unsatisfied by my presence, and you're upset I've acted out of line and broke some rules, I want you to know I will not let anyone ruin you or your soul."

His honesty would normally piss me off. Because no one has that sort of right to make judgments on my behalf of what is good or bad for me, or who I can risk being around. But, something about his honesty, his revelation, sinks deep into me, touching the protective wall I've put around me and my soul without cracking it.

"You broke rules? How devilish," I say, trying to ignore the rest of his admittance.

"Divine intervention is taken seriously, Faith," he says.

And he's done a lot of it. "Oh."

"But it's a risk I'm willing to take for you."

"Why?" I have to ask. It's hard to process an angel's instant devotion and love. They're so pure and good, that I know he's not lying or trying to manipulate me. But I want to hear it. I need his reason.

He opens and closes his mouth, struggling to find a response. Then he doesn't. All he does is slide his fingers through mine and bring my hand up to his chest to feel his racing heart.

Staring out at the ocean, I lean over and rest my head on

his bare shoulder. As much as I want to pry, to put meaning behind his confusing words and actions, I can't. There's no point. Come nightfall, everything might change. Worrying about my Demon Watcher's intentions, getting angry about his divine intervention, are tiny distractions against the calamity about to unleash the moment the sun sets. The softness of his wings brushes against my arm as he folds them around me.

"I'm not so sure you should risk anything for me," I say after a moment. "Not if—" I pause. I hate even thinking about the possible fate of Dad and what it means. "I can't have you trying to intervene. I don't want you to get hurt. I'm afraid of what my demonic side will do."

"I'm afraid as well," he admits.

"You are?"

"I can't lie, Faith."

"Shouldn't you try to encourage me to keep my crap together? Tell me that maybe it's not as bad as it seems? That I will conquer all odds and overcome this horrible situation. That I'll be stronger because of it?"

"I didn't think you liked that kind of thing," he says.

I can't help but laugh. It's not a shoulder-shaking, hilarious, uplifting laugh—more of a strangled, breathless cross between a groan and a suppressed sob. "I don't think I can do this. What will happen to me if I lose control? You can't expect me to sit back and accept this is how things are."

"That's the last thing I expect from you. And if you lose control..." His words fade off.

"You'll save me?" Such a stupid way to put it, but I can't even tell it how it is. Because to think that an angel, especially one who has admitted how much I mean to his existence, could murder me to take my soul is horrifying. Almost more so than making a deal with a demon.

"I'm not to intervene with what happens to your soul. You're not human, Faith."

And angels can't risk messing with Hell-bound souls of demi-demons. The consequence of intervening could cost Ezekiel his wings.

"It's a good thing I wouldn't ask you to or anyone else for that matter."

He slides his arm around my back. "Thank you."

"You're welcome? I think?" I straighten my neck. "You make it sound like you might consider it if I asked."

"But you're not going to ask."

"Now I might."

He chuckles, the new lightness to his voice wrapping around me, making my dark thoughts seem like only shadows. "Heaven help me," he says, but he continues to smile, and I know he's joking.

"Careful. One angel is enough for me," I say. "No need to bring the army to me."

The smile disappears from his face for a second but returns just as quickly. I wish I could decipher his reaction. These feelings. Everything about him.

"What?" I ask. "Don't think I missed that weird look."

He laughs. "Very perceptive. If I didn't know any better, I'd think a little angel blood snuck through from before your father's descent."

Confusion puckers my brows, the lightness circling my soul suddenly vanishing with his words. "What did you say?"

He shuts his eyes for a second, like he realizes the mistake he made by saying such a thing. Such an insanely, crazy thing. There is no way that Dad was ever an angel...right? I'm half demon. My mom loved a demon.

A tear slips onto Ezekiel's cheek, and he hangs his head. "I'm sorry, Faith. I can't say any more."

I scramble out of his arms and away from him. "You better!"

"Faith," he says again, pleading with his voice. "Please."

"No! You can't say something like that and expect me to forget. You can't do that to me. This is my life, Ezekiel. He's my dad. I deserve to know. After everything you've done and everything you and those angels put me through, give me this." I slide my fingers into my hair, pushing it from my face. I look up at the crystalline sky like it'll open up and let me glimpse Heaven for answers.

"I'm sorry," he says, shaking his head.

I release a loud scream, kicking the sand. Power ignites in my fingers, the blue sky turning into darkness. Lightning strikes overhead, and the clouds burst open, sending a waterfall of rain over my once peaceful dream.

Ezekiel stands, his black wings unfurling on his back, a new hardness to his eyes I haven't seen before. I step away, fear piercing my heart. He no longer looks like the beautiful, endearing angel I've grown used to. He looks like one of Heaven's many warriors, avenging and powerful, so godly that I drop to my knees.

"What have I done?" he asks, but not to me. He's throwing the words to the universe like someone will respond.

But my dream remains quiet, the darkness all consuming.

Ezekiel disappears before me, leaving me on my knees in the wet sand.

For the first time since meeting him, I feel alone. I feel his absence in my soul.

It leaves me broken, and my very soul scatters on the imaginary wind.

HELL TO PAY

"FAITH, FAITH WAKE up. You have a visitor."

Cadence's voice pulls me from my sleep, and I snap my eyes open. Confusion overtakes me as I glance around the small dorm room. I rub my eyes, half expecting to see Ezekiel in the corner of the room, but it's just Cadence.

I listen for a moment, not hearing any familiar angelic sounds. Ezekiel isn't here. He really did leave. And it takes everything in me not to frown at the sadness his absence leaves behind.

I suck in a breath, noticing the lamp on my night table is on. "What time is it?"

"Midnight," she says.

I fly from my bed. "What? Oh, my God. Why didn't you wake me? Is it my dad?"

Cadence reaches out and hugs me. "He's okay for now, Faith. But Cami's waiting for you outside. She wants to talk to you."

I cover my mouth so I don't sob. "This is it, right? She's the one who's going to tell me Dad's fate? Stupid angels too scared to face me."

Cadence pulls me to my feet. "No doubt about it. Let's keep it that way, huh? Now, get dressed. I can't believe you're still wearing that angel's disgusting shirt."

My cheeks heat at the mention of it. Why does it feel like once I change, Ezekiel's absence will feel real? Why do I care? Because while he claims to care about me, he doesn't. If he did, he'd tell me about Dad and what he meant about his angel blood.

"I don't need to change," I mutter, pulling away from her and to the door.

Swinging it open, I nearly plow into Christopher who stands outside with his hand ready to knock. I startle, jumping back. He greets me with a smile, holding his hands up in surrender. I snuff out the sudden pulse of demonic power glowing in my hands. I really need to be careful.

Cadence slides between us. "I'm so sorry. Faith doesn't do

well with surprises. You'll have to excuse her."

I cringe, wishing she didn't make it sound like I'm an un-controllable child just coming into my power.

"I see you found your way back to your room," Christopher says, stretching to look at me from over Cadence's head.

"Unfortunately," I say, moving her out of the way to face the werewolf.

She releases an audible—at least audible to me—breath. "You know each other." It's not a question. "Thank God."

"God had nothing to do with it," I say to Cadence, smiling.

She rolls her eyes. "You sound like..." She glances at Christopher. "Never mind. Be quick. Night's running out, and Cami needs to head back to Moonlight Shores."

The sudden appearance of Christopher almost made me forget. I nod to Cadence, and she struts from the room with a glance at me from over her shoulder. I nearly push past Christopher to follow her, but he reaches out and runs his fingers across my shoulder.

"I hope I didn't get you into any trouble," he says, glancing around the small dorm room.

I shrug. "Just annoyed an angel."

"Good," he says, smiling wider. Something dark flashes in his eyes that I didn't see before, and I wonder if it's because I'm now aware of the darkness lingering in his soul. And it excites me. I can't help the attraction still pumping through my veins.

We stand, staring at each other for another moment, and I

free myself from his gaze. Unlike with Ezekiel, I don't feel locked or imprisoned by Christopher's stare.

It makes me like him even more.

"Walk with me?" I ask, motioning to the door. "I have a meeting with..."

"With the alliance leaders?"

"Um, no. A demon," I say. "You know what? Why don't you stay here and wait for me?"

He laughs, taking my hand. "I'd be a terrible hunter if I were scared of demons. I'll walk with you. I'm heading out anyway."

"Where to?" I ask.

"Secret," he says. "I was going to ask if you wanted to come..."

"I do." My automatic response surprises me. I'm pretty sure I'd go anywhere as long as it's not here. "But I really need to see what's happening with my dad first. Have you heard anything from Joshua?"

His smile fades, and he doesn't respond.

Panic erupts in my heart. "What? Did they find something?"

"A hellhound. It was—" He snaps his mouth shut. "I'm sorry, Faith. It was at your house."

"What?" That doesn't make sense. Why would a hellhound be at my house? A mixture of fear and relief rushes through me. Fear, because if there was a hellhound sighting, it would mean that one of the missing wolves—Aria even—was broken and

Hell-bound. But it also means that there's proof Dad wasn't involved. He's been with the angelic army.

"Yeah, it was guarding your property after sunset," he says.

I'm conflicted, stuck between wanting to laugh and cry. I hold my face expressionless instead. "This is proof my dad didn't do it. He was with the angels. They'll have to release him." I pull my hand away from him. "I'm sorry, Christopher. I have to go."

"Faith, wait," he says.

But I'm already running to the stairs to catch up with Cadence to meet Cami. I thought her being here came with bad news, but maybe she's here for something good. Maybe she's here to tell me that everything is going to be okay, and I'll get to see Dad again soon enough.

I run the entire way to the front door and slam my hands against the glass. A red mustang idles right outside the building. Cami leans against the passenger's side door, her wild dark hair cascading down her leather jacket in untamable waves. Her vivid eyes flash green like a cat's for a split second, and she offers me a small smile.

"Cami!" I call. "How's my dad? When are they going to release him? Someone told me a hellhound was spotted at my house, which means it's impossible my dad did this. He was with the angels."

Cami's stern expression gives nothing away. She doesn't react to my words at all. "Get in the car."

I freeze, something strange in her voice sending my heart

racing. It's like she's closed herself off from the world, acting like the pureblooded demon Hell turned her into. And the only time I've ever seen her act so emotionless was...I can't even remember.

Without arguing, I climb into the passenger's seat. She slams the door closed and walks around the hood to get behind the wheel. Without hesitating, she stomps the throttle, sending grass and dirt spraying behind us. I jerk back in the cool leather seat at the force and quickly sling my seatbelt on and buckle it in place. She drives just as crazy as my dad, if not more so.

"Where are we going?" I ask, finally summoning the nerve to break the thick silence filled with background noise from the rumble of the engine, the AC blasting through the vent despite the windows being down, and the muted sound of rock music still sneaking through the speakers.

"Just for a drive," she says.

"You're doing this because of the hunters, aren't you?" If it was something good, she'd have already told me. She wouldn't have whisked me away from all listening ears and curious eyes. She might be doing it for everyone else's benefit.

"Yes," she says simply. "I've been put in a tough position, and they don't need to know whose side I'm on."

"My side? Won't that put you in a dangerous situation with the angelic army?"

She stomps the throttle, zooming us through the open gate and to the main stretch of road that leads us away from the Hunter's Academy. She glances in her rearview mirror once, and then shoots a glittering bolt of electricity into her backseat.

"My watcher's not here," I say, my voice low.

She darts her eyes to me and back to the road, her steely expression morphing as she lowers her eyebrows, probably at the tone of my voice. "Just making sure we're alone."

"Where's Evan?"

"With Zach and Dylan. They're with Raphael. Things are kind of tense right now," she says.

"Obviously."

Instead of laughing at the sarcasm dripping in my voice, she purses her lips. "I need to be straight with you, Faith. Your dad is in a lot of trouble. It's taken me threatening to unleash Hell upon the world to get the angelic army to stop from proceeding with their desire to kill him."

A sob sneaks from my throat, and I cover my mouth. "But he didn't do anything wrong."

She reaches out and touches my knee. "It doesn't look so good, and I don't know how much longer I can hold the army off."

"But you're the most powerful demon in the world," I say.

She sighs. "With a Heaven-bound soul."

"That you can't put on the line." Of course she can't. I wouldn't want her to. Whatever the angels think Dad did—whatever bad blood they have—should not fall upon the demon who nearly lost everything. Who sacrificed so much to give me a life—even only a few short years—with my dad. "I understand. I don't want you to. But, I know he's innocent, Cami.

The hellhound—"

"Was not new, Faith," she says, cutting me off. "Nor was she completely broken."

My brows furrow. "What? How could that be? Dad released all the hellhounds he had after the war. You were there. That was your deal, and Dad wouldn't have broken a deal." Deals are as sacred to demons as wings are to angels. The only ones ever breaking a deal with demons are humans.

She taps her fingers on the wheel. "I don't know what to say. I want to believe Raphael, but—"

"But nothing. He didn't do it," I say.

"The evidence is piling up against him. Hellhounds don't wander far from a demon's home. The werewolf—she was thought to have been killed in the uprising. She's been missing for five years, Faith."

I slam my palms on the dashboard. "I would know if there was a hellhound in my house!"

Cami swerves at the pitch in my voice. "I know, Faith. I know that. But demons are tricky."

"But I know my da—" A bright flash of light erupts before us, causing Cami to slam her brakes. She squeals to a stop, the scent of burning rubber wafting through the air. I don't get to finish my words—and maybe this divine intervention was to stop me from lying to myself. Because the longer I'm away from Dad, the more I realize how much I really don't know. How much he's kept from me—for reasons I'm unclear of.

"Damn it," Cami says, slamming the car into park. She's

out of her seat before I even have a chance to unbuckle my seatbelt.

Electricity dances from her fingers as she flings her hand out, sending it into the nearest tree. It lights the dark road brighter than the ethereal golden wings of the angels in front of her. The small group takes a step back, and then she points at them.

"Another body was found." Through the hum of the idling engine, I listen to a familiar angel with golden curls.

Cami sends another bolt of electricity into the trees. "Isn't this proof enough?" I don't have to read her lips to be able to hear her angry voice. Each word sinks deep into me.

I sit straighter in my seat, a spark of hope lighting in my heart to consume the darkness.

"Means nothing," another angel says. "Murdered by a human under the contract of Raphael."

My chest clenches, and I unbuckle my seatbelt.

"Are you certain?"

"We have the human."

"I want to question them," she says.

"Are you really more concerned about saving a demon who clearly doesn't deserve another chance? Have you lost sight of our purpose? The werewolf killed was only a girl. She did not deserve such a fate."

Shadows edge my vision at the soft whisper of the angel's voice trickling to my ears. My whole body tenses, heat flourishing from my heart and up to my face. My blood pounds in my ears as my heart works in overdrive.

Before I have a moment to think about what I'm doing, I climb from the passenger's seat and behind the wheel. My knuckles turn white from my grip, and I take a deep breath. Wind whips through my hair from the open windows.

"Cami, the demon spawn," one of the angels says.

Without thinking, I throw the gear in reverse and stomp the gas pedal. The car zooms backward and away from the angels, and Cami yells out my name. But I don't stop. If I stop, they'll try to take me back to the academy. They'll lock me away. I need to get out of here and back to Moonlight Shores.

Jerking the wheel while stomping the brake pedal, I drift the car around, sending it skidding into the dirt. A low growl sounds through the air, and a beautiful white wolf launches from the forest and directly at me through the open window. I release a yelp, its big paws landing on my legs and its huge head blocking my view of the road. I expect it to turn its head toward me to sink its sharp teeth into my face, but it scrambles back and onto the passenger's seat and barks.

Angelic light explodes in the tree behind me, and I react by stomping the throttle, spraying dirt into the trees as I drive forward and back onto the road. I expect the entire angelic army to block my path. I expect Cami to unleash Hell onto the car to stop me. But none of that happens.

Glancing in the rearview mirror behind me, I spot her pointing her finger at one of the angels and waving her arms. A familiar angel lands beside her, and Zach, her own Demon

Watcher, expands his black wings. He wraps his arm around her and launches into the air. The other angels follow suit, leaving me alone to disappear in the night.

And I can't help wondering what was so important that they'd abandon me, the girl crazy enough to steal a demon's car.

The wolf whines next to me, and I release a shuddering breath. "I hope you're okay with long rides, because I'm not going back to the academy, Christopher." After spending so much time with Aria and the Moonlight Shores pack, I've grown accustomed to recognizing werewolves in their true forms.

The white wolf barks, his hazel eyes shining.

"I can't sit around there anymore. I need to go back an—" I can't get the words to form. I can't even fathom the idea that the body of the girl found was Aria.

Because if it was, someone will be at the receiving end of my wrath.

I'll give up my Heaven-bound soul for it.

Whoever is responsible for putting me in this mess— putting my dad, my best friend, all those innocent were- wolves—they'll have Hell to pay.

ABANDONED

"YOU'RE SUPER BADASS, you know?" Christopher says, shrugging into a too big dress shirt that looked ready to go to the cleaners in the trunk of the Mustang.

Unidentifiable stains splatter the front of it, and I almost ask Christopher to stick with only the baggy slacks because the shirt smells like Hell—not the alluring fragrance of upper-level demons. I'm pretty sure the gag-inducing, dry stains are remnants from a lower level demon that no one left outside in the day for the sun to take care of.

"And you're insane that you followed me. Why are you even here? My dad is being held for torturing your pack." I peer around the dark gas station, expecting angels to rain down on me in all their nauseating gloriousness. But there isn't a single streak of light or discarded feather in sight.

"My former pack. I'm a traitor, remember?" Christopher strolls toward the passenger's side door.

"Doesn't explain what you think you're doing," I say. "Hard to believe you're here from the goodness of your Hell-bound soul." There. I put it out there. Because I'd be crazy to trust Christopher no matter how cute and friendly he is. In this demonic world, looks are deceiving. Few people can be trusted, and at this point I don't think I trust anyone outside my instincts, and even that's questionable.

Christopher's easy-going smile fades. I expect him to turn on me this second. The last thing Hell-bound people like is to be called out. It's not like they have control over which direction their soul heads. Sure, being a cold-blooded murderer is guaranteed to unlock the gates of Hell, but something as little as bad intent can trigger it. It's whatever the soul desires, but it's also something that can change and be made up for. Heaven forgives no matter how much Hell despises the idea.

His serious expression melts into a glower, and he reaches into the trunk and yanks out a tire iron, holding it up like a bat. "Faith, beh—"

"Don't even try anything. I can melt your face off." I take an automatic step back, igniting power in my hands. Christopher is stupid and brave, but that's what it takes to work for the Hunter's Alliance.

A growl sounds through the night, sending dread right up my spine. Slowly, I turn around, afraid to turn my back on Christopher, but not as afraid as I am of the smell of burning flesh. The putrid smell of sulfur soon follows along with the scratching sound of nails against pavement.

Fire lights my face aglow, the hellhound launching directly at me, not giving me a second to use my demonic power against it. I fall back, hitting the ground hard. The hellhound's fiery paws sear through my shirt and burning pain explodes in my shoulders. Frothy black saliva foams from its mouth, a glob drips on my face, burning my cheek.

Ramming my hands up, I shove power right at its chest, trying to knock it off me. It howls and snaps at my face. I squeeze my eyes shut, preparing for the pain to ensue, praying to whoever is listening to make it quick. Being burned and torn to shreds wasn't how I expected to end my mortal life.

The crunch of metal against bone sounds through the air, and the hellhound's weight falls away from me. I scramble to my feet in time to see Christopher transform into a wolf in front of my eyes.

The hellhound growls, shaking its head from the force of the tire iron Christopher hit it with. Circling around, the hellhound stalks me, just watching and waiting for the perfect opportunity to attack. If it weren't for the sparking red orb swirling between my palms, it would have come at me full force again.

A low growl sounds from my right, and a white wolf saunters up next to me, rubbing the side of its body against my leg. Something about Christopher's werewolf presence beside me calms my racing heart. Just being a wolf after dark is dangerous for him, yet here he is in all his animalistic beauty, standing with me, staring evil right in the face. He might be Hell-bound, but I can feel a part of his soul radiating with something good enough to draw my Heaven-bound soul to his.

"Get back!" I yell, straightening my shoulders and holding out my arms to make myself look bigger.

It's been years since I've been around hellhounds, but I'll never forget all the nights Dad spent teaching me how to tame the beasts. But this is different. I know the hellish monster before me was once a werewolf, now broken and lost by the hand of a demon. Knowing what used to be under all the burning flesh and evil makes it harder for me to want to kill someone who has a chance at redemption. The werewolf the hellhound was before was forced into a Hell-bond and didn't have a choice otherwise. Sending it to Hell seems cruel, but living a fate such as this might be worse.

"I don't want to hurt you," I say. "I know someone who can help you."

The hellhound creeps forward, and I shoot a blast of power at the ground in front of it. Leaping over my blast, the hellhound flies through the air, taking advantage of the second I need to summon more demonic power.

Christopher growls, jumping right at the hellhound, and the two beasts—one broken, one possibly a step away—collide with each other and tumble to the ground. The hellhound smolders, singeing Christopher's white fur, snapping its frothy jowls, trying to take a bite out of the werewolf's neck. I summon more power, watching fur and burning flesh scatter across the empty parking lot.

I rush closer to the fight, now turning into an all out war of who will tear who to shreds first, and try to find an opening. If I blast my power at the hellhound and miss, I could hurt Christopher, *kill* him.

But he might die either way, all on my behalf.

"Help!" I scream. "Ezekiel, please. Please, help me." The last thing I'd ever resort to was to beg for my Demon Watcher's assistance. He might've left me alone in my room and then again in the car with Cami, but I know he wouldn't abandon me. But I also never thought he'd stand by and watch a werewolf succumb to a hellhound. "You can't pick now as a time to not use your divine intervention."

Holding my breath, pushing away the sound of the fight, I listen for my watcher—the sound of an intake of breath, the thump of a heartbeat, the ruffle of feathers—but to my despair, I can't hear him. I can't feel him. After telling me that his existence revolved around me, how he lived purely for me, he's not here. He lied. The purest being in the universe lied.

I've never felt so abandoned.

A high-pitched wail rips through the night. The hellhound

snaps its jaws on Christopher's front leg. I cringe at his bone breaking, the horrifying crunch sending me running forward. I slam my palms into the side of the hellhound, my skin burning even with the power that comes from my fingers.

The hellhound yelps, tumbling on its side, skidding across the pavement. Christopher struggles to get to his feet, his front leg still smoldering and bleeding from the hellhound's bite. I stand between the two beasts, using my own body as a shield to Christopher.

I raise my hands, preparing to throw all the demonic power I have at the beast, hoping that it's enough to send it to Hell, because it can't stay here. Not in this form, not if it refuses to back down.

The hellhound stands, wobbling on its legs, and I expect it to either run or try to attack me again. Its hackles rise, the flames licking across its slimy, blackened skin in orange waves, an eerily fascinating sight.

The hellhound bows, dropping its head to the ground.

I stand in horrified shock at the action. Not because the hellhound gave up, but because it gave up to me. From my knowledge of hellhounds, it's out of character and instinct for a demon-broken creature to affirm a person or demon outside its own master's dominance.

"No," I whisper, frozen in horror as the hellhound slinks forward and rolls over to expose its stomach at my feet. "This can't be happening."

But it is. This hellhound is acting identical to how Dad's

pack acted toward me. They understood that I wasn't their demon master, but once Dad showed me how to handle them with the power in my veins, the demon blood I share with Dad, they treated me no differently than him. They bowed to me like the hellhound. And there is only one explanation—one my heart can't bear as it shatters in my chest, each beat sending pieces of my broken heart to scatter across the ground with the rest of the wolf fur and hellhound slime.

"Heaven, this can't be," I whisper. "Please, this isn't Dad's doing."

The hellhound nuzzles its head against my jeans, singeing the fabric.

This isn't some other demon's hellhound. It's Dad's.

Heaven was right about him.

And in this moment, as I stand here falling apart, now gripping the back of the broken werewolf by my dad's hands for support, I know this is over. He'll be sent back to Hell, and even I can't save him.

HELLHOUND

VIC STANDS TALL in the doorway to the rundown house I was certain I'd never see again. But I didn't know where else to go. Returning to Moonlight Shores isn't an option with how badly Christopher is injured. It's not like I can drop him off at a hospital in his werewolf form, and I'd be crazy to attempt a call to a human vet. What he needs is his pack. After everything he went through to protect me, it's the least I can do.

A low growl sounds out from behind me, and I cringe. There was no losing the hellhound no matter how fast I drove.

It continues to follow me like I'm its demonic master, which might end up being the death of me with the way Vic tenses, reaching for the blessed dagger on his belt.

I hold up my hands. "I didn't know where else to go."

"That's a—"

I nod. "I'll explain everything, but please, Christopher's hurt. I can't carry him alone."

Vic glances at the hellhound, hiding in the shadow of a tree. "I can't go out there."

Turning to glance over my shoulder, I hold my hand up. "Stay there."

Slinking back, the hellhound hides behind the tree, just waiting. I don't know what I'd do if there wasn't cover to obscure it. The hellhound, in all its fiery glory, is a glaring beacon for the angelic army to see from above, and the main reason I know I must stay far away from Dad. Even if he did break this werewolf, I still refuse to give a reason for the angelic army to send him to Hell. I don't care if it threatens my soul. I can't betray Dad. He had to have his reasons for going against the deal he made with Cami and the angelic army years ago.

"You're commanding it," Vic says. It's not a question.

"You're safe, please. Just get Christopher."

I don't blame the Traitor Pack's leader for hesitating, but I'm about to summon Hell power to get him moving. Luckily, I don't have to. He steps forward, still clutching his dagger, and follows me to where the Mustang idles next to the curb.

His sharp intake of breath confirms how bad Christopher

really is. Christopher's white fur, now stained with blood, covers wounds I can't see. And the fact that he isn't changing back into his human form makes it all worse. He doesn't deserve such a fate, even if his soul is Hell-bound for whatever reason that may be.

A tear escapes from my eye, dripping onto my cheek. Vic scoops up Christopher in his arms, and I follow behind him, leaving the car running in case I have to rush out of here. If Christopher dies because of that hellhound, one created by Dad, I must leave. The werewolves will know. I bet they can already smell it all over me.

"Get talking, little demon," Vic says, crossing the threshold into the house. It hums with the same feeling I got from the walls of the Moonlight Shore pack's mansion. It's been blessed. Of course it has. Werewolves aren't stupid. Even if there is a stronger punishment for demons who break werewolves, it still happens. *I can't believe you, Dad...*

I suck in a breath, looking around the living room. Commotion breaks out from the hallway, and the werewolves I met earlier, along with the witch, swarm the room. Their cries of concern make it hard to think. I can't block out the noise. Each heartbeat hammers in my ears, giving me the worst headache. The panting, the shoes on the threadbare carpet, the cracking of knuckles...

My head swims with fog I can't seem to push away. Someone clicks on a stereo, and obnoxiously loud music blares through the air, taking away the sound of the voices. I wince, covering my ears. My stomach rolls from dizziness, and I reach out to grab onto something, anything. In return, a hand locks onto my wrist.

"Whoa, careful," a feminine voice says. "You okay, Faith?" It's Kristin, the witch.

I open and close my mouth, trying to push words out. It takes me an excruciating minute to remember how to use my voice. "It's too loud. I feel weird."

Kristin steps into view, grabbing my arm. "Guys, she's having a bad reaction to my protection spell."

I blink. One second I'm standing in the middle of the room and the next I'm sitting on the couch with no recollection of how I got here. My whole body screams, pain starting from my fingers and working its way up my arms. I cough, and drops of blood splatter across my jeans.

"Quick, Faith. Drink this," Kristin says, handing me a glass of water.

I bring it to my lips, taking a small sip. My mouth burns like I've poured a bottle of hot sauce into it. I cough and spit, choking on whatever the witch gave me. Fear squeezes me so tightly, I ignite power into my hands.

"Whoa, calm down," Kristin says.

"You poisoned me!" I scream.

"I'm helping you."

The world spins, and I can't keep my head up. My chin touches my chest, my body turning slack, refusing to move with the command my very soul demands from it. My eyes burn, a fog clouding the world.

"You better take her outside before she explodes or something," a masculine voice says. It's Vic.

"Give it a second. Her soul and blood are fighting. That goodness is ruining her."

"My bet's on the demon blood. If she's anything like Raphael, damn."

"I'll take that bet."

I can't tell who's talking. All I know is I've been given something and now I'm paralyzed.

"Faith." The soft whisper trickles to me from the fog. I expect to see Ezekiel in all his angelic glory here to save me, but instead, I catch sight of Christopher lying naked on the floor, a ratty blanket slung over him.

"You betrayed me." I'm not even sure I said the words out loud.

A vicious howl sounds from outside, the hellhound slamming into the invisible barrier protecting the werewolves.

"It's not what you think," Christopher says, struggling to get to his feet. His arm bends in a weird direction, clearly broken. "It wasn't supposed to be like this. I'm trying to help you."

Squeezing my eyes shut, I summon all the Hell power I can manage. Instead of thrusting it at the werewolves, now scattering for anything to hide behind, I chuck it right at the barrier. It sparks, zinging with my power. The hellhound breaks through, launching into the house.

The last thing I see is the fire of my dad's hellhound setting the dark room aglow in beautiful flames.

"Faith?" Ezekiel's voice cuts through the fog clouding over everything. White sand covers my bare feet, but I can't see my surroundings. The usual dream beach Ezekiel creates for me is hidden behind the same spell that stole my consciousness.

I search my surroundings, taking a few steps forward. I get nowhere. Nothing changes. "Ezekiel, are you there? Why did you abandon me?"

"Where are you? What is going on? Your soul, it's—" He doesn't continue, almost like saying the words out loud will confirm what he feels.

What I feel. That my Heaven-bound soul is in jeopardy, and not at my free will.

A figure looms in the distance, the silhouette of wings expanding out. The fog makes it nearly impossible to see my watcher, but I know he's here. He might not be with me physically, but he's with me now. It's like a part of my very soul connects to him—everything about our strangely intense relationship burning far below my mortality and his eternity. It exceeds his duty to watch me. Our connection runs soul deep in ways it shouldn't. It's why he left. He doesn't have to tell me for me to know for sure. I can feel it in the emotions swirling from him— the pure emotions now laced with something darker, demanding, inviting...

"I—" As his deepest hidden desire breaks through the fog to hit me like a bolt of electricity, I struggle to say I'm with

Christopher and went against his angelic warnings. That I was so concerned about Dad that I blatantly gave in to my demon desires for true justice to be served. I'm afraid to reveal how badly I messed up by taking things into my own hands, allowing Christopher into my life with his Hell-bound soul and gorgeous smile. How I went against everything, even knowing my dad was responsible for the hellhounds. I chose a demon, with his hellish actions, because I love him. And I'll still fight for Dad regardless.

But I fear I'll crumble for disappointing Ezekiel. I knew I was attracted to him, but I also knew whatever I was creating between us in my soul was as wrong as my choice to stand behind Dad. I knew Ezekiel could never reciprocate anything. He wasn't capable of it—at least I thought that to be the truth.

Until now.

"Forgive me for failing you, Faith. I should have never left you, knowing that night was upon us. And now I'm so afraid." Light erupts in the distance. Ezekiel's angelic light shines brightly, fighting the fog. But he's too far. I can't even hear the whisper of his wings.

I feel the weight of his guilt trickle to me, even from the distance keeping us apart. If I lose this battle I had no idea I needed to prepare for—the battle within myself—I can't stand knowing he will blame himself. "Ezekiel, you didn't fail me. I'm the one failing. The angelic army set you up for a lost cause, and you can't take the blame for what happens to me."

"You are quite the battle, but you are not a lost cause to

me. Now, you better use that infuriating demon stubbornness and resist whatever is causing your soul to shift. I mean it, Faith. If I lose you, I—"

"Okay," I say, cutting him off, knowing I can't resist what's happening to me. It's too late for me. Too late for Dad. I should find comfort that we might still have the chance at an eternity together as a family, but it should have never come to this. We deserved more than this. I deserve more than to be pushed by Heaven itself into falling from the grace that was supposed to protect me. The grace that proved I was more than a demon's daughter. The grace Ezekiel loves in me in ways I can't comprehend. In ways I'm not sure I want to. Not now. Not after everything.

Ezekiel's light grows brighter, but instead of cutting through the fog, it dims the rest of the world around me. All I can see is the halo of his figure burning so brightly, trying so hard to push the darkness away. But the darkness persists, and my world fades.

All I can see now is his light.

"We were supposed to meet in Moonlight Shores." The guttural, masculine voice pulls me from the dark recesses of my mind. "Bringing her here might've ruined everything."

"Are you kidding me? She came on her own. How was I supposed to know she'd put me before her dad?" Christopher's voice sends my heart racing in a horrible, end-of-the-world kind of way. "It was bad enough I had to risk exposure with not only the demon but the angelic army, and then a damn hellhound? I thought the pack was lying."

What is he talking about? What am I ruining?

"I'm sorry, Chris. I didn't take her good soul into account. You just sprung her on me so suddenly, I had assumed Raphael had claimed her. She is his daughter after all. But we won't have to worry about it much longer. Her soul just needs a little push." It's the girl—Kristin. "You've already got her halfway there. She's perfect right now and won't resist."

Perfect for what? Christopher got me halfway there? If only they knew it wasn't in the good of my soul that Christopher ended up back here. I did it for selfish reasons, trying to prolong Dad's fate and hide the hellhound.

Inhaling deeply, filling my lungs with now clear air, I summon demonic power from the depths of my burning blood. Pain zaps through my hands, and I scream out. It's like I put my hands in an electrical socket.

A warm hand touches my face. It takes me a minute to realize I can't move. I'm bound, and my hands are submerged in some sort of liquid.

"Faith, calm down. It's okay," Christopher says.

I swear if someone tells me to calm down one more time today, especially while being restrained, I'm going to burn the world down. Calm is the last thing I want to be. Calm doesn't put control into my demonic instincts.

"Don't touch me. Get away." I cringe away from him, and he jerks back, respecting my demands.

He rubs his hand over a makeshift sling, holding his injured arm to his chest. How can he still look like he's worried about me while purposefully holding me hostage and stopping me from being able to protect myself?

"I'm so sorry we had to bind you, but you're dangerous. You get it, right?" he asks. "I'm going to release you now. Just don't melt my face off. The hellhound bites are bad enough as it is. Your beast got Malik pretty good. It's going to take the rest of the night for him to recover."

Of course I know I'm dangerous. I thought I hated when people cowered away from me, but now? I like it. I want to see the werewolf who claimed to like danger, who tempted my evil side, to fall to his fear.

Stop that. You don't want people to fear you. The tiny voice of reason slams the door on the dark, foreign thoughts seeping from the shadows on my soul. Confusion puckers my brows as I regain control. "I—I don't understand."

"Demi-demon 101, kid. Never surprise someone who can kill you with a wave of the hand." Vic saunters from the hallway, blisters covering his left arm, though he acts like it doesn't bother him at all. "Ya hungry? In pain? Need to punch a wall?"

I shake my head, trying to yank free from the chains holding me hostage. "I want to leave. Please, I need to go. My da—"

"Is in a helluva lot of trouble," he responds. "Which puts me in a helluva lot of trouble."

"All of us, really," Kristin says.

I blink, not sure what is going on. How is my dad's trouble

related to all these people's? I shake on my chair again, frustration pouring through me.

Christopher eases closer, holding his hand out to me like you would to let an animal smell you, get used to you—test them to see how they'll react. I consider snapping my teeth at the werewolf for treating me like I'm less than human, but I freeze.

"I'm not going to hurt you, Faith. I'm not a monster, and I didn't go through all that trouble to be with you tonight to lose you," he says. "Can you please hold still and stop fighting. And no power. Shit hurts."

I glare into his hazel eyes, trying to see the Hell-bound soul Ezekiel warned me about, but all I see is a look of pure sympathy. I've seen the worst monsters in my lifetime, and he's right. He's at the end of my list with an imaginary scratch through his name.

Christopher's bottom lip puffs out slightly, and he leans forward because I'm stationed in a corner. I stiffen as he slides an arm around me, resting his head on my shoulder to unlock the chains with one hand, chains which hum with the buzz holy objects do. They don't hurt me or burn like they would a full-blooded demon, but they react to my demonic power.

The sound of Christopher's heartbeat thrums evenly in my ear, and his warm breath tickles the hair on my neck. The chains loosen, and I yank my hands up and out of the liquid.

"That's holy water you're dripping everywhere, Faith. Don't ignite your power until you've dried your hands unless you're into getting shocked. And please, don't blast anything. Your beast ruined my couch," Kristin says.

Christopher hands me a towel, and I stare at the dirty sling holding his arm because of the hellhound bite he received while in wolf form. My gaze trails from his injured arm and to his shoulder, peppered with blisters and puncture wounds I can see through the rip in his shirt. A purple bruise shadows his jawline, and I can't stop my hand from reaching out to brush my fingers along it.

"Looks bad, right?" he asks, stepping back and putting space between us. "Hurts like Hell."

I stand awkwardly, realizing the rest of the boys I met earlier aren't in sight. "Is everyone else...?" I don't want to ask if the hellhound killed anyone, because it'll mean it had done so on my behalf.

"They'll all heal," Christopher says. "Nervous about your pet."

"The hellhound...is it?"

"Your beast is alive but subdued. I already knew you'd be upset being bound, but I know how territorial demons are about their possessions." Kristin crosses the room and opens a door. The hellhound lies unconscious in the bathtub with the shower running, keeping the flames out. No wonder the other werewolves aren't here.

"I'm not a demon, and that hellhound definitely isn't mine," I say, grimacing at what she said. It's obvious I'm not a demon for the fact that I was here last in the day, something demons can't do.

Kristin arches one of her bold, perfectly shaped brows. "We won't judge you, Faith. Everyone knows the broken will submit to their masters and kin. I didn't think Raphael still had it in him since the war, but I guess old habits die hard and all that jazz."

I open my mouth to tell them that Dad isn't responsible, but what's the point? The lie would be for my benefit. How he got away with it, I have no idea. *He didn't get away with it.*

I turn to Christopher. "How could you not want to murder me? You're a werewolf." I motion toward the bathroom. "That could very well be your fate."

A smile plays on his lips. "It's nearly guaranteed at this rate."

My mouth drops open, and I step back, crossing my arms. "What? That's not funny." But it kind of is to me. Joking about turning into a hellhound is as bad as joking about landing your soul in Hell. Why do I appreciate his humor?

"Neither is the deal I made with your dad, who will surely return to Hell, taking me with him if we don't stop those featherheads from punishing all of us before our contracts expire," he says.

A million thoughts whoosh through my mind. If what he says is true, then he's not an enemy like I thought. He and his pack of traitors could very well make the best allies. Even if the only reason they don't want Dad to die is to save their own souls, I'll take it. I don't care about their reasons. It's more than

I can ask for.

"I did not survive all these years, barely survive the demon war, which your father helped lead, if I might add, to just get sent to Hell for something as small as missing wolves," Kristin says.

"He didn't take them," I say.

"I don't care if he did or not," she says. "And neither does the angelic army. They've had it out for him since..." Her words trail off, and she leaves clues to my past unsaid. I really don't like how all these people have this information about me and my dad, like it should be common knowledge. Maybe it is. Maybe it's why Dad isolated me all these years.

"Since he fell from grace, right?" I ask. Unlike Ezekiel, this pack of traitors don't follow the same angelic code. They can tell me whatever they want without consequence. And I'll take advantage of them and what they know.

"Who told you?" Kristin asks.

"My Demon Watcher."

The witch closes her eyes. "The nephilim who stole you from us earlier?"

I purse my lips together.

"Guess I forgot to mention that, too," Christopher says. "Faith's too good for a half breed."

The witch sucks in a breath. "Your watcher is pure?"

"And on his way."

Vic swears.

"Do you want to save your dad, Faith?" Christopher asks,

moving closer to grab my hand.

"Of course I do."

"Then come on. We gotta take care of that pure soul of yours if our plan to get Raphael is going to work."

HELL-BOUND

"**I**'M NOT KILLING anyone," I say, dragging my feet as Christopher guides me down the hall and to the back of the house.

Depending on the circumstance, since Heaven likes their gray areas for redemption, murder is on the top of the list of ways to guarantee you're Hell-bound. If I was to purposely and knowingly take a life for these reasons, Dad would be jumping for joy. He'd be planning my descent with a huge party at the Morningstar. He'd...he won't be doing any of those things.

I'm still not convinced I should even listen to these people despite their willingness to help Dad. They knew the consequences for dealing with demons. They knew that if something happened, they could end up in Hell before their contract expired and they didn't have some special way to redeem themselves. Angels rarely offer redemption to those who make deals, and some souls, after working with demons, are far too tangled with Hell to be free.

"How do you feel about maiming someone?" he asks.

He talks like turning my soul toward Hell isn't a big deal. Maybe because his is already heading in that direction. Either way, it shouldn't feel so normal trying to think of ways to push me to the side of evil. Maybe this is what my soul wants. Maybe it's what I want. Because the more I look at Christopher, watching him smile, notice how he will stare at my lips intently like they're something he wants to taste... What is wrong with me? Dad would ground me for eternity for flip-flopping on crushing on a werewolf and my own Demon Watcher.

I link my fingers together and flick my gaze to the ceiling. "Well, I'm not morally opposed if I'm in danger."

"Heaven really does have its halos locking your soul in place, huh? I would think being raised by a demon would guarantee—"

"I was raised by my grandma. Dad took over a little late."

Christopher turns to look at me, stopping me from heading toward the back of the house. He trails his gaze from my eyes and back to my mouth again, a look not lost on my beating heart. "Hmm. I think I know what we can do."

Faster than I have time to react, Christopher spins me through an open door and into a bedroom. My back presses to the cool wall, his body stepping up so close to me that all I see is him. He rests his hand with his palm flat on the peeling paint next to my face. If he was able to move his other arm, I'm sure he'd teasingly block me in.

I smirk, heat crawling up from my chest and into my face. I don't know if it's the way he looks at me, his eyes filled with such desire, or because I'm alone in a bedroom with a hot boy whose existence excites the demon within me, but something comes over me. I wrap my hands around his waist and spin him so he's the one with his back to the wall.

Closing the distance, I lean into him not even caring that his injured arm is trapped between us. He releases a low growl in his throat, his smile widening as he looks at me, thinking about a million ways to get me to turn my soul away from Heaven. But this? As much as Dad would disagree solely to try to persuade me otherwise, isn't on the list. Not between me and Christopher.

Our mouths hover so close that I breathe in the small, vanilla-scented gasp that escapes from his full, pouty, demon-tainted lips. "You're supposed to corrupt my soul, not the other way around," I say, still keeping a sliver of space between our lips.

Another throaty growl vibrates against my mouth, and he kisses me, using his free hand to pull me closer, locking his fingers to the back of my neck. He pushes us both from the wall, never letting even an inch of space get between us. My mind races, thinking about how crazy this is. How thrilling. How much my inner demon would like nothing more than to rip the shirt right off him so I could graze my fingers along his stomach, feeling his muscles quiver and ripple in response to my skin against his.

"This isn't going to work," he says, still holding onto me, moving his lips from mine to my jaw.

"I don't care," I whisper, because the last thing I want to think about is my purity and the state of my soul.

His lips move back to mine and he sucks my bottom lip between his teeth, nipping me just hard enough that I dig my fingers into his back. "I really don't want to care either—I almost don't—" His fingers brush the hem of my shirt and slide up to the bare skin of my side. "Damn it, you're so beautiful. Sexy."

I smile into his lips, tugging his shirt up before I singe the fabric that gets caught on his makeshift sling to rip the rest of it free. I hadn't realized until this moment that I needed this distraction. To feel someone so close who wasn't trying to mess... But he *is* trying to mess with my soul. Everything he says isn't because he wants to be with me or because he likes me. He's using me like everyone else.

I freeze, pulling my hands from the curves of his sides to place them on his chest, blocking him from leaning into me again. "I—I can't do this."

Christopher releases a long breath, stepping back to slide

his free hand into his sandy blond hair to push it from his face. He turns his back on me, and I stare at all the scars peppering his skin. Long slashes run across his back, puckered skin from sharp claws. Scatters of circular scars form perfect bite marks across both his shoulders, on his side, and I can't stop myself from sauntering closer to rub my hand across his imperfect skin that tells the story of his life—a story far exceeding his age in the amount of damage he's procured.

Aria only has one tiny scar on her forearm from a wolf nip. Christopher looks like his entire pack tried to tear him to shreds.

"I shouldn't have brought you here, Faith. I knew I shouldn't have, that this was too much to ask from you, no matter whose daughter you are." Christopher says it to the wall instead of my face. "I've made my mistakes and decisions, and I knew the consequence of my deal with a demon."

I reach out and touch my hand to his shoulder. He reaches up and rests his hand on mine. "I don't want my dad to die, but you have to understand."

"I'm an asshole for asking you to try to turn your soul for me—I'm nothing more than a selfish coward who deserves an eternity in Hell. It's just—I had only months until my contract expired with your dad. I had hoped to find myself back in good grace working with the Hunter's Alliance."

I purse my lips together. "Was whatever you got worth it?"

His shoulders slump. "It got me a life I wasn't going to have."

"But was it worth it?"

He spins to face me, a dark look crossing his face. "I don't know."

A knock sounds on the door, and it swings open before Christopher responds to whoever is on the other side to come in. Kristin stands in the doorway, a frown crossing her face. She looks us up and down and shakes her head. "We have to go. We'll figure out your soul on the way."

Christopher steps forward, blocking me. "Faith's not coming with us."

The witch narrows her eyes. "But her dad."

"We'll stick to our original plan. I can't put her soul on the line."

Kristin steps into the room, and I expect her to wave her hand and unleash some sort of paralyzing spell to capture me so I'm forced to go with them. I brace myself even, ready to fight back.

She sighs instead, surprising me. "I wish you weren't ever forced into this position, Chris. Heaven sure missed a good one in you. But, why don't you let Faith decide what she wants to do."

I peer between the two of them. "Of course I want to help my dad, but my soul? Heaven doesn't mess around with Hell-bound demi-demons. Not since the war."

"It's the easiest way for us to intervene," she says. "Just long enough to get the angelic army on someone else so we can release him. You'll have your whole life to return to good grace, and if we free your dad, he'll guarantee it."

"Can I think about it on the way?" I ask.

She presses her lips together. "Yeah, fine. It'll give me a few hours to convince you." She looks at Christopher. "And maybe even wereboy can still get the chance to corrupt you after all."

Christopher laces his fingers through mine. "You have to move the demon's car. The last thing we need is someone to tear down Kristin's house while we're gone."

I don't *think* Cami will tear a house down, especially since I'm the one who stole her car, but I can't be certain. Pissing off a demon calls for disaster no matter how good her soul is or whose side she fights for. Not to mention, if another demon caught sight of it, that is a new kind of trouble within itself. Demons thrive to test each other's power.

"You sure you don't want to drive?" I ask, opening the driver's side door.

He grins. "I should, huh? Might be my last chance to do something freaking insane."

He laughs while he says the words, but it's forced, like he wishes he didn't even have to consider that the end for him might be nearing. I don't want to think about it, either. I just met him, and I... My heart clenches, because even if I like Christopher, I can't see any type of future with him. He's a werewolf, and I'm a demi-demon. It's as crazy as thinking Ezekiel could be more than my guardian.

The thought fades with the flash of the hellhound zooming

from the house to bound in my direction. Christopher tenses, and I push him behind me, igniting my hands with my demonic power.

The beast skids to a stop and whines at my side, nudging its nose into my jeans. I cover my hand with the hem of my shirt and quickly pat its head. Without fire resistant gloves, I'll burn myself. Even with my hot power, I'm not immune to the intensity of fire, especially hellfire.

"Good boy," I say, dropping my hand.

The hellhound howls.

"I mean girl."

Christopher places a hand on my shoulder to peek at the hellhound sitting in front of me. "It's not so bad when it's not trying to rip me apart."

I glance down at the female hellhound again, because he's right. I used to treat them like pets long ago, the familiarity of the beast's presence more comforting than it should be.

And then I notice the eyes. Panic rushes through me seeing the flecks of gold in the hazel color—completely broken werewolves have eyes like burning coals as Hell strips them from their humanity. But this hellhound, with her human eyes that shine up at me, still clings onto her humanity. She's half broken and aware. And those eyes—I know those eyes from anywhere. I've looked into those beautiful eyes every day for the last two years.

Those eyes belong to Aria.

I cover my mouth with my hand, suppressing the scream

already ripping through the air at the realization that my best friend, the girl who had never judged me, who had always been here for me, despite who my dad was, is now held captive in a fiery body, chained to Hell, and at the demon I love, the demon I trusted all my life, my own flesh and blood's hands.

Christopher spins me around, gazing me over in shock, looking for injuries he can't see. Injuries I feel burn through me, splitting my heart between my love for my dad and my love for my best friend.

"It's—" I can't even manage to say the words out loud. I don't understand. How could this be?

"Faith," the familiar voice comes from behind me. I didn't even hear Ezekiel land. He's come to my rescue, and now? I don't need to be rescued. But he'll see our plan. What if he... I can't think about that now. Because Aria.

Ignoring both Christopher and Ezekiel, I kneel down, not even caring that the front of my shirt smokes and smolders. I throw my arms around my best friend, trapped as a hellhound, trying to push all the goodness of my soul into her to save her.

"Aria," I say. "I'm so, so, so sorry. My dad, he—"

"He couldn't have done this," Christopher says. "This is proof. The bodies showing up in Moonlight Shore are being murdered by a tainted human the angels think belongs to your dad, but Aria's been broken, and only a demon can do that, right?"

I honestly don't know. I thought so. But even half broken werewolves have some sort of loyalty to the demon who broke them.

I rake my fingers through my messy hair, pushing the blond strands away from my sticky cheeks. Sucking in a deep breath, I stand and face the only person around who could give me the answer.

"Help her, Ezekiel. Please. She's not fully broken. I know you can do it." If Ezekiel frees Aria from the demon hold possessing her, she might have information that can save Dad. She might be covered in flames, but she's my miracle.

A warm hand slides around my waist as Christopher holds onto me from behind. Ezekiel glances from me to Christopher. My watcher stiffens, an indecipherable look—possibly a cross between pain and disappointment, sheer torture even—wipes away the softness of his handsome features. He expands his wings out, and Christopher jerks away in surprise as Ezekiel reveals himself to the Hell-bound werewolf.

"Holy shit!" Christopher yells, shielding his eyes, cowering behind me like Ezekiel's presence is worse than the hellhound. No one likes surprise appearances, especially not me, so I can't imagine what's going through the werewolf's mind. He's used to demons. Angels? I bet he's never seen a full-blooded one.

Aria howls, her black, frothy jowls dripping like burning oil to the grass, setting it on fire. An angel's presence surely sets off all sorts of turmoil through the Hell coating her skin. It takes everything in me not to scream at Ezekiel to disappear again for her sake. But I need him. I need him to bring back Aria's humanity no matter how painful it might be. She doesn't deserve this fate. She's also the answer to saving my dad while keeping my soul in Heaven's good grace.

My watcher steps forward, heavenly light blasting from his hands and directly at Aria. He didn't even give either of us a chance to prepare, not like you can ever prepare a hellhound for an angel's light to try to snuff out their burning skin. Commotion sounds from around me, hollers and howls, a high pitched scream. Aria's massive body falls into me, and I stumble, hitting the ground. Her flames dim, but the heat of her oily body burns the skin of my stomach, unprotected by my shirt.

I scream, trying to push her off me, and Ezekiel's light hits us both in a steady stream. My vision shadows from the light, but Aria remains in the demonically broken form no matter how much of Heaven Ezekiel pours into her.

Something's wrong. It's not working.

Christopher locks his fingers around my wrists, dragging me out from underneath Aria, and the hellhound drops to the ground, smoke pouring from her hot skin and into the cool night. My chest heaves, and I pat my stomach like I can put out the burns decorating my once smooth skin.

"Let me see her," Ezekiel says, light still radiating from his skin, creating spots in my vision.

Ezekiel holds out his arms to me, his wings sending a gust of wind so powerful that the flames on Aria's back ignite again, leaving her burning and now weak on the ground. My watcher doesn't give Christopher much of a choice. The werewolf can't pull me away fast enough before Ezekiel closes the space completely.

Ezekiel drags me from Christopher, his dark eyes embodying the same emotions I felt when he touched my soul in my spell-induced dream. I curl my arms around his waist, my whole body drawing to him, needing to be close, to feel his goodness wash away everything horrible in my soul. I had no idea I could even miss him, but now that he's here, I realize I missed him more than I ever thought possible. Ezekiel's so far inside my soul that I can't imagine what it was like without him before. And it scares me.

"I don't understand," he whispers, touching his cool fingers to my now pink stomach, cooling my hot skin. "It should've worked."

I sniffle, resting my hands over his so he presses his fingers to me more firmly. It helps ease the pain radiating through me. Ezekiel leaves me all sorts of confused, but in this moment, I know he only tried to help Aria because I asked. His worry is palpable through his trembling fingers.

"Faith, don't let him get to you," Christopher says from behind me. "He's one of them. He'll ruin it for all of us."

I snap my head up to look at the werewolf. "He's my watcher, Christopher. He's only looking out for me. It's okay."

The light radiating from Ezekiel pulls my thoughts from Aria and Dad, from everything crashing down around me. It reminds me what I want out of my life—and as much as I love Dad, he'll understand why I can't jeopardize my soul for him. For some reason, my dad chose to turn his back on Heaven. He chose to fall for reasons I can't understand. And might not ever get the chance to learn.

"Faith, please. I'm begging you," Christopher says.

Christopher reaches out, touching my hand. I turn and look into his watery eyes. His desperation runs hot through him, and if there was ever a soul on the planet that deserved an ounce of mercy, it's this beautifully, nearly broken werewolf.

Ezekiel stands, pulling me up with him, and I don't resist. It's like his arms are what I needed all along, like it's the first time I've been able to truly breathe all night. He did say Heaven created him solely for me, that my existence was his purpose. And I feel it. But, just because I feel it doesn't mean it's truly good for me. All the good around me seems to get broken now. My perfect life with Dad. My best friend. And now this? The universe must need to remind me of my place with Hell in my veins. Nothing good should come of Hell, especially not me.

The thought alone wants me to ask Ezekiel to set me down. I'll ruin him. My existence could hurt him in the end no matter what. I'm a losing battle, my soul teetering, people needing me to make the fall, Dad needing me. Christopher and his traitor pack. Aria.

But Ezekiel? He needs nothing. All he wants is for me to be okay. For my soul to survive the night and to stay strong against the pressure of the damned reasoning with my good side and alluring my demonic half.

Ezekiel flaps his wings once, sending my hair flying. "We should go. This isn't your place, Faith."

Christopher kneels in the dead grass, shrugging his hurt arm from the sling so he can press his hands together like he's about to pray. "Please, you can't take her. I'm begging you. She's my last hope."

Ezekiel radiates with Heaven's light. "She asked for divine intervention."

I shift up so I can press my forehead to my watcher's cheek. I run my fingers along the downy inky feathers of his wings, just caressing them as if they're part of my imagination. Ezekiel's jaw tightens, his lips disappearing into a line.

"Ezekiel..." My words get lost to me. I don't even know what to say to convince him of what I need to do. In a world so wrong, this—being here to help the traitor pack and my dad— feels like the right thing regardless of what side my soul falls to.

"Faith, please. Don't ask this of me. You know I can't force you to leave unless you say the word. But staying here? It's not good for you. The wolf pup wants to use you. And Aria...we can find help for her, because it's not in my power to save her the way you want me to."

I press my lips together, contemplating his words. "I have to try. It won't feel right if I don't. I wish you could under-stand."

"I'm trying," he says.

A black feather from Ezekiel's glorious wings catches on a breeze and drifts into the night. The fear I carry in this moment is not of him but because I'm afraid for him. For what I'm do-ing to him by asking such a thing as to let me make the choice myself. He's conflicted, and asking him to help me, to not intervene so I can help my dad, could very well put him in an unfair position.

Ezekiel draws his eyes from Christopher, pleading at his feet, to me. His dark stare holds me, like it's all I need to survive all this. Just when I think I'm going to lose myself, Ezekiel tilts his head back and toward the sky, putting a painful inch of space between us. "What do I do? I know I'm not to intervene unless necessary, but this position is—I'm unfit to be in it. Please, guide me. I can't stand the silence." His words are too quiet that no one normal could hear them apart from me, and I know he's not talking to me or himself.

I follow his line of sight, expecting the sky to open up and for God to peek through with orders—an army of angels even—but nothing happens. Even I, with exceptional hearing, am greeted with lonely silence. The sound of no one listening. The feeling that no one is there.

I slide my hands around Ezekiel's neck and rest my head against him. His heartbeat thrums in my ear, the rhythm racing the tighter I press into him, feeling every rippling muscle of his body. He flaps his wings, stirring up the dead leaves and dirt, picking up the smell of burning hellhound, but he doesn't launch us into the air. He respects what I want.

"I don't understand any of this, but I don't want you to intervene, Ezekiel," I say, never in my wildest dreams imagining I'd be the one comforting an angel. "I know you're worried about my soul, but I'm worried about you, too. I—"

He leans back to gaze down at me, reaching up to touch my cheek. "Your life and safety is important to me. Your beautiful heart. The light in your eyes. I don't want you to risk anything for—" He doesn't say Christopher's name, but I know it's what he means. "I'm sorry. My judgment is clouded. I—"

"I want to risk this because I can't sit back and not help no matter who I'm helping. I know Heaven will forsake me if I oppose them for my dad, but he's not the only one at risk. I'll suffer with guilt for the rest of eternity if I don't try something to help these people."

"Who want to corrupt you."

Tears sheen my eyes. "I know you don't think I'm a lost cause, but I don't think I'll ever win. How am I expected to turn my back on people who've asked for my help because their eternities depend on my dad? If helping them turns my soul to Hell, but not helping them feels like I'm still ending up in Hell, how am I supposed to even decide? And Aria? Look at her, Ezekiel. Your light couldn't touch her, and you know my dad didn't do this. Can't you tell them and buy me enough time?"

He shakes his head. "I can't leave you. Don't ask me to. I'm in this position now because I left you."

"Are you in some sort of celestial trouble?"

"I'm being tested," he says.

"Then do what you need to do. I'm not going to ask you to risk anything for me."

His eyes glass over, and he glances toward the sky again. "Thank you," he whispers. But it's not to me.

I frown. "You heard something?"

He brushes his lips against my cheek, surprising me. "Only you, Faith. You're my answered prayer."

16

CONFLICTED

"**A**N ANGEL, DEMON spawn, hellhound, witch, and a pack of werewolves get into a van—"

Kristin leans forward in her seat and smacks Vic on the back of the head, causing him to howl in laughter. "And Vic's terrible joke killed us all."

"There aren't even enough seats," Lou says, peering into the van. "I'm not sitting next to the beast."

"That's my best friend you're talking about," I say.

"I meant the angel," he says with a smirk.

"Faith and Christopher can play lapsies. Aria can run, and

featherhead can fly," Vic says.

Christopher grins at me from the backseat and pats his legs, motioning me to get in. I suppress the soul startling revelation from Ezekiel to the back of my mind and beam a smile right back at Christopher, the memory of our attempted soul corruption flitting through my mind to suffocate all things angelic like a defense mechanism. Fire blooms from my chest and up my neck, and if Ezekiel didn't hook his arm around me and lift me off my feet, I'd have cozied in with the werewolf for the long ride.

"Faith stays with me," Ezekiel says, resting his chin on my shoulder. The whole avenging, I'm-yours-for-eternity-whether-you-want-me-to-be-or-not, attitude rises with the expanse of his black wings. His muscular arms lock me in place in a hold not unlike the sacred bindings every damn person who isn't demonic seems to favor in this world. But, this is better. Despite the coolness of his skin, heat radiates between us...probably from the constant overactive thrum of my heart trying to throw itself in his direction.

I clear my throat, averting my gaze to the ground. Everyone's eyes are on me, anticipating what I'm going to do next. "I'm not flying and risking more divine intervention."

"Then I guess you can play lapsies. But with me."

Oh, unholy Hell. I'm a goner. My demented demonic blood automatically twists the purity behind his words in ways it shouldn't. He's worried about my soul in the presence of the Hell-bound, but he should be more concerned about what his innocence does to me.

I'm a dead girl. Dead. Dead. Dead.

Saved by an angel.

Every passing second feels like another year between me and Ezekiel. How is it that his presence can get to me so? I never had this problem with my other angel friends. They've always felt like that—friends, family. There is nothing friendly or familial in this intense relationship born from the annoyance of being assigned a full-blooded angel. Ezekiel was supposed to be safe. But he feels utterly and completely dangerous. And I like it.

Christopher scoots over to make room for us, and Ezekiel slides in, still holding me. Being carried around by an angel is nothing compared to sitting in Ezekiel's lap, leaning my back against his chest, which thankfully is hiding behind a clean shirt. I should really ask him to switch, since I still haven't changed yet. He could shield me long enough to do it without an audience. The thought of undressing in front of each other in such a small space, though innocent in intent, makes me shake my head and close my eyes. Maybe I should've risked divine intervention. Flying is unpleasant enough to stop me from imagining...*Damn it.* I could use one of Dad's discouraging rants about boys right about now.

"Is this okay?" Ezekiel asks, resting his arms around my waist like a seatbelt. He's probably better than one.

I swallow, trying to form words instead of listening to the thrum of his heart, now projecting louder than everyone else's, because his body touching mine is all I can concentrate on. "You know, I thought you'd be uncomfortable as Hell considering how you feel like steel and concrete most of the time but—"

"You thought *I'd* feel like Hell? Come on, you know I'm made of Heaven," he says, chuckling at his dumb joke.

Except I laugh, and I hate that he's made me laugh at something so stupid. And my laugh, isn't even a laugh, it's a giggle. I slap my hand over my mouth to stop the light, breathless sound. Luckily, no one comments on how ridiculous I sound. If anything, they're probably now annoyed that I'm not feeling the weight of a hellish eternity on my shoulders like the rest of them.

I lean forward so my back isn't touching Ezekiel and turn toward Christopher. I'm suddenly feeling all sorts of awkward. Not because I'm in Ezekiel's lap, because there's nothing awkward to me about that, but because Christopher sits right next to us. I'm torn between liking the Hell-bound werewolf and yearning for Ezekiel, probably because I can't have him. I shouldn't like Christopher for that matter.

I'm being torn apart for no reason other than my humanity hates me and wants to punish me for being part demon. How dare it make me feel every little piece of my being with such intensity. If only it wouldn't be catastrophic to shut it off. The possibility is there, but Dad warned me against it. Feeling human is a gift he doesn't want me to take for granted, especially being it's one of the reasons I was born. To give him the ability to feel the world like I do. He doesn't feel it as deeply as I do. If he did, he'd understand why I'd even contemplate such an act.

"He only wants you for what you have to offer him," Ezekiel says. "Don't let it confuse you, Faith. I can see you're attracted to the pup."

I expect a growl to escape from Christopher, but he continues to look at the road ahead when Vic puts the car into drive. The glow of Aria's flames flicker outside the window, the hellhound managing to keep the same speed as the vehicle. Even if we lose her, she'll find me. She might have a demonic master, but our friendship brought her to me, and there's no way I'm letting her go so easily.

"You seriously aren't giving me relationship advice, are you?" I ask, trying to keep the annoyance out of my voice. Dad could give better dating advice than an angel, though last time we had The Talk, he swore I'd better stay single for all of eternity and threatened to be That Dad. I told him he already was. "You wouldn't know anything about those sorts of things."

"And how do you know? I'm not from another world."

"You sure about that?" I ask.

"I wasn't born a full-blooded angel, so yes. I'm sure."

"A nephilim?" I want to devour every little detail he reveals to me. Getting an angel to talk is probably a harder task than turning a Hell-bound soul toward Heaven. "You were a nephilim."

He nods. "I've ascended."

"Obviously. When?"

"The uprising."

I cringe at his words. If Ezekiel ascended during the Demonic Uprising, it would mean we lived during the same time—on opposite sides of the war. How he could even want to be here with me, say these types of things to me...

"Ezekiel. You—"

"My mortal life on earth does not affect my existence now," he says, cutting me off. "And I exist for your humanity, so of course I know about everything that comes with it. I do wonder if it'd be easier if I didn't, because the knowledge makes this incredibly difficult to ignore." He shifts me to dangle my legs to the side.

"Huh?"

"Your desire."

I blush. When he puts it that way...

"The wolf's, too. He looks at you in ways that leave me...I—I prefer he didn't look at you in any way."

Oh, God. I suppress the urge to ask for Heaven's help. Ezekiel's honesty will be the end of me. I can't tell if there is more behind his words. They sound innocent enough, like he would prefer there be no attraction between Christopher and me for the sake of my good soul, but it *feels* differently. Personal. Like he doesn't want anything to escalate for his own selfish reasons. But a selfish angel? Never. I can't wrap my mind around it.

Christopher clears his throat, and I peek at him scrunching his brows. "You're really shielding Faith, watcher?"

Talk about a private conversation between me and Ezekiel.

He made us both disappear altogether. I guess it's better than Ezekiel expressing his feelings about me and my desire for everyone to hear.

And then the thought settles into me. What I know about angels from the demonic side of things is that they don't open up. They remain distant and secretive. Non-intrusive. Ezekiel is all sorts of intrusive, pointing out my mortifying emotions, even telling me how they make him feel. The fact that he recognizes them even after his ascension? Ugh. I hope he doesn't feel them like he can my soul, though the two seem tied together.

I release a breath, my whole body shuddering with the action. This open and honest conversation with Ezekiel makes it hard to remember where I am. Who I'm with. Maybe that's Ezekiel's goal. He said he understood my humanity. I'm sure he remembers what it's like being human. I wouldn't put it past him to use it against—for me? I don't know. He's using it in ways that turn me into a mess of confusion.

"It's creepy, you know?" Christopher adds.

I smile.

Who needs divine intervention with a cute werewolf distraction?

Reaching out, I touch the werewolf's shoulder, breaking Ezekiel's shield preventing him from seeing me. Christopher jumps, startled.

I hold my face expressionless, though there's a hurricane of emotions battling through me, mixing everything together, threatening to sink me in my own confusion. "I'm sorry, Christopher. It's a private conversation." Now I feel guilty that I like Christopher and Ezekiel feels it. It's ridiculous. I shouldn't care. I shouldn't want to smile and cry at once.

"They're talking about you, kid," Vic says, glancing in the rearview mirror. He couldn't hear me and Ezekiel, but it's obvious.

Christopher rubs his good hand across his eyes. "This is so weird."

"He wouldn't be able to handle the idea I'm always around, Faith," Ezekiel whispers, pulling my attention back to him. I wonder if he's trying to get into my head because of all my emotions. One way would be to attempt to hold my undivided attention by pissing me off or making me swoon. Ezekiel does both.

I smirk, trying to keep things light before I bury myself against Ezekiel and all his observations that put doubt into me about the werewolf I barely know. But it's not like I exactly know my Demon Watcher either. Not how I want to. "Are you sure it's not the other way around?"

"Maybe that, too. I—I'm sorry. I can't lie to you. I should've never brought it up. Don't ask me anything else." He releases a small breath in my ear. "I was not prepared for this." He's talking to himself.

I frown, unable to see his eyes, so I shift again, straddling him in the seat. My knee hits Christopher's leg, and his mouth drops open as I come into view again. My whole face burns with embarrassment. All I wanted was to face Ezekiel and ask him a million more questions despite the fact that he asked me not to. But his sudden vulnerability ignites the darkness in me, and I want to use it against him for answers.

"Whoa, little demon. Your idea of lapsies is way better than I imagined," Malik says from the third row. I look up at his blistered face, still smiling even with the injuries caused by Aria.

Lou punches him in the leg, causing him to holler. "Dude, don't talk to Faith like that. That's an angel. It can't be anything less than pure."

"Yeah, and you don't want to piss Christopher off. He's holding hope to live to see tomorrow so he can ask Faith out on a real date," Randall, the nearly always silent pack mate says from his other side.

Christopher groans.

Ezekiel remains silent, probably thanking Heaven for this weird werewolf intervention that stops me from asking my watcher more questions.

Damn angel putting me in this extremely awkward position, both physically and mentally.

"You don't have to comment on anything they say," Christopher says, reaching out to touch my hand.

I suck in my bottom lip, sadness washing over me. Ezekiel pointed out that Christopher liked me, though he didn't like his intents for my being here, but now that Christopher's pack mates confirm that I'm not having one-sided, humanity driven emotions, it digs into a part of my soul. The fact that I haven't even had to think about tomorrow, because tomorrow not coming isn't an option for me, not like with the traitor wolves and the witch, gets to me. And I hate that they even have to consider it not being an option.

I take Christopher's words to heart and don't say anything. My previous embarrassment melts away, a darkness cooling the warmth rushing through me, and I lean my head on Ezekiel's shoulder. He hugs me without saying a word, incredibly in tune to everything I'm feeling.

The van suddenly feels awfully crowded the longer I'm in it.

"Hope is good," is all I say in response. "It's all we can ask for, right?"

"Maybe saving Raphael's life will get you a pass to date—"
Christopher growls, cutting Malik off.

He was only saying what I'm sure the whole pack was thinking. If we somehow manage to save my dad, it doesn't change the fact that I'm a demon's daughter. Attempting to date a werewolf, a demon hunting werewolf at that, isn't exactly something I'd want or could ever reveal. It'd be day dates for life.

Ezekiel rests his hands on my back, his soft breathing whispering in my ear. "He doesn't stand a chance."

"I didn't think angels got jealous," I say, turning my attention back to my watcher.

Ezekiel doesn't respond right away. "How much do you know about angels?"

"My knowledge about angels has nothing to do with it." I

pull away and look at him, knowing he's shielding me from everyone's view and listening ears again. "God, you're so hot and cold."

"And you drive me crazy," he says, leaning closer. His eyes trail from mine to my lips before averting to stare out the side window.

"The feeling is mutual," I say.

"I didn't say it was a bad thing," he says.

"Neither did I."

The smile Ezekiel flashes me shines brighter than all the heavenly light in the universe. I close my eyes, just soaking in everything good and pure about him. He makes it easy to forget we're in a car full of people, all Hell-bound, with huge expectations of me. Distracting Heaven to free my dad is a lot to ask, but Kristin swears she will get it right with magic. All it takes is one spell. One drop of Dad's blood, and no divine intervention.

I should be scared, terrified, but Ezekiel numbs the bad feelings. And as long as I don't look at Christopher, who now leans forward in the seat, his head resting on his fisted hand, nothing seems dire.

"Keep smiling like that and you're going to get in trouble." I reach up brush my thumb over Ezekiel's cheek. "Hellish trouble."

"Is that a threat?" He still continues to smile. "Because I'm not afraid of Hell or demons or werewolves for that matter."

"You're just afraid of me and the possibility of my soul corruption," I say. "Why?"

"I've told you. You are my purpose."

"That's sad."

"The only thing sad about any of this is that you keep looking over at the werewolf, when I'm trying to keep your full attention."

I tilt my head back and laugh. "You're so pure that it literally hurts my soul every time I think of you. You know that, right? My poor demon blood boils with the idea."

I expect him to frown, to say something about the Hell coursing through me, constantly putting me and my soul at risk. That I'm over-thinking things, putting too much of my silly emotions behind things so menial that it's laughable. My intense attraction, no matter if it's caused by the soul deep connection we share, his beautifully handsome face, or how I want what I can't have, is just that: Attraction. A distraction from the rest of my life.

"Faith." He whispers my name so softly I only hear it because I'm reading his lips, feeling his breath shape the silent words without the sound. He closes his eyes for the first time, not trying to peer into my soul for some answers that remain hidden from the rest of me. "Help me. Guide me."

"What?" I ask, confusion wiping the smile off my face.

"I can't," he says.

He opens his eyes, a strange look hardening his features. I realize he's not talking to me at all. I only heard his words because I'm so focused on him, so much so that a single breath is loaded with everything on his mind. He might be able to read my soul, but I read his desire like it's sewn across his chest in bold, red letters.

"You can't do this?" I ask, trying to decipher the meaning behind his words. "I'm not asking you to do anything. No divine intervention, remember?"

He brings his hands up from their spot on my back and touches each of his palms to my cheeks. "You're so beautifully human."

"I'm only half."

"And beautifully demon, too."

"Ezekiel, you're acting weird. I mean, you're always questionable, but I—"

Without warning, he leans forward and brushes his lips to mine, so feather soft, I'm not even sure it happened. I sit frozen, stunned, my heart racing, my blood rushing. All thoughts lost to me as I replay the moment over and over. My poor heart can't handle this as it is split between doing the right thing and wanting the right thing for me.

I touch my fingers to my lips, trying to determine if the world is real, if I'm not suddenly in some fantasy I keep having.

"I—" I expect the van to flip, for the ground to open up and send us all into the fiery pits of Hell. I expect lightning to strike Ezekiel, burning his wings off his back. That thought alone sends my mind spinning.

But nothing happens.

Neither of us moves or breathes or blinks.

"I'm sorry," he whispers. "I had to see."

"See what?"

"If it's real or if I'm getting lost in your humanity."

"I don't understand what that even means."

"There's a reason the angelic army recruits humans and half breeds for jobs such as this."

"A job," I say. Of course I'm a job. It's what I've always been. I don't even know why I let myself get carried away on the brilliance of his wings. Christopher was right. In the end, Ezekiel is one of them. He's on the opposing side of my very essence even if my soul is good.

He shakes his head. "I didn't mean it like that."

"Maybe you should've." Because really, that's what I *should* be to him. Nothing more.

"Please, Faith."

I sit up straighter. "Tell me? Did you get the answer you were looking for from that *meaningless* kiss?"

"I did, and—"

A tear slips from my eye. "Don't. You say you can't. But *I* can't. This whole world is so twisted. I'm not supposed to be kissing werewolves, and definitely not angels. My best friend shouldn't be a broken beast who you failed to save. I shouldn't even have to consider the good grace of my soul to rescue my dad. This is messed up." I scramble off Ezekiel's lap, half bent to do so, and standing awkwardly in between the seats. Power ignites in my hands, threatening to explode through the van. "This is messed up!" I scream. Not at Ezekiel or anyone else in the car for that matter.

"Faith," Ezekiel says.

"I can't do this! I don't deserve this! Do you hear me? Do you even care?"

The van swerves, and I lose my balance, falling forward into Ezekiel. My whole world shakes, the noise of metal scraping against metal stinging my ears, stealing all the rest of the noise away from me.

Ezekiel grabs onto me, pulling me to him despite my screams, and the whole world spins, the van rolling over and over and over again until it jerks to a stop. Groans and whimpers sound through the air, and I lie on the roof, looking up at everyone dangling from their seatbelts upside down.

Blood drips from above me, splashing on my forehead.

I peer up and meet Vic's eyes.

His open, empty, lifeless eyes.

What have I done?

DEVOTED

EZEKIEL DRAGS ME from the car. I don't even know how he managed to get out, but here he is, kneeling next to me, wrapping his black wings around my body like he can somehow keep every piece of me from falling apart.

I push him back, crawling forward to the smashed window. Glass digs into my hands, stinging my palms, but I shimmy in to see the damage I caused. Kristin falls from her seat, thudding on the roof. Christopher struggles to unlatch himself with his broken arm. The backseat with the rest of the wolves is too quiet. I'm afraid to look.

"Damn it, Faith. Your soul has better shifted with the damage you caused," she says, looking around the roof for something. "See my bag anywhere?"

Christopher thumps next to me, releasing what sounds like a bark. I help him flip over, trying my best to keep his arm in place so he doesn't hurt it even more. He sits up and turns his gaze to me. My eyes water. I can't help it. Guilt pours through me, and my head swims with so many thoughts, I can't even count the breaths of everyone to see if anyone else died by my doing.

Christopher reaches out and touches my cheek. "Are you okay?"

"I need my bag!" Kristin yells. "Vic's soul."

"It's back here," Malik calls from behind us.

"Randall? Lou? You guys all right?" Christopher asks.

Silence.

I close my eyes and concentrate. Three heartbeats plus my own. "They're dead."

Kristin releases a frustrated scream, scrambling from her place in the front next to Vic's dangling body. She pushes past me, cursing up a storm to Heaven, and retrieves her bag. Another bang sounds through the air, and Malik hits the ceiling.

"Your angel better stay away. I know for a fact they're too far gone for redemption," Kristin says, yanking a few opaque vials from a leather bag. "And I'm not letting these souls go to Hell so easily. I don't care if I have to renegotiate my contract. I'm not letting them descend."

A low growl reverberates through the air, crawling up my spine. Heat erupts on my ankle, and I'm ripped from Christopher's side and out of the van again. But not by Ezekiel. Aria flips me over with her snout and snarls in my face. These werewolves might be traitors but that doesn't stop her fiery heart from caring. Since she still has contact with Christopher, she obviously knows the others.

I cower, bringing my hands up to block her from sinking her sharp teeth in my face. She's never lashed out at me, and I'm sure I'm beyond her forgiveness. "I'm sorry," I say. "I didn't mean—"

A blast of Heaven's light radiates through the dark night. Aria whimpers and slinks away from me. Ezekiel stands above me, wings out, and he reaches out his hands to pick me off the ground. I thrust my leg up, kicking him in the stomach, pushing him back so he can't.

"No!" I yell. "You can't help me. Look what I've done."

Tears sparkle from his eyes. "You didn't do this."

"You're right. If you hadn't—if I didn't lose control, I—"

He points into the distance. "Look, Faith."

A man stands in the middle of the road with his arms across his chest. Strolling closer, he moves with a dancer's grace, his footsteps nearly soundless as I listen for something identifiable. He's all shadow in the darkness, and his eyes reflect the light like cat eyes, sending a rush of fear over me. But something's different. My soul screams he's a demon, and he looks familiar, but I can't pin down who he is from this distance.

There are too many demons in the world to keep track of them all.

A low growl hums through the air to me. I push from the ground, gathering as much molten power as I can between my hands. Demons recognize my dad's power, and this one should realize I'm not to be messed with...unless word got out that Dad is in the hands of the angelic army.

Any time there is a shift in power between demons, they start gathering, waiting to take the opportunity to rise.

I glance over my shoulder at Ezekiel, realizing that Christopher, Malik, and Kristin have exited the van. "Protect them," I command. "I mean it, Ezekiel."

"Okay," he says, surprising me, not even putting up a fight.

Like boots stepping on gravel, a weird crunching sound echoes through the silent air. The man jerks his head from side to side, his body writhing and contorting right before my eyes. His bones snap, and his insides shift and move in a sound not unlike water shaken in a plastic jug.

I gasp, tensing. The man isn't a demon at all. He's a werewolf. But I don't understand. He feels demonic.

Launching forward, the wolf charges toward me. My heart rams against my ribcage, and even though I steel myself for his attack, surprise breaks my concentration, and my demonic power flickers out.

The sleek blond fur of the wolf is unlike the other wolves of the Moonlight Shores pack. I've seen Joshua in his wolf form a dozen times over the last few years, and there is no mistaking him now.

Howls sound through the air, coming from all different directions. Wind whips through the air, Ezekiel flapping his enormous wings behind me. I expect him to rush forward at any second to scoop me up to fly into the air. I brace for it—self preservation runs hotter than anything else rushing through me.

A guttural growl sounds from behind me, and a fiery blur rushes past me and in Joshua's direction as he runs toward us. Aria charges the blond wolf, a trail of smoke drifting in her wake. I take an automatic step back and right into Ezekiel's arms.

We stand frozen, watching the scene unfold in front of us. Aria, in all her hellhound glory, prepares to attack Joshua. I didn't command her to do so, but with every fiery step she takes, I see an end to my life on earth. The angelic army will no doubt punish me, blaming me for the act against the wolves even though they attacked first. And I know why.

My dad.

I've always known that the Moonlight Shores pack held my being a demon's daughter against me, because they would never forget the years of servitude and suffering Dad put them through. But Aria was my friend despite it. Joshua allowed me into their home. And now I know why. They've been waiting for this chance to make sure the demon responsible for all the bad in their lives pays the price they think he deserves. And I can't help wonder if this was all a set up.

But how can I hold it against them?

How can I blame them for wanting to send Dad to Hell?

Joshua, in his beautiful wolf form, launches into the air at the same time Aria does. One Hell beast and one unforgiving pack leader are about to tear each other to shreds all because of demons. Because of me. Family against family. Blood against blood. This is how the world works when it comes to good and evil. It's what the angelic army expected of me. I'm proving them right.

I suck in a breath, my chest clenching, refusing to let me breathe out. Aria misses Joshua, and skids across the gravel behind him. But she doesn't charge to attack. She rushes to rub the side of her flaming body against his. A sizzling sound, like a spark setting dried paper ablaze, buzzes in my ears, and I bring my hand to my open mouth.

Joshua's body lights up, the flames of Hell licking through his fur and skin, turning the beautiful blond color black and igniting him like a torch in the dark night. Ezekiel tenses, squeezing me tighter, flapping his wings to take off.

Something collides into his back, sending him reeling. I tumble from his hold, somersaulting across the rocky pavement. We were both too distracted to see another werewolf coming. A flash of white fur dances in my peripheral vision, and Kristin screams out.

I scramble to get to my feet, summoning as much Hell into my hands as I possibly can. Christopher, in his wolf form, drags Kristin back. Rage rushes through me, and I throw my power in his direction. I should've known. Once a traitor, always a traitor. Ezekiel was right. The wolf was using me.

My power hits the side of the van, melting the metal into a lava-like mess on the asphalt.

"Faith, behind you!" Ezekiel yells, an arc of heavenly light escaping his outstretched hands. It hits the hellhound sneaking up on me, sending it flying back.

Ezekiel runs toward me, and I throw another orb of power at the hellhound refusing to give up. My Demon Watcher slings his arm around my waist. I cling onto his shoulders, squeezing my eyes shut from the cool wind created by his wings.

Then my eyelids turn red.

Ezekiel yells, spinning around, gripping me so tightly around my chest that I can't breathe. A hellhound smashes into us, and Ezekiel lands on top of me, covering us with his wings. The scent of burning flesh trickles through the air, and all I can hear is my own racing heart.

Heavenly light radiates from Ezekiel, but it sputters out, and he sucks in a sharp breath. Black feathers scatter through the air, drifting on the wind, glowing red as they burn up and disappear.

"My wing," Ezekiel says, still lying on top of me.

Fear courses through me. "Oh, God. It's burning."

"I've been bit. I can't fly us out of here."

Another growl rips through the air, and Ezekiel's knocked off of me. Hot hands grab my hair, yanking me to my feet. I swing my arms out, but someone else grabs me from behind. My shoulders scream, and I summon demonic power into my hands.

"Try anything stupid and I'll gnaw your hands off, Faith," Joshua says.

Confusion washes over me. I don't understand. This is impossible. Hellhounds don't transform back and forth into werewolves. They disappear alongside their demon masters with the sun.

"Hey, Uncle Josh, you promised no unnecessary harm." Aria's voice sounds through the night, stabbing me right in the heart.

I suck in breath after breath, but air refuses to enter my lungs.

"Aria," I say, tears stinging my eyes. A thousand thoughts threaten to send me to my knees. "I don't understand. You were a hellhound."

She steps closer, stark naked, touching her hand to my face to pinch my chin. "I'm sorry, Faith. I really am."

"Please," I say.

She presses her lips together. "I love you. You're my best friend. But, this has to be done. Raphael's going to ruin you like he ruined us. It doesn't have to be that way."

"Please. He's my dad."

"And Raphael broke mine. My mom is dead. Lost to Hell. Look what he made us do. Look at the beasts we've become. Better to serve ourselves than to bow to him or any demon for eternity." She jerks, her bones snapping, and she turns into the beautiful platinum wolf I know and love. But that wolf is gone in an instant. Flames consume her, turning her back into a hell-hound.

"I don't understand," I say again to no one. Betrayal sinks deep into me. Aria says she loves me. She claims to be my best friend. Yet here she is, breaking me to pieces. Drawing Hell straight from my veins. Playing on everything we had.

"Faith." It's Ezekiel.

I turn to him, looking for answers. "Save her."

His brows lower. "I don't know how. I've never seen such a thing. She can change at will, which means—"

Aria swiftly transforms back into her human façade, snuffing out her flames, her skin still steaming. "I don't need help from those who've denied us mercy and allowed this to happen. I don't need to be saved."

I bow my head, fear and hopelessness burying me in a mountain of everything I'm about to lose. Now I'm about to lose Dad after I've lost the one person I thought was different. The one who I thought could look past everything. Obviously, I was mistaken.

"I can't believe this. Who are you?" I ask. "What demon got to you? I swear I'll—"

"A demon? No. They think they're all powerful, but power taken from Hell isn't the same as power given by Hell. Heaven isn't the only lover of sacrifice."

"You don't know what you're doing, Aria. Hell? You're willingly bowing to Hell? All because of the past? My dad isn't the same demon."

"This isn't all about Heaven's Traitor. This is about getting what I deserve in this eternity, which is more than being treated like an animal," she says. "I'm doing this because you're my best friend, Faith. You deserve better than Raphael. You deserve greatness. You'll forgive me once that bond to the demon is broken."

Everything hits me at once, and the only reason I'm still standing is because Joshua holds me in place. Her admission is too much. Heaven's Traitor? What does sending Dad to Hell even accomplish? She can already take on an unleashed hellhound form. A form even angels fear.

Joshua drops me, and I crash to the pavement. I don't even attempt to get up as the edges of my vision shadow. Curling my knees to my chest, I hold myself, the world crashing and burning around me—not by my own hands or my dad's. By the girl I would have stood up to the world for.

Aria's betrayal cuts deeply through my soul, spilling out everything good I held on to. My demon blood seeps into my spirit, filling up the emptiness.

"Faith, please. Resist," Ezekiel says.

But I'm not so sure I can.

"Resist."

"It's the only way," I whisper.

I let Hell into every part of me. I embrace my demonic self.

Because this is who I am.

A demon's devoted daughter.

But something unexpected happens. The goodness of my

soul fights back. But with fighting back, I'm weakened. I feel almost completely human.

I'm lost.

SACRIFICE

"FAITH." EZEKIEL'S VOICE drifts into the darkness holding me prisoner. "You need to wake up. They're opening the door."

I don't respond.

"Please."

His pleas wrap around me like the whisper of his wings, but he doesn't touch me. A hot hand encircles my wrist, refusing to let me go. As hard as it is, I peek through my eyelashes and up at Christopher.

I tense.

"Seriously, Faith? You're going to let one little decision on Chris's part ruin him for you?" Aria asks. "You've forgiven your dad. Hypocrite."

Christopher pouts his bottom lip. "I'm sorry, Faith. This wasn't—"

Aria elbows him. "It's better than trying to rescue a monster. Or did you forget Raphael broke your entire family?"

Christopher's jaw clenches, and he tilts his head to look at the ceiling. "I wouldn't forget that."

"My dad owns Christopher's soul," I say, trying to sit up.

Aria glares daggers at me. "And I have it covered. When Christopher told me he was planning to help you, I knew he'd fail. One of the most powerful demons couldn't break your soul, and he's your blood. But demons aren't the only ones who deal in souls."

"Angels won't—"

The back of the trailer whines open, and Joshua climbs up. He crosses the space to Ezekiel, who doesn't even shield himself. Joshua pushes Ezekiel forward, purposely ripping Ezekiel's black feathers out, some of which still smolder from being bitten by a hellhound. Wincing, Ezekiel expands them, pushing the pack leader back, and then his wings disappear.

"Try to shield yourself or intervene and I'll tear her throat out," he says, pushing Ezekiel hard, making him stumble.

I scramble to my feet, preparing to launch at the pack leader, but Christopher yanks me back. I slap Christopher across the face. He spins me, wrapping his arms around me like his hug could calm me down. I want nothing more than to ignite my power to burn this whole place down with everyone, including me, in it. The tiny morsel of hope I carried now obliterated the longer I think about everything unfolding around me.

"Faith," he whispers, breathing into my ear. "Please."

I ignore the traitor wolf. "Don't touch my angel!" I scream.

Aria scrunches her nose, peering between me and Ezekiel. "Whoa, I thought you hated that guy. Now, you're standing up for him?"

"I swear if you touch him I'll—"

"Oh, crap. You like him?" It's hard to separate all the feelings I've had for Aria for our entire friendship. She still sounds like my best friend. But something no longer feels right.

My heart thuds so loudly that her surprise turns into a pout.

"Whoa, not like him. You *love* him. Damn, Faith. I always knew you were messed up, but this? What in the Hell? That guy isn't capable of reciprocating. He's only out for that pretty soul of yours with nothing to offer in return."

Love is a strong word—a dangerous word—to use to define my feelings for Ezekiel. It's not something I had ever expected out of my attraction to his divinity, especially in the short amount of time since he revealed himself to me. But my heart knows better than to deny it. I love Ezekiel in a way that far exceeds mortality. It's not how I imagined my love for someone to be. With Dad and Cadence, they complement each other. With Cami and Evan, they balance each other. Those loves have been my only references. But Ezekiel? He was made for me, like Heaven stole a piece of my very being to give him.

This love is pure, so real that I feel like I can summon it into tangible form not unlike my demonic power. It's how I imagine an angel loves, so deeply, unconditionally, unending. Love unattached to the hot emotions that come from my humanity. This is the kind of love where I can't stand the idea of him being hurt. I'd gladly give up everything, do whatever they want, anything, just so I know he's okay in the end.

This isn't normal, human love. It's heavenly. It only takes an instant to occur.

Dad's warned me about it dozens of times. I thought he was joking. I can't help think that maybe it has to do with his blood, a fallen angel's blood in my veins. He wasn't always demonic. I know that now. It's why Heaven's so adamant about their purpose to send him where they believe he deserves to be.

And now I'm mad at the whole universe rising up against me.

But even with the anger burning around the love I want to deny, I'm afraid of what my love would do to Ezekiel. It's a double-edged blessed dagger, and it'll go through the both of us all the same.

"You wouldn't get it, Aria," I say, a little too late. Because she wouldn't. I don't think she even gets the severity of the situation she summoned upon herself.

"You say that like I'm incapable of understanding love. I'm no less human than you are," she snaps. "Though everyone seems to think so."

"I always thought you were more," I say.

Joshua closes the distance between me and him and yanks me from Christopher. "Shut up. I know what you're doing and you'll not get into her head, little demon. It's bad that she cares enough to have asked that you do not suffer. But you should suffer. You stood by and did nothing while Raphael broke so many. How Heaven still wants your soul is beyond me."

Fury slithers through my veins as fast as my demonic blood pumping into my heart. "I was a kid when I discovered your pack! You can't hold that against me. I didn't know any better."

"Yet you defend him now when you do know," he says.

"Because people change."

"Demons can't."

"Faith, you're wasting your breath," Ezekiel says. "You can't save those who willingly give their eternity to Hell."

"But demonic contracts can be broken," I argue. I know this. "Dad said angels intercept souls worthy of redemption all the time."

"There isn't a contract involved." It's the first time Kristin says anything from her corner of the trailer. I didn't even know she was there. "This was caused by a trade. A sacrifice. A spell."

"Say another word, and I'll cut off your tongue," Joshua says. Darkness consumes him. He's no longer the man I knew. I wish I would've seen it earlier. I can't believe I cared enough to even want to help him.

"Then cut it off," she snaps.

He elbows me, knocking me back, rushing toward Kristin. I squeeze my eyes shut, bracing for the horror about to unfold.

"Uncle Josh, no!" Aria yells. "We need her to say the words to release the souls promised. Don't let your temper get in the way."

"What?" Christopher says.

Aria looks like she doesn't want to answer him, but she leans close, pressing her lips to his ear. "Be thankful, cousin. You were supposed to be one of them but the witch's soul will take your place. One of Raphael's chosen. With Raphael's blood and humanity, the Hell energy created by the souls attached to him, and the portal the angels will open to Hell, we'll own both the night and day without worry of angels or demons. Eternity on earth is ours like we've always deserved."

My blood cools like ice water slides through my veins instead of my demon blood. I can't believe my ears. This isn't about getting the justice they believe they deserve in punishing Dad, this is about power, about rising beyond the mortal bounds. Everyone has a place in the universe, whether it's Heaven or Hell, but few get an eternal existence on the mortal plane. The Demonic Uprising was proof how holding souls upsets the balance of the universe so much so that humanity nearly lost, but this? It can't be much better. Unleashed beasts of Hell not only put humans at risk, it puts the angelic army and even other demons at risk.

Where do I fit in with all of this?

I suck in a breath, repeating Aria's words in my head. A

virgin demon spawn definitely wasn't on the list, thank God, but Dad's blood and humanity are. I don't think the angelic army is going to let there be any demonic bloodletting, so I know where my place is. It's how Kristin was going to cast a spell to free Dad. But I almost wish it was a virgin demon spawn—that I can change. Dad's blood flowing through my veins? I'm doomed. No blood transfusion can save me.

Aria turns her attention to me, realizing I heard everything she told Christopher. I don't have time to even react before she launches at me and smashes me into the trailer wall.

Stars burst in my vision, and Ezekiel unfurls his wings.

The last thing I see is the scattering of burning feathers drift to the ground.

"Ezekiel?" I ask, calling through the mist covering the dream beach. "Ezekiel, are you there?"

No response.

Kicking sand, I stroll down the beach, trying to see through the mist that sends my hot skin steaming. It can't end like this. I can't spend whatever time I have left alone in my own head.

"Ezekiel!" I scream.

I search the desolate beach, realizing that the ocean I love, the expanding sea that reminds me of home, is now a desert. Gnarled trees reach toward the sky, the trunks like silent screaming faces of the lost. Instead of the bright sun overhead, moonlight casts beams of white light on an onyx path that appears before me. The world around me, one seemingly created from my worst nightmares stretches into a dark, lonely abyss that sinks to my soul.

A flash of light falls from the sky like a star plummeting to earth. A thud breaks the silence muting the world apart from my breathing, and a glowing black feather lands on the ground before me.

Then another.

And another.

I follow the glittering trail of feathers, spotting a body lying on the sand in front of me, obscured by the fog. A pain so intense rushes through my very soul. I was afraid of this—of something happening to my Demon Watcher because of me, and now it has. Now that I see him lifeless before me in a world that was supposed to be made of my wildest dreams now a nightmare, I can't take it. I'm not sure I can survive this much longer.

"Ezekiel!" I scream, rushing to get closer. The faster I run, the farther he seems to be. Nothing I do, no matter how hard I try, gets me within reach of my angel. I remain lost on the onyx path surrounded by the desolate sand of a night desert.

Dropping to my knees, I twine my fingers together, tilting my head up toward the ethereal light of the moon hovering in this empty world. "Grandma? I need help. I don't know what to do. I'm lost."

The world hushes around me like the night holds its breath. The silence embraces me, but it's not an empty silence. It's heavy and so quiet it's loud to my ringing ears. It's the sound of someone listening. Of someone answering my pleas—my prayers.

I expect the sun to rise up to push the darkness away. I expect my grandma's soul to materialize in front of me, to take my hand and lead me to wherever it is I'm going. Because in this moment, my soul feels suspended in Purgatory, like at any second, I'll find out exactly where I'll go.

But nothing changes.

Except the silence.

A gasp echoes through the air, the ruffling of feathers sends a wave of pure hope through my very essence, and the sun does rise.

I blink at the sudden light, blinding me and realize it's not the sun at all.

Glorious black wings outstretch toward the midnight sky. Ezekiel's celestial light pushes the mist and darkness away. With open arms, he rushes toward me, closing the distance so I don't even have to take a step.

His wings wrap around me the same time his arms do, and he lifts me off my feet, pressing his forehead to mine, a smile lighting up the universe brighter than his inner grace.

"You're okay," he whispers, his lips nearly brushing mine. "Your soul—it was so weak. I wasn't sure if you would hang on."

I hug him, burying my face to his shoulder, reaching out to graze my fingers across his beautiful wings. "Is this an illusion? Your wing..."

"Is fine. I'm fine."

Tears spill from my eyes. "I don't understand."

"You're my purpose, Faith."

The weight of his words settles heavily on my soul. No matter how often he says them, I still can't wrap my mind around them. "That is still as sad as the first time you've said it."

He chuckles. "You're more than that, too."

I frown. Not because of the depth hidden in his words, but because of the truth to them. "Yeah, I'm the key to destroying the world, too."

His forehead crinkles. "This isn't about revenge for your father's past, is it?"

I shake my head. "How much do you know about witches?"

"They're mortal vessels of power—cursed or blessed—linked through bloodlines not unlike werewolves. Demons nearly massacred them all because they saw them as competition when it came to souls, and when some witches willingly give souls..."

"You mean sacrifices?"

"There's no power for demons in souls who willingly give themselves to Hell without a contract."

"Oh."

"But I don't want you to worry. The werewolves can't use your soul, even by the spell of a witch, unless it's Hell-bound either by an action of your doing, your choice, or a contract with a demon—none of which affect you as long as you knock it off with your soul corruption."

I groan.

"Freewill is a powerful thing, Faith, but words are empty without meaning behind them. You're lucky you didn't really want to risk the safety of your soul. Also, I should mention that if you think experiencing human desires will—"

I close my eyes, making him snap his mouth shut. It's like he has so much to say and not enough time. "First you attempt to give me relationship advice and now you're really going to go there with a sex talk? Can we save this to give me something to look forward to later?"

His face reddens. "I—"

"Because, you know, the wolves aren't after my soul, and I'm pretty sure an eternity talking about sex with you is the universe's way of making up—"

"Wait, what? Your blood?"

I pout. I can't think of a better way of combating my panic than making him blush. "The Moonlight Shores pack isn't looking for a way to combat demons in their mortal lives, Ezekiel. They're using my dad's descent to Hell as an opportunity for immortality."

"That would mean—"

"The angelic army will technically be the ones responsible for this mess if they open a portal."

Ezekiel tenses. "This isn't good."

"Yeah, I think I prefer the implications of sex on my pure

soul with you instead."

He's trying so hard to remain serious that it makes me laugh.

"Now's not the time, Demon Spawn."

He's still holding me so close that I can feel the beat of his heart against mine. "I'm just afraid I won't get this opportunity aga—"

He tilts his head forward, and I snap my mouth shut, half expecting to be interrupted with a kiss, but he stops a hair short. I could close the space between us, make the move that I never realized how desperately I wanted to do at my discretion instead of being surprised by him during a ridiculously confusing conversation in the van next to—

A screech rips through the air, the noise exploding in my head, making me cringe and thrust myself from Ezekiel. His light dissipates, throwing me back into the mist of the desolate desert night world.

My whole body screams in pain, like my soul slowly tears away to distance itself. I thrash, jerking to try to get whoever is holding me to let me go. Hot hands squeeze my wrists, and I swear whoever is holding me will cut them off if I don't use my power.

"Stop! Faith, don't. Don't use your power." Ezekiel's pleas strike me through the heart, the despair in his voice the only thing keeping me from testing my luck. From fighting until my very last breath.

He yells out, the pain in his voice making me pull myself

together.

The hands let me go, and my back slams into the concrete floor. I gasp, spitting and coughing, the air whooshing from my lungs. It takes everything in me to open my eyes. My body wants nothing more than to react and fight without me even having to try.

"Shut up, Zeke," Aria says, her voice echoing through the air.

"Do what you feel you must to me, but please, don't hurt her anymore."

I blink my eyes to clear my vision. Aria stands in front of Ezekiel with a dagger outstretched, pointing at his chest. Angels aren't immune to pain or torment. They bleed like mortals just like demons do while in the earth realm. It takes a blessed dagger and extreme injury to kill lower-level and mid-level demons, but for a mortal to send an upper-level demon to Hell is more complicated. Sometimes impossible. It required getting past the power protecting them. For angels? I don't want to think about it.

"Well, if you hadn't tried to intervene, I could've made it quick. You think I want her to suffer?"

Something warm trickles from my wrist and into the palm of my hand. The pain cutting across my skin was real. It wasn't from Aria holding on too tightly. She cut me. I'm bleeding. I don't know why I thought I'd have more time.

Ezekiel's gaze darts to mine. I press my bleeding wrist to my jeans, trying to staunch the blood seeping from me. Aria follows his line of sight and points the dagger in her hands at me. I scramble back so she can't get to me and my blood.

I hold my hand up to summon power.

"Faith!" Ezekiel yells. "Don't. If you summon Raphael's power, it'll activate your demon blood for her. That's what they need."

"So, you want me to bleed out?"

Aria steps closer, and I back into the wall. "That's exactly what he wants. Take one for the team for Heaven. Prove to them you're worthy of that infuriatingly good soul of yours. Show them their actions against your father are warranted and even though they're quick to send him to Hell, you're not the devoted demon daughter they thought. Come on, Faith. Life is full of sacrifices. Why not sacrifice everything for those who will never show you mercy."

I hate that I see reason in her words.

"Faith, she's lying. They won't let you die—"

Aria spins around and throws the dagger at Ezekiel, hitting him in the shoulder. He yells out, blood pouring from the embedded blade.

"Stop it!" I scream. "Stop!"

Aria narrows her eyes at me, her lips twisting to the side, an idea lighting the darkness in her gaze. I tense as she crosses the room to Ezekiel and laces her fingers around the hilt of the dagger. She twists it, causing Ezekiel to yell out again.

My head spins, the sound of his pain burning my ears. I can't stand it.

"Faith, don't let her break y—" Ezekiel grinds his teeth, trying not to yell, but Aria pulls the knife out to sink it into his side.

But it's too late.

Launching from the floor, I fly across the room. I can't bear to see my Demon Watcher suffer. I can't wait for them to push me to my breaking point.

Dad would be furious if I did nothing. If I gave up.

I don't want to die for Heaven.

I definitely don't want to die for Hell.

But for Ezekiel? I'll die for him.

"Faith!" he yells. "No!"

All I see is the beautiful glow of my demonic power light his dark eyes.

HEAVEN'S TRAITOR

EZEKIEL BLASTS ME with white light—light so pure it consumes my demon power before it even leaves my palms. Electricity stings my hands, and I yelp, the shock more powerful than I thought possible coming from him.

Aria shoves the dagger into his stomach, and the amount of blood pouring from my Demon Watcher leaves me reeling. Hell really got to her. The girl I knew would never dare hurt someone, especially an angel. And I wish I knew what went wrong, what I could've done to stop her from giving her soul away.

Rushing forward, I jump on her back, locking my arms around her throat. She runs backward, knocking me into the wall. Ezekiel steps forward, light streaming from his hands. He hits her with his heavenly light. She screams.

I cringe at the high-pitched wail followed by the sound of shifting bones. Aria tears through her clothes, her light gray fur growing from her skin to burn away as she lights up like a torch. She rushes the wall, using it to propel herself at Ezekiel. A blade is one thing, but summoning Hell into herself will inflict unbearable misery on an angel.

Holding my palms out, I imagine pulling power from the pits of Hell. Ezekiel turns his angelic light from Aria and onto me. Aria crashes into him, pushing him back. But I don't stop. I create a ruby orb of liquid fire in my hands.

"Faith!" Ezekiel yells.

With all my strength, I release it at Aria, the force strong enough to knock her flaming body off Ezekiel. My hair floats around me, caught on the energy from my power. I heave, my stomach twisting. Darkness presses against me, threatening to eat my soul.

Aria's flames snuff out, her tar-like, greasy body now lifeless on the floor. Ezekiel stands above her, blood dripping from his chest, smoldering her Hell-consumed body. A scream rips from my throat, my fear and anger slipping out of me and leaving total shock and grief behind. The girl I trusted most, the one who treated me like family, the one who loved me despite of who I was, is gone forever. I'll never see her beautiful smile, hear her laugh, watch the sunset glitter off her platinum hair.

This can't be happening.

She betrayed me in the worst way possible, but my heart refuses to stop caring, to stop loving her. It refuses to give up hope that maybe this was all a nightmare.

But it's not.

Aria is dead by my hands.

I've sent her to Hell for eternity.

My soul fissures, puncturing me worse than the cuts crossing my skin. Tears sting my eyes, and I drop to the floor, hugging the still smoldering body of my best friend forever trapped in the body of a beast. If I could open a portal to Hell, I'd jump in and fight Lucifer himself to try to bring her back, even after everything. Because even if Hell got to her, it could never change the fact that I loved her like family. That in the end, her betrayal still doesn't warrant an eternity in Hell. She had her reasons like I have mine.

"Ezekiel, please. You have to save her," I beg, linking my fingers together. "Please, she can't be lost."

Tears sparkle in his eyes, like rainbow prisms catching both the heavenly light that radiates from him and the Hell fury still clinging to me. He closes the distance, locking his arms around me in a hug.

He yanks me from Aria, touching the pink skin of my flesh from the heat of her hellhound body, trying to ease the pain. But the pain on the surface is nothing compared to the agony in my entire being. "Faith, I can't. Her soul is already gone."

Aria's lost to Hell forever, and there's nothing I can do.

Dad might be responsible, but Aria still made her choice in the end.

I still can't help feeling like I've failed her. I never saw the signs. I never saw any of this coming.

"God, why?" I can't stop myself from asking the question out loud, like maybe I'll get a response in the form of a miracle, anything, to give me a reason not to curl up on myself. The night's not over. Dad is still alive. I can't lose another person to Hell. I can't.

"You think he's listening, the daughter of Heaven's Traitor?"

My body reacts, and I summon power in my hands to throw at the silhouette of the woman standing in the doorway. Red eyes glow from within the shadows crossing her face. The Hell clinging to her sends a storm of panic through my chest, and I scramble away from Ezekiel to face the witch.

"He's not. And have no fear, Aria is not lost. She'll be heavily rewarded for the sacrifice she's made to pull Raphael's blood from you," the woman adds.

Ezekiel grabs my shoulders, pulling me back, but he's not fast enough.

Fire bursts from my stomach, and I clutch the bejeweled handle of a dagger unlike anything I've ever seen. Each red gemstone shifts and moves like molten lava is trapped under the surface, glowing brightly against the onyx metal.

Ezekiel thrusts one of his hands out, sending light into the shadow, but nothing happens. The room remains dark. There aren't shadows here. My vision is failing, warm blood pouring from my wound, spilling across the floor.

"Drop her before I force you to fall by her side," the witch says.

I moan, igniting a burst of demonic power in my fingers. "No." I expect the words to ring loud through the air, but they only come out a whisper, a small gasp.

"I'll gladly face Hell before I let you even touch her," Ezekiel says.

Two smoldering hellhounds blur through the shadows, their Hell light drawing my focus from the woman's glowing red eyes.

"Heaven's unfair to put you in this position. Another righteous angel to fall for humanity. For a demon's kin. An angel so brave and willing can serve Hell so perfectly."

I summon all the strength I have left to create a single orb of my dad's power within my fingers, but it's not enough. Ezekiel will perish with me if I don't do something more.

"Ezekiel, please." The fire of Hell burns through my very skin from the wound giving the witch exactly what she needs. "I can't have that on my soul."

"I'm not letting her take you," he says.

I reach back over my shoulder, crying out in pain but refusing to stop myself from touching his cheek as he holds me up. The hellhounds growl, inching closer and closer, following the woman's lead.

"Ezekiel, leave my blood and body, but take my soul, okay? It's yours. Stop the angels from opening Hell. Please, I'm dying. I'm begging you for this one thing. Save my dad."

"Faith," he whispers.

"Just do it."

The hellhounds launch in our direction, and Ezekiel wraps me in his wings, setting off a light unlike anything I've ever seen. It touches my very essence, stealing away my pain, leaving my skin buzzing. Peace and hope wash over me, tears rimming my eyes. It's like my whole being submerges in everything good and pure in the universe. I'm lost to love and happy to be.

The second the feeling blooms it washes away, leaving me cold and empty.

I scream. But it's too late.

Ezekiel disappears, and I drop to the floor, my body sliding on my own blood. Reality sets in, and flames block my vision before a woman comes into view. She reaches down, ripping the blade free from my stomach, making me wail out again.

The hellhound to her right lifts and drops his paws right on my wounds, burning my flesh, staunching the blood. My vision turns red, and I jerk under the pain. The world flashes in and out as my stupid brain holds onto consciousness. I'm still alive.

The witch bends down, shoving her fingers into my mouth. She pours a vial of hot liquid down my throat, causing me to cough. "Blood to blood from light to dark, heal this body, heal this heart. A demon's kin now free of grace, will stand by my side in her rightful place."

Dizziness washes over me. "What's happening?"

"Can't be wasteful now. Your angel just loved you too much," the witch says, reaching out her other hand. She digs her sharp nails into my shoulder, yanking me up. "But Hell loves you more."

Another pair of arms catches me before I fall. I groan, confusion gripping me. Christopher wraps his arms around me, hugging me to him. My legs dangle. I'm too weak to even stand up.

"She's beautiful, isn't she?" the witch adds, grabbing my chin to look into my face more closely.

My head lulls, and I don't respond.

"And such a fighter—martyring herself to save that blessed angel. He'd have made the perfect demon." She squeezes my face, forcing me to look into her red eyes. "But you'll do fine. Hell will open its gate for you, daughter of Raphael, Heaven's traitor."

I open and close my mouth, sucking in a breath but unable to form words. "H-H—"

She grins, pressing her fingers to my lips. "Shhh, my soon-to-be beautiful demon. We're running out of night."

"Ezekiel, help me." My voice gets lost in the fog surrounding me. I think I'm asleep—I know I'm not dead.

Silence.

"Ezekiel? Please."

"Faith."

I close my eyes, listening to the voice, letting it fill my mind. But it's not Ezekiel. I've been abandoned.

"Faith, wake up!"

My world shakes, my whole body curling in on itself, pain the one feeling I have left. Not only does my body hurt, my mind, my—a cold emptiness sinks through me—my soul? It's gone. How I'm alive, still gasping for breath, still capable of wishing death would come for me is beyond me.

I cough, groaning. The burns on my stomach explode at the pressure forcing my skin to shift.

"What in the name of Hell?" Kristin's voice wraps around me, her strangely comforting familiarity something I never thought I could ever appreciate. "Oh, God. Your eye."

My hand jerks up to touch my face. I half expect to feel my eye hanging from its socket with the way she makes a gagging sound deep in her chest. But I still feel it under my closed lid. Though something is wrong. Everything is blurry. But not. The mist? I see the strange desert from my dream. The one with the gnarled trees with the screaming faces, the onyx path, the beams of moonlight.

Ezekiel? A huge expanse of wings cuts through the fog, but just as quickly as I see them, a halo of light glows through my vision and the figure disappears.

"What's—" I heave again, my insides threatening to spill out. Blood coats my blistered and still burning palm from when my power and Ezekiel's made contact before I could expel it.

Kristin rubs her hand across my back. "I need you to pull

your damn self together, Faith."

I brace my palms on the cool tile floor. It's not unlike the one Aria tried to bleed me out in. There's only a single door and no windows.

My stomach clenches again, and I throw up. Black bile sprays in front of me, and my stomach refuses to stop convulsing until there's nothing left. Kristin doesn't move back, continuing to pat my back.

"I never thought you'd bleed black," she says.

I wipe my mouth on my arm. "I don't."

"Well, you are now."

She holds up my arm, showing the still oozing cut on my wrist. My usual red blood, no different than any human's I've seen, now drips black.

"I think—I think I'm dead," I say. "I don't know. I should be dead. I—"

Kristin shifts, kneeling next to me. She grabs my chin, turning my face back and forth like she can peer into my body to see what's happening on the inside. "Open your eye again."

I hadn't realized I had one closed. The second I open it, the mist swirls in front of me, layering over the world like a second skin—a filter—showing me something that's there, but I can't usually see. It's so strange.

Reaching out, Kristin grazes her fingers over my heart. She sucks in a breath. "Holy shit. Where is your soul?"

I blink my foggy eye, closing it to block myself from the strange world. "Ezekiel took it."

"Holy shit," she repeats. "He didn't sever your mortal binds. What kind of angel messes up like that?"

"I was dying, but the witch, she—" My whole body tenses, and I clutch my head. "Oh, God. I'm soulless, but I shouldn't be here."

"You're not entirely soulless. I see a spark clinging to you. Where is your watcher, anyway? I didn't think they ever left their charge's side until death."

Tears burn my eyes as her words sink in. "He thought I died. He disappeared."

"Well, he didn't portal to Heaven, obviously. If you didn't die, he couldn't have gone all the way," she says. Those feelings I felt, the goodness of the world flowing to me weren't Ezekiel or death. It was Heaven. I know it.

I groan, my head throbbing. "How do you know all this?"

"Your dad," she says. "I'm his soul keeper—of the living variety, of course. And honestly, I'm pissed off he chose to keep you from me all these years. I touched Hell to create the spell to help him and your mother have you. I mourned you and Grace when the alliance came to save her soul. And then when Christopher showed up with you at my house, I—" She moans, clenching her fists into hands. "He's a dead wolf."

"I'm pretty sure we're all dead," I say, opening my blurry eye.

The mist circles the room, and a figure pops into view in front of me. I startle, releasing a small cry, and push myself to my feet. I wobble in place. My legs threaten to give out on me, but I manage to take a small step forward.

Ezekiel stands tall before me, his inky wings unfurling, and a breath of wind blows my hair behind my shoulder. His dark eyes shine with ethereal light. He captures me in his intense gaze, peering at me from this strange world. Raising his hand, he holds it up. I mimic his movement, and our fingers spark at the sudden touch.

"Kristin," I say, waving my hand out behind me. "Do you see him?"

The witch gets to her feet, brushing her arm against mine. "What are you talking about?"

"Ezekiel, he's right here."

He reaches out his hand, cupping my cheek with his freezing fingers, like he's touching me through some sort of veil. But the world he's in? It's not Heaven. No way. It's not here on earth, either.

"I think he's in Hell," I whisper. "It's so cold and dark and desolate. So empty. Oh, God."

"Sounds nothing like Hell. I've touched the place, and it was loud and full and hot and—" She shudders. "Inviting but repulsive at the same time."

"Faith." I can't hear Ezekiel say my name, but there's no mistaking my name on his lips. "I'm trapped until the veil thins."

I crinkle my nose. "Where? Where are you trapped?"

"You have to fight. Don't give up. Don't let them kill you."

"I don't understand, Ezekiel. How can I save you?"

His fingers slide to my chin, and he leans closer, like our souls collide between the living and mist world. He brushes his lips across mine, but I can't feel more than a tiny shock. "Save yourself." I almost feel his breath whispering the words.

"You have my soul," I say.

"But you carry the blood of a demon. If the portal to Hell opens, you'll go with your father, and I'm stuck here. I'll be responsible for bringing you back. The angelic army—they'll never allow it. I have possession of your soul, which means you don't. You'll return without your humanity, without anything left of you. You'll be no different than—" He flaps his wings, swirling the mist around, unable to finish his words. "I can't lose you to Hell or Heaven."

"Then give it back," I say. "I want my soul back."

Tears sparkle in his eyes. "I can't. Your words were binding. I—I've failed you. I couldn't bear to end your life myself. I thought you were dying. Your soul was already pulling free."

I suck in a deep breath, panic gnawing away at me. "Give it back, Ezekiel. Give me my soul."

"You said to leave your blood and body. I was saving you, Faith. Please, forgive me. I couldn't—"

Power ignites in my hands. "Give me my soul!"

"I—I can't. Please, Faith. Fight. Save yourself. I can't—I lo—"

Throwing my power, I hit Ezekiel in his ethereal form peeking through the veil. The mist explodes in light, and I cover my eyes.

Kristin yanks me back, and we crash into the wall. The mist swirls and moves, and then I cover my blurry eye.

Sobs wrack my chest, and I gasp, folding in on myself. I can't believe this is happening. If what Ezekiel says is true, if I die, the witch would be right. I'll return a full-blooded demon all because I gave an angel my soul, and she stopped me from dying, leaving me in this soulless state.

Kristin exhales a long breath. "Whoa. Don't you ever do that again."

"Do what? Try to break the veil to punch my watcher for not murdering me and saving my soul properly?"

She grabs my throbbing wrist, shaking her head. "Yeah, exactly that. That prison realm is the only thing protecting humanity from demons. It's imperfect, but at least the days still belong to us."

I frown. "What?"

"Raphael never taught you about the Veiled Realm?"

"That's the alliance's term for the night. It's silly. He'd ground me if I started using hunter terminology." Saying the words out loud about Dad puts a deep cut in my chest. I haven't heard the term Veiled Realm in years. It's not even a real place. It's what the Hunter's Alliance calls the night. If we're not human, we're said to be part of the Veiled Realm because we live among the human world, hidden in disguise. Ordinary humans don't even realize all that happens, how fragile their state of being is. But that can change in an instant. Once you get dragged into the demonic world, you don't ever leave. You're officially on the other side of an imaginary veil.

"I swear I'm going to save Raphael only so I have the opportunity to smack him for turning you into a porcelain doll he bubble wrapped, shoved in a box, and locked in a safe. You have so much potential, Faith. I'm afraid you'll never get to meet it."

"Well, I better figure it out, because Ezekiel says he can't return here until the veil thins. If the Moonlight Shores pack and that witch use the portal to Hell, the angels will send Dad to Hell through, I'm apparently screwed."

"If you can access the Veiled Realm, that means you'll be able to access the veil when it closes off to make the prison realm that entraps demons. All of earth is screwed if you return as a demon and can break it," she says.

This is so much to take in. The world I'm seeing? The misted night world with the screaming gnarled trees is the same world that holds Dad hostage by day. The only ones able to travel in and out are angels. But now me? I don't understand. *Dad wasn't always a demon...*

"Then kill me," I say. "Take my life. Finish me. I—I can't have this hanging over me."

Kristin doesn't respond. She doesn't get the chance.

The door swings inward, and a figure hovers in the doorway. Before I know it, Kristin flies across the room. She plows into Christopher, knocking him off his feet. The surprise leaves him stunned.

"Faith, run!" Kristin says.

I jump to my feet, summoning the strength through my demonic blood to carry me from the room.

I hit the solid body of a werewolf. Joshua grabs me by my hair and lifts me off my feet. I swing out my arm, punching him in the face, turning his head sideways. He holds me up, my scalp screaming with the rest of me as my torso stretches out with the movement.

He wraps his strong fingers around my neck and squeezes.

I don't use my power. I don't fight back. All I do is summon the courage Dad instilled in me.

And then I pray.

UNANSWERED PRAYER

HAVING A PRAYER denied is something I should have expected as the daughter of a demon, but this is the first time it really mattered to me. All those little prayers I've been wasting on mundane things, like sneaking out without getting caught by Dad, or praying a gutted demon wouldn't spray across one of my favorite dresses, all stole from this very second when I need divine intervention the most. When I need all of Heaven to hear my words. To step in and do what they should have done all along.

But maybe praying for death isn't the kind of prayer that

can be answered.

Maybe because a part of me doesn't mean it.

I've strived to live my whole life. To see another day. To grow old even when everyone I know and love around me never will.

But another, huge, burning, bleeding, world ending part of me wishes I could get it over with and gasp my last breath. Hear my own heart stop beating. Because I don't want to touch Hell, to visit the devil himself—who Dad jokes about being Uncle Lucifer—because I wasn't meant for this fate. I never agreed to this. *You don't pick fate, Faith. The universe always has a plan.*

I push away my grandma's words of wisdom, because I'm pretty sure she never realized how plans can fail. How one stupid breath of words could ruin me.

"My beautiful demon, so smart. So feisty," the witch says. "But it's not quite time."

"Go to Hell," I say.

She laughs. "My time will come, and it'll be so very welcoming for everything I've done."

Joshua drops me to the ground, and I cringe, tucking my knees to my chest. He kicks me, sending me reeling and into another wall. The witch touches his arm, clicking her tongue while shaking her head. She motions for him to grab onto Kristin.

"Christopher, take Faith. I know you'll be gentle. You understand what's best," she says.

"Yes, Mary," he says.

Christopher carefully slides his arm under my legs and around my back, picking me up into his arms like a small child. His heartbeat pounds so furiously, it blocks out all the other noise around me. He swallows, his Adam's apple bobbing in his throat, and I try to twist myself, but he locks his arms tighter but doesn't hurt me.

"Christopher," I whisper. "Please."

He stiffens without responding.

"Hush, little demon. Don't speak," the witch, Mary says, running her sharp nail across my cheek. "No need to break this wolf. He is yours. Consider it a gift from me to you to have your own beautiful beast by your side on your return."

I turn to look at Christopher, the mist circling us as I open my blurry eye. Through the dark world covering the overhead lights, I see an emptiness in Christopher's eyes—he stands tall, still holding me, but in the mist his usual hazel eyes burn like coals, Hell peeking through my new distorted vision.

"No," I whisper.

"Bound to your father, bound to you. Blood is blood black and true. The demon within will gladly take, this beautiful wolf, yours to break." Mary's sing-song voice, such a musical sound, draws my attention from the mist. A flash of light stands tall behind her—Ezekiel. But I close my eye and he disappears. "The veil it thins with Heaven's light, the grace of God to steal the night. Your time on earth will soon be gone as Hell whispers an alluring song. Blood is blood, red to black. Hell will take your body back. Your power will flourish bold and true, your demon within will come breaking through."

My head spins, her words swirling in my ears, stealing the sound of Christopher's heartbeat. Stealing the sound of Kristin's screams. Stealing every sound around me. Her mouth no longer moves, but the chant continues to ring in my ears.

"Demon born now blood so black, the portal to Hell will take you back. The veil it thins with Heaven's light, your soul will soon take the night. Demon born and Heaven bound, hear my whispers, fall for the sound. A soul now gone, was light and true, now settles and Hell will enter you. Blood is blood, black and true, the demon within will now break through."

The entire world shifts, burning bodies dart around me, the walls of the room disappearing. Shouts and growls, screams and cries, steal the sound of the witch's incantation. Feathers dance through the air, burning and drifting with the flap of wings. Pain burns around me as Christopher's arms set ablaze.

"Bound to a demon, bound to you, the portal to Hell now breaks through. With blood so black and night so thin, Heaven's cries will not win. Demon born, a creature of Hell, hear my whispers, hear my spell. Break the bound that entangles you, let your demon now rip through."

I scream, writhing as burning pain licks my flesh, eating me alive in Christopher's arms. His growl reverberates through me, muffling the sound of the witch's words. My back hits the ground, and I scramble to my feet, disoriented. The mist swirls through the air, the onyx road winding before me, but I freeze in my tracks.

"Faith!" Dad kneels on the ground, surrounded by angels, one with wings so white and blinding it stings my eyes.

Flaming vines jut from the dirt, wrapping around his chest, chaining him to the ground. A flaming sword cuts through the mist, fading with the sudden light of the rising sun.

I summon power within my fingers, the mesmerizing demonic orb turning from red to a black so dark it steals every ounce of light. I take a step forward to blast the angels away, but a hellhound flies forward, rushing past me.

Blinding light erupts from the angelic army, shooting the flaming beast with the purest energy in the universe, sending Christopher tumbling to the ground. It's in this moment that I know he was never against me. The traitor wolf would've remained by my side to descend into Hell to rise again if he was against me.

The flames of his back disappear, and his oily body lurches forward, refusing to back down. He's standing up to Heaven to save my dad. To save my life.

"Stop!" I scream. "God, make them stop!"

The angels ignore my pleas. They refuse to hear my prayers. The Moonlight Shores pack of hellhounds charge the angels. Fear courses through me. They'll never see what is coming. They'll assume the beasts are to protect Dad. They'll open the gates of Hell all unaware of Mary—of me.

I brace myself.

"Bound to your father, bound to you. Blood is blood black and true. The demon within will gladly take, this beautiful wolf, yours to break." Mary's hand touches my shoulder, spinning me around. "Demon born, a creature of Hell, hear my whispers, hear my spell. Break the bond that entangles you, let your demon now rip through."

Amid all the chaos, the flying feathers, the burning world, stands Ezekiel in all his heavenly glory. His black wings expand on his back, ethereal light shining in his eyes. He rushes straight through the angelic army and Dad, not in the same world. He flaps his wings, yelling my name, outstretching his arms.

The mist drifts around us, stirring on the wind of his wings now blowing my hair behind me. The world around me freezes, fire and light, the sun and night, Heaven and Hell all vying for my attention, but I refuse to turn away from Ezekiel and his glowing essence—my soul. I can feel it, see it, it calls to me.

"Faith, fight!"

"Blood to blood, black and true, let the fire of Hell enter you."

Pain explodes through me, and I gasp, the strange onyx hilt of the witch's blade sinking deep in my chest. One second, I'm standing amid the mist of the Veiled Realm, watching the events of earth unfold, and the next I'm standing at a fiery gate, the voices of the damned singing my name.

I blink again, and it disappears.

The mist cuts through, and Ezekiel's angelic essence shines like rainbows light up against the mist.

"Demon born, a creature of Hell, hear my whispers, hear my spell. Break the bond that entangles you, let your demon now rip through."

"Faith!" Ezekiel screams. He rushes me, flying right through me. None of his angelic light can reach me, the veil still thinning, the gate to Hell still cracking open. "Faith, fight!"

I hear his words over the whisper of the witch's spell, threatening to end my mortal life—threatening to force my descent. Threatening my blood and demon bond.

Summoning all my power, I light up both the mist and the coming dawn, drawing the angelic army's attention to me. I rip the witch's dagger free, throwing it with the perfect accuracy Dad taught me at the nearest hellhound lunging at the angels. It drops to the ground in a burst of flames.

A familiar figure rises from the ground, blood coating her face, and Kristin expands her arms, shouting words I can't hear over the whoosh of Ezekiel's wings, over his cries breaking through the veil. Another hellhound drops to the ground.

Mary steps in front of me, blocking the entire world from my view. Behind her, Ezekiel gathers light, his black wings shining so bright the feathers look white. But he can't touch her. The veil still holds until the sun rises, and the angels still refuse to let Dad go.

A blazing sword lights the fading night.

"Blood is blood, red to black, Heaven will never give your soul back. Open the gates and descend. Unleash your demon from within."

"Faith!" It's Dad.

An angel with the purest white wings aims the sword.

I jerk my arm out, blasting my power at Mary. It hits an imaginary shield, setting the night aglow in red light. Ezekiel throws power at the witch from behind, and our power collides in a sparkle of fireworks igniting soundlessly through the air.

Mary thrusts her arm forward, digging her sharp nails into my chest, wrapping her hot fingers around my heart through the wound she inflicted.

I gasp, the fire of Hell burning from my core and through the rest of me.

"Blood is blood, the perfect gift. Your soul and body make the shift. Hell rises into your bones, the demon within will take you home."

I scream, wrapping my fingers around the witch's wrist. The world fades in and out, fire and darkness flashing like a strobe light, threatening my consciousness. One second I see nothing, the next the world, and then lastly Ezekiel's eyes, glistening in the Veiled Realm.

With my last bit of power, I release Hell's fury at the witch, burning before me, smiling through the smoke and flames. Glass shatters, ringing in my ears—but it's not glass. It's the veil. Heavenly light entwines with my demonic power, and I thrust my arms out, pushing Mary forward and into the prison world.

Light radiates from the east, cutting through the darkness. I rush forward, slamming my power into Mary, the air around us shimmering. Ezekiel charges us, thrusting me forward, his heavenly light burning my eyes, pushing against the darkness threatening my soul.

Mary's screams rip through the air, and I push power at her, setting her aglow in demonic light. The mist disappears, Heaven and Hell colliding between me and Ezekiel, and I fall to my knees.

"Faith." Dad's voice whispers through the air. He stands tall, the angelic army surrounding him. Outstretching his hand, the blessed light of the morning wraps around him, stealing him back into the sunlight prison world.

I can't believe I did it. I can't believe I saved him.

I blink up at a figure haloed in the light above me. Ezekiel stands over me, his black wings outstretched on his back. He kneels down, taking me into his arms, and the purest form of love settles through my skin, touching me in the empty spot my soul left behind.

"Faith, please. Faith hold on. Don't leave me."

But I can't hold on.

I lose myself to Ezekiel's light, and we both disappear.

21

SAVED

"BLOOD IS BLOOD, red to black. The power of Hell will take you back."

Thrashing, I scream out, igniting demonic fury in my hands. Mary's voice rings in my ears, and fire burns over me, licking up my legs to consume me.

"Faith—Faith, wake up." Cool hands touch my cheeks, and the fire dissipates, leaving my skin smoldering, but the cool touch glides down to my legs, snuffing out the imaginary heat from my memory.

Opening my eyes, I stare at Ezekiel. His dark gaze holds

me, searching my face. He shifts me in his arms, curling me closer against him. I blink, a weird, warm haze clouding my vision. I struggle to look over the expanse of his black wings, but he rests his hand on my face, trying to block me from seeing something.

"What's—" I cough, clearing my throat. "What's going on? Where's Mary? Where are the angels? Am I dead? Did you save me?" Question after question flies from my lips. "My soul. You gave it back. God—" My stomach heaves, and I groan.

"Shhh," Ezekiel whispers. "You saved yourself. Everyone's gone for now. The pack kept the army busy, and I was able to get you away with the witch's help."

I attempt to pull away, but Ezekiel still doesn't let me go. "I—"

"Hold her still a moment longer," a familiar voice says. "I'm almost done."

"Kristin?" I ask. "You're alive."

"Of course I'm alive," she says. "You saved Raphael, and by saving him, I get a little more time to fulfill my contract."

Something hot sears the back of my hand, and I scream out.

"Hold her tighter," Kristin says.

Ezekiel wraps his arm around me, snuggling his face into my neck. His black feathers brush my nose, and I catch sight of a strange brown haze surrounding us again. With my free arm, I slide my hand around his neck, pressing his wing down.

My heart falters. Outstretched before me is a strange world.

Dead trees tangle together, surrounding an eerily familiar black road. The haze looks hot, like I should be sweating, but Ezekiel's cool skin wraps around me.

"Ezekiel!" Kristin yells.

He stretches his wings wider, obstructing my view. "Faith, please. Don't look around."

"Where am I? Is this...?" I can't even utter the word.

"We're still alive and on earth," Kristin responds. "Thankfully."

"I was dying," I say. "I felt my soul return to me."

Ezekiel sucks in a breath. "Forgive me, Faith."

"What?"

"She'll get over it, featherhead," Kristin says. "She has no better person to hold her soul than you."

"What?" I ask again.

"Look at me," Kristin says, ignoring my comment.

Anger rips through me as Kristin and Ezekiel ignore my questions, as they blatantly dance around me without giving me the answers I seek. Swinging my arm out, I punch Ezekiel in the shoulder, forcing him to release me. Kristin grabs my other arm, but I ignite demonic power in my hand, and she scrambles back.

The world glows around me in a brown haze. I peer up at the bright sun overhead as it crawls across the sky at a pace too fast to be normal. A guttural sound erupts through the air, and I spot a lower-level demon slinking through the dry grass, ignoring us as it walks in circles.

I catch sight of a glowing body a few feet away, the inky black skin of a hellhound burning and smoldering, but without the true flames of Hell engulfing it.

It lies lifelessly on the ground, shadowing the edges of my vision.

I spin on my feet, staring at the gnarled forest of trees, strange faces screaming from within the dead bark. Fear and panic encircle me, lacing around my pounding heart. Without having to ask, I know this is the sunlight prison realm. But this isn't the same version as the one I saw last night within the mist. This is what it looks like during the day. That would mean I'm—

"Grab her!" Kristin says.

Ezekiel hooks his arms around me, yanking me off my feet. He dips me, tilting my head back, and Kristin pours something into my eyes. I thrash, my vision blurring, my eyes burning at whatever she dumped on my face.

"Blood is blood, from black to red. Steal the sight from her head. Close the veil, lock it away. Steal her sight, hide the day."

The world blinks out, like someone turns off the lights, and I scream. Panic courses through me, and I freak out without my vision. Strong arms grip onto me, and Kristin repeats the words three more times.

Suddenly, bright light cuts through the darkness, and my vision clears.

Ezekiel hugs me to him, encircling me with his wings. His cherry blossom scent tickles my nose, and I heave a shuddering breath, just relieved to see again. He doesn't let me go until I stop gasping, his wings hiding me once again from the world.

"I know this is a lot to take in, Faith, but you're okay. Your soul is in the best hands. Ezekiel will guard it for eternity no matter what happens now." Kristin's voice cuts through the sound of Ezekiel's ruffling feathers. "You're incredibly lucky."

"Forgive me," Ezekiel whispers.

He loosens his hold, finally allowing me to stand on my own two feet. A frown hardens the usual soft features of his face, and I don't back away. I stare up at him, bringing my hand to touch his wet cheek, gliding my fingers to smear his tears.

I swallow the burning in my throat, holding onto him, getting lost in the glittering kaleidoscope of tears shining his eyes. "For what?"

He cups his hand over my own. "For loving you too much. For failing you and putting your whole eternity at risk, because I'm a coward. Because I couldn't bear to end your beautiful human life."

Tears rim my own eyes, and I release a soft laugh. "I can't hold that against you, but I'm confused. Am I alive? Dead? A demon? I saw the sunlight prison realm."

"You're still demi-demon and very much alive," he says. "But what I did—there are consequences. When the hellhounds bit me and we—"

"You took me into the Veiled Realm?" I ask.

He nods. "I knew better, but I didn't want to fail you. I

had to do something to help you, and I used your blood, derived from Heaven and tainted by Hell, to get through. It opened your soul. It weakened the veil to you, Faith. And now that your body touched Hell and your soul Heaven, you're in danger. The whole universe will try to get you."

"But we're not going to let that happen," Kristin says.

"I don't understand," I say. "Why are you helping me?"

"I know this will sound weird, but I—you're a part of me. I helped create you. I can't see you perish. Not again." The witch steps forward and wraps her arms around me, sandwiching me between Ezekiel and herself. "I used a spell to hinder the sight of the daylight prism realm, but you'll still have access to it. This will help you leave."

I frown. "What?"

"You can't stay here. The angelic army saw. You saved Raphael."

"You can explain to them—"

"Faith," Ezekiel says. "Your existence goes against everything we know. They won't understand. The world is ever-changing, but the angelic army remains the same. There's no trial or pleading for you. This is the only way."

"But I killed Mary," I say.

"A wolf broke for you," he says.

I frown. "She did that."

He shifts me, and points to a naked body on the ground. "It was your blood."

My stomach heaves as I take in Christopher's broken and

damaged body. Bringing my hands up to my face, I cover my eyes, and the world shifts again. Christopher's human body shifts into a smoldering form of a dead hellhound, smoking in a world away from my own.

I scream and drop my hands. He returns to the naked boy on the ground. Bringing my hands up, I notice the puckered, blistered skin on the back of my hand. An oval with a circle has been branded into my skin, reminiscent of an eye.

Kristin reaches out and grabs my wrist. "This was the best I could do. I'm sorry you still have to see Christopher's soul, but he's bound here by contract."

I turn away from her and kneel on the ground in front of Christopher. Ezekiel tugs his shirt over his head and places it over the werewolf's steaming skin. I study him, expecting him to gasp and wake up, to ignite in flames, to do something, but he's gone. Except his soul, I see it shining around him. It remains.

I suck in a breath. "Oh, God. I never wanted any of this to happen. This is what my demon blood does to—"

A cool hand touches my shoulder. "This isn't your fault."

"He tried to help," I whisper.

"I regret the moment of doubt I had toward him. I knew he wouldn't turn against me for Hell willingly. He would've never sided with the pack that tore him apart over and over again because he saw how the world was changing. Raphael saved him, you know. But dealing with demons always comes at a price. He's at your dad's mercy, since he couldn't complete the contract," she says. "But it was worth it to him."

A tear leaks from my eye and splashes onto his cheek. "I'm sorry, Christopher. I wish I hadn't doubted you. I wish my dad never put you in this position. I wish Aria didn't betray you. I'd give anything to make this right. I can't bear to know that he'll spend eternity in Hell—"

"Faith," Ezekiel says. "Look."

I watch in horror as Christopher's soul breaks free and starts to fade.

"What have you done?" Kristin asks.

"I don't know."

"Stop him. He can't go to He—"

Ezekiel reaches out and runs his hand over Christopher's soul. Kristin screams, launching at my angel, but I block her. I can't help it. Because I don't feel the panic of Hell opening. I don't see the flames or hear the damned whispering. All I feel is love and peace, hope and light, and everything Ezekiel embodies washing through me as he holds my soul. And now Christopher's.

The world melts into nothing but pure light, and a figure materializes before me. The cute werewolf with the sandy hair and hazel eyes reaches out and touches my cheek. No pain or suffering, no sorrow or heartache breaks through the light.

I smile. "I didn't think I'd ever see you again."

"And I never thought a beautiful, feisty as Hell demi-demon would be the one to save my soul," he responds, shifting on his feet. "But damn it. I really wanted that date first."

I blush, laughing.

"The angelic competition for your attention is pretty tough, though. I'm sure you'll forget about me over the next eighty or so years."

I sniffle. "I'll never forget you. I just wish—"

Christopher steps forward and hugs me, resting his chin on my shoulder. "Don't. She was too far gone. I know better than anyone that you can't save them all."

"But we save who we can." Ezekiel materializes next to me, touching a hand on both of our shoulders. "And it's time to go, Wolf Pup."

I suck in a shuddering breath. "Eighty years," I say. "I won't forget."

Christopher laughs. "Make it a hundred. I want you to live as long as possible, okay?" Leaning forward, he brushes his lips against my cheek. Unlike from our short time alive together, this moment doesn't ignite anything put pure love and hope and goodness between us. "Bye for now, Faith." He turns to Ezekiel. "Take care of that beautiful soul of hers, featherhead."

And like that, he's gone.

Christopher disappears, stealing the light away.

When I open my eyes, I'm in Ezekiel's arms. His face lingers so close to me that every breath I breathe is of him. His breath gives me what I need to survive. I don't know if it's because Heaven still lingers in my bones, or I'm so very grateful for something as simple as breathing, but I close the distance between us, brushing my lips to his.

His whole body reacts to mine, and he devours my kiss, tightening his arms around me, wrapping me in his wings. He steals my breath away while still allowing me to breathe, deepening our kiss until the love he has for me turns all consuming. I run my fingers through his hair, traveling my hands to the back of his head to his shoulders.

I lose myself to every emotion he ignites in me, letting him destroy all the bad threatening my very existence. Because with Ezekiel, I know I'll be okay in the end.

With Ezekiel, I'll get to live.

"Oh, unholy Hell." Dad's voice rips through the air, yanking my attention away from Ezekiel. "Release my daughter before I blast you back to Heaven."

I tense, pulling away from Ezekiel to stand protectively in front of him. I blink in confusion, twilight stirring the air around us. With Ezekiel, time slows and quickens, and I can't keep track. With him, time is just for us.

"Raphael," Kristin says.

Dad turns to look behind him at the witch. "I'm gone for a few days, and I don't even know what is going on in the world."

Kristin smirks. At lightning speed, she swings her arm out and slaps Dad across the face. "You bastard demon!"

Dad smiles. He could've stopped Kristin from even raising her hand, but he allowed the witch to hit him. "You already knew that, my little witch."

She raises her hand up to smack him again.

I step forward and stand between them. "Stop."

Dad spins me around and hugs me against him. "You're grounded for eternity for that impure action with the angel, but you have no idea how proud I am of you. To take on the angelic army for me? Your soul—" The color drains from his face as he stares at me. Reaching up, he runs his finger under my eye, making me close it. "Oh, God."

It's the first time I've heard him utter such a thing.

Stepping back, he covers his mouth with his hand, narrowing his eyes at me like he can summon my soul—which isn't in my body—to the surface of my skin. His eyes widen, shifting wildly, and he shakes his head.

"It's in good hands, Dad," I say.

Igniting Hell fire, he launches a ball of liquid power at Ezekiel. I jump in front of it, catching it in my hands to snuff it out.

Dad yells, screaming incoherently at the sky.

"It's not his fault," I say. "He was trying to save me. I—" The events of the last few days spill from my mouth, and I tell Dad about everything from Aria and the Moonlight Shores pack and Mary to the Hunter's Alliance and the Traitor Pack. I spill my soul about Heaven and Hell and the Veiled Realm. I tell him everything.

Dad covers his face with his hands, running his fingers up into his blond hair to lace around his head.

Kristin steps forward and touches her hand to his back, a gesture I've never seen one of his contracted souls ever do. It's the first time I've seen anyone show him sympathy apart from me and Cadence.

"I've done what I can to protect her, but she can't stay, and you can't follow her. Not unless you want to test your power against Heaven and Hell," the witch says. "It's the only way."

Dad drops to his knees, bowing his head. In this moment, he looks so utterly human, I can't bear it. This is worse than seeing him tormented by the angelic army.

I close the distance and kneel next to him. He throws his arms around me, pulling me to him until I'm cradled in his lap like the child he saved after Grandma died. He pushes my hair from my face and kisses my forehead.

"I love you so much, Faith. You're my entire existence. Everything I've done has been for you," he whispers. "And yet here I am, unable to protect you still."

"It's a good thing you taught me how to protect myself," I say.

He laughs, but it's a stressed, almost heaved noise. "I don't want to let you go, but the witch is right. You can't stay."

"I swear on my existence that I'll protect Faith," Ezekiel says from behind me.

Dad sighs. "You are your mother's daughter."

"I'm your daughter, too," I say.

He hugs me and turns to Ezekiel. "Is my daughter worth it to you, watcher? Are you sure you're willing to do what it takes to see she's safe?"

Ezekiel nods. "You have my word."

Dad gets to his feet, pulling me with him. "If anything

happens to her—"

Ezekiel expands his wings. "Faith is my purpose, Raphael. I exist for her. I love her. I'm *in* love with her."

Dad peers at me for a long moment, studying me, a mixture of emotions crossing his usually cold and calculated face. "Be good to him, Faith. He never stood a chance with you."

Tears blur my eyes, and I nod.

"I'll figure this out. Don't even think this will take eternity," he says.

I hug him once more. "Good, because I don't have that here."

Kristin clears her throat, and I pale at the sight of the bejeweled onyx dagger glowing in her hands. It's the same one Mary stabbed through me, the one she tried to send me to Hell with. Dad wraps his arms around me, and it takes me a minute to realize he's holding me in place.

"Be quick, Kristin," he says. Pressing his lips to my ear, he whispers, "I love you forever, my daughter."

"Blood to blood, from black to red, take Faith and kill her dead. Summon her soul, forgive her sins, open the veil and let her in. Bound to a demon, a spawn now born, a soul is split a body torn. Bound to an angel, bathed in his light, protect Faith, give her the night." With her chant, Kristin sinks the blade into my heart, and I scream, writhing in Dad's arms.

"Faith, be strong," he whispers.

"As demon blood coats the ground, let Heaven and Hell hear the sound. A demon's daughter's final breath, a pure soul now put to rest. Blood to blood from red to black, a body will burn as Hell takes her back."

Fear pours through me as my skin heats. Pain shadows everything. The world spins, and Dad eases me to the floor. Mist surrounds me, swirling through the air, stealing the world, stealing Kristin and Dad.

Blinding light erupts before us, and the angelic army touches down in front of him and Kristin. Familiar angels stretch out their black wings toward the sky. A familiar voice screams through the air.

Cadence throws herself at Dad, wrapping her arms around him. Cami turns into Evan's arms, and Zach and Dylan cover their mouths. My body ignites in fire before them, and a sudden quiet fills the air.

I can't watch the people who love me most cry beside Dad and Kristin, but I can't look away. I can't bear feeling like my existence betrays them. Red power dances across my vision, and Dad stands, sending power toward the sky. But I can't hear his scream.

The only thing I can hear is my final breath sounding through the veil.

I turn to look at my body disappearing in the earth realm, engulfed in flames. My ears pop, and my legs wobble. Ezekiel holds me up, the world going in and out of focus. For a split second, I see the world through both our eyes. He forces me to turn away, hugging me.

"This isn't the end," he whispers, wrapping his wings

around me.

"That's what I'm afraid of," I say, frozen in place, fear coursing through me.

Because this is only the beginning.

Epilogue

UPRISING

"IT DOESN'T LOOK bad." Ezekiel rests his hands on my shoulders, peering at my reflection in the mirror. "You still look as beautiful as ever."

"You're obligated to say that." Leaning forward, I stare at my eyes in the mirror. I don't ever think I'll get used to the white now overtaking my iris. I look like a mid-level demon's poor attempt to create a human façade.

I pop the cap to my contacts container and dip my finger into the cool liquid. Ezekiel tugs my hand back, spilling my solution and blue contact on my makeshift vanity table. I sigh and spin, pressing my hands to his muscular chest while glaring.

"You don't need it," he says. "But especially not today."

I frown, narrowing my eyes. "What's that supposed to mean?"

Ezekiel smiles, unfurling his beautiful black wings. They expand through the room, touching each wall of the tiny apartment, making it hard to resist his commanding presence. Reaching into the back pocket of his jeans, he pulls out a tiny card.

"This appeared on the kitchen counter. Materialized out of thin air," he says.

My heart pounds, racing in my ears. I read the address over and over again, like if I read it enough, I could magically close my eyes and end up there. A breeze from Ezekiel's wings pushes me forward.

"Well, hurry up. Get your shoes on. You can't expect me to carry you all the time," he says, pointing at my boots.

"*Me* expecting that from *you*?" I ask, laughing.

He grins, holding out my leather jacket.

I'm already running out the door, charging ahead of Ezekiel. The whoosh of his wings sounds through the air, and a shadow crosses over the ground in front of me. He lifts me off my feet, yanking me into the air, throwing me in front of him. My stomach rises into my chest, and I release a small scream. He catches me, burying his face in my shoulder.

"Damn it, watcher. You know how much I hate that," I say, sliding my hand around his neck, snuggling against him.

"You'll never outrun me, Demon Spawn," he says, brushing his lips against my cheek. "But I love when you try."

I tilt my head back and laugh, my voice ringing through the air. The world blurs around me as Ezekiel flies us over the unsuspecting city far below. Covering my eye with my hand, I watch the city morph into a forest of gnarled trees, an onyx path, and a dry sandy landscape that stretches on for miles where there's usually ocean.

Ezekiel descends, darting toward the earth so fast that I turn away to peer at the beauty of his wings. A few black feathers catch on the breeze and disappear into the sunlight.

His boots touch soundlessly on the hard asphalt, and I jump from his arms, losing my balance. I somersault across the ground, turning from street pavement to onyx ground with every blink. I hit my back on a wall, and my breath whooshes from my lungs.

I cover my face with my hands, and a figure stands above me.

"Faith." Dad mouths my name, not greeting me with his usual smile.

I scramble to get up, glancing at the world around us, a fear settling into my bones.

"Dad," I say back. "What's wrong?"

"Faith, the werewolves are rising," he says, his voice breaking through the barrier. "The angelic army is on high alert, the truce between Heaven and Hell is fissuring."

My heart pounds so hard in my ears. "What?"

"I'm afraid for you with that angel."

"Faith, what's going on?" Ezekiel asks, his warm hand sliding into mine, though I can't look away from Dad.

"Demon born, a creature of Hell, hear my whispers, hear my spell. Break the bond that entangles you, let your demon now rip through. Blood is blood, red to black. The power of Hell will take you back." Mary's voice pierces through me, sending me reeling and away from Dad.

The sudden chant rings in my ears, stealing both Dad and Ezekiel's words. I scream out, blasting demonic power in front of me. "Do you hear her?"

"Faith, listen to me." Dad's voice cuts through the air. "I know you trust—"

"Blood to blood, red to black, you might have a soul, but they'll take it back. Body and blood, separate now, there's no hiding from Hell, it'll make you bow."

I drop my hands from my face, spinning around, fear coursing through me.

"Ezekiel," I yell. "Ezekiel, she's here! Mary's here!"

"Blood to blood, demon bound, all needed is a whisper, a sound. The veil that hides you won't last long, Hell comes back, forever strong. Angels fight and angels cry, your Demon Watcher will surely die. Heaven and Hell fight for you, but your demon within will break through."

Arms wrap around me, lifting me from the ground.

"I got you, Faith," Ezekiel says. "We're okay. Mary's gone. She's not here."

But I think she is. Those haunting words were more than a memory. I don't say the words out loud to Ezekiel. I'm afraid to speak at all as Mary's spell swirls through my mind.

"Faith," Ezekiel whispers. "What should I do? You want to land and find your dad again?"

I release a breath, shaking my head. "No—I—God, help me."

"It's okay, Faith," Ezekiel says. "You're safe. I'll always protect you."

Angels fight and angels cry, your Demon Watcher will surely die. The chant rings in my ears. I'm not so sure I'm the one in need of protecting.

I touch his cheek, gazing into his mocha eyes. "And I'll protect you."

To be continued...

Other Young Adult Novels by Ginna Moran

PARANORMAL

Destined for Dreams Series
Demon Within Series
Finding Nate Series
Going Ghostly Series
Spark of Life Series
When Souls Collide Series
Demon Watcher Series

CONTEMPORARY

Falling into Fame Series

STANDALONES

Life After Lila

ACKNOWLEDGEMENTS

FIRST AND FOREMOST, I'd like to give a heartfelt thanks to Sarah, Katie, and Jan for all the time and energy you all spent bringing this novel to fruition. You three are invaluable bookstars. And Katie, an extra thanks for expressing an interest in reading a book about Faith. She really did deserve her own story.

Another thanks is owed a few friends of mine—Jazmin, Amy, and Malory. Without your unending support, I'd constantly swim in self doubt. I appreciate all your kind words of encouragement and excitement.

Lastly, a shout out to my family. Thanks for letting me sleep in after I stay up all hours writing. Thanks for having patience when I ask for five more minutes a dozen times in a row, and thanks for believing in me. Much love!

ABOUT GINNA MORAN

GINNA MORAN IS a writer from sunny Southern California. She started writing poetry as a teenager in a spiral notebook that she still has tucked away on her desk today. Her love of writing grew after she graduated high school, and she completed her first unpublished manuscript at age eighteen.

When she realized her love of writing was her life's passion, she studied literature at Mira Costa College in Northern San Diego. Besides writing novels, she was senior editor, content manager, and image coordinator for Crescent House Publishing Inc. for four years.

Aside from Ginna's professional life, she enjoys binge watching television shows, playing pretend with her daughter, and cuddling with her dogs. Some of her favorite things include chocolate, anything that glitters, cheesy jokes, and organizing her bookshelf.

Ginna Moran loves to hear from her readers so visit her online at www.GinnaMoran.com. You can also find her on Facebook, Twitter, Instagram, and Snapchat (@GinnaMoran). To stay up-to-date on new releases, sign up to her newsletter. You'll not only get a FREE story, but you'll be able to participate in monthly giveaways!

Ginna Moran is currently hard at work on her next novel.

www.ingramcontent.com/pod-product-compliance
Lightning Source LLC
Chambersburg PA
CBHW051642180726
48284CB00006B/1833